BELOVED RECONCILIATION

Book 3: 1932–1945

Margaret Maxwell McLaughlin

Margaret McLaughlin
10 Ladyslipper Lane
Forestdale, MA 02644
margaretmclaughlin50@comcast.net

This is a work of fiction. Names, characters, businesses, places, events, locales, and incidents are either products of the author's imagination or used in a fictitious manner. Any resemblance to other actual persons, living or dead, is purely coincidental.

Cover design and interior formatting: Kristen vonHentschel

ISBN: 979-8-9937919-0-6

Printed in the United States of America

Contents

Preface...vi

Acknowledgements ix

Cast of Families... xii

Una's Introduction to Part 3 xvii

Part 1 – 1932

Chapter 1   Rough Sailing – Sunday, January 3, 1932.....................3

Chapter 2   The Football Match – Sunday, February 3, 1932 6

Chapter 3   The Nurse and The Professor – February 17, 1932...11

Chapter 4   A Second Chance Reunion – February 17, 1932......15

Chapter 5   Playing Parts – Sunday, March 20, 1932 19

Chapter 6   Larger Than Life – March 27, 1932..............................24

Chapter 7   The Women's New Circle – March 30, 1932...............28

Chapter 8   Many Windows – April 30, 1932 33

Chapter 9   Years Need Not Part Family – May 15, 1932.............36

Chapter 10   Beyond the Cackling Goose and
Brawling Bull – May 30, 1932 40

Chapter 11   Following the Workers – June 15, 1932 44

Chapter 12   Reality Returns – June 19, 1932 49

Chapter 13   Touché – June 19, 1932 53

Chapter14   Who is an Activist? – June 27, 1932 57

Chapter 15   Jon's Compass Editorial – June 27, 1932....................61

Chapter 16   Today's Gallery – June 28, 1932 70

Chapter 17   A Poppy and A Prayer – Sunday, July 17, 1932.........75

Chapter 18   Horse Chestnuts in View – Sunday, July 17, 1932 79

Chapter 19   Time On Their Sides – Sunday, July 17, 1932 83

Chapter 20   Finally, the Wedding – August 13 , 1932 87

Chapter 21   No! No! No! – October 5, 1932....................................91

Chapter 22 Well Saved – October 5, 1932......................................94

Chapter 23 The Sack and Bonnet – November 5, 1932.................97

Chapter 24 Colorful – December 31, 1932.....................................100

Chapter 25 Beyond Proclamations – December 31, 1932 105

Part 2 – 1940 – 1941

Chapter 26 Looking Ahead – January 1, 1940...............................111

Chapter 27 Red Poppies – January 19, 1940..................................113

Chapter 28 Fates or Coincidence? – January 19, 1940 116

Chapter 29 St. Thomas' Staircase – January 19, 1940 119

Chapter 30 Flashes – January 19, 1940...122

Chapter 31 Lilies for Lily – January 21, 1940 125

Chapter 32 Sunday's Well Poisoned – February 18, 1940...........128

Chapter 33 The Halo – March 24, 1940...132

Chapter 34 Lovers on The Lough – March 24, 1940.....................136

Chapter 35 My Wild Irish Rose – March 24, 1940 140

Chapter 36 Cigar Talk – May 24, 1940 144

Chapter 37 The Mule's Kick – May 24, 1940.................................150

Chapter 38 A Pause In The Beyond – June 30, 1940 155

Chapter 39 The Kiss – September 1940...159

Chapter 40 Monday Memorial – September 9, 1940.....................162

Chapter 41 A Winter Proposal – November 1940.........................167

Chapter 42 Engaging Traditions – February 8, 1941....................171

Chapter 43 Triage – Wednesday, April 16, 1941 175

Chapter 44 The Second Coming – Sunday, June 15, 1941 179

Chapter 45 Unpredictable Predictability – October 3, 1941 183

Chapter 46 Voices Raised and Recognized –
December 6, 1941 190

Chapter 47 Inside and Out Parallel Lives –
December 20, 1941 197

Chapter 48 Tempus Non Fugit – December 31, 1941 202

Part 3 – 1945

Chapter 49   First Day – January 1, 1945..211

Chapter 50   The Kharma Tea House – February 1945.................215

Chapter 51   The Star – February 1945...220

Chapter 52   Train of Thoughts – July 13, 1945.............................229

Chapter 53   Interview 1 – Charlie Magee, July 20, 1945..............234

Chapter 54   Interview 2 – Thon McCormick Irvine,
July 25, 1945..239

Chapter 55   Preparing for Interview 3 – Anna Crossley Lawson,
July 27, 1945..245

Chapter 56   Interview 3 Part 2 – Anna Crossley Lawson,
July 30, 1945..251

Chapter 57   Interview 4 – Netty McNeill Campbell,
August 4,1945..256

Chapter 58   Interview 5 – St. Stephen's Wolf and Fox,
Sunday-August 5, 1945..260

Chapter 59   Summery of Seasons – Sunday-August 12, 1945.....265

Chapter 60   Beyond and Before – Sunday-August 19, 1945........270

Preface

For those of you who have read or listened to Beloved Reconciliation Book 1: 1820-1916 and Beloved Reconciliation Book 2: 1918-1923, forgive me again for repeating myself here. For those of you who have not, I hope the following is helpful in understanding why this work was written.

Many of us actively seek how the past informs our current beliefs and actions – or inactions – in being peacemakers. Many of us don't, yet wonder nonetheless. I must admit that in this year of 2025, I find it particularly critical to learn how our ancestors resolved conflicts non-violently. Women and men as peacemakers are needed more than ever. This Beloved Reconciliation Book 3: 1938-1945 is a both a guide and plea for such people today.

This series started and continues because of my father, Edward Nelson Maxwell. He was one of my first peace-makers, although, our family would admit he also had quite a temper. Born in Belfast, Ireland, in 1908, he experienced the Easter Rising in 1916, the partition of Northern and Southern Ireland in 1921, and the Free State civil war in 1922. Regretfully, he never talked to me about the impact these historic events had on his childhood before emigrating to America in 1929. He rarely talked about his personal life either, except that he boxed boys who were harassing his older brother James, graduated from Belfast Royal Academy, proselytized on soapboxes outside Fisherwick Presbyterian Church, and lacked funds to go to college so ironed men's suits in the laundry room of a Belfast linen mill.

It was my maternal grandmother, Heywood Crawford Irvine Smiley born in 1884, who was my first formal teacher about Irish life and non-violence. Living with my family throughout the 1950s and 1960s, she would enthrall me during our afternoon "teas" with stories of tours around the Belfast Lough in the family sailboat Snow Pea and her courtship with my grandfather after she caught his eye while singing in a Bangor Presbyterian church choir. They emigrated to America in 1918. She was the quiet yet consummate mediator during my family disputes but never shared how she acquired such a skill from "back home."

Fast-forward to 2017 and a study carrel in the U.S. Library of Congress. I had just retired from a thirty-year career in international development with a focus on girls' education and women's rights. I was determined to move beyond those topics to write a biography of my father. Once I learned that his own father, Robert Maxwell, had signed the 1912 Ulster Covenant to take up arms against all Catholics if Home Rule passed, I was resolved to understand the attitudes supporting such a stand.

It was a small book by Tom Hartley on the Belfast Milltown Cemetery that convinced me to embellish the biography with a few historical facts about Irish history. I quickly realized there is no such thing as a "few historical facts" about a family, or about Belfast, or about Northern Ireland, or about the Republic of Ireland that do justice to six hundred years of conflict.

Sitting in the library's neoclassical grand reading room, next to the U.S. Supreme Court and across from the U.S. Capitol, the biography transformed itself into an historical fiction about the Irish struggle for independence from Great Britain. For the past eight years, I have read Irish books, plays, and poetry – I must regret, however, not in Gaelic Irish; I've studied research papers, speeches, scholarly histories, and newspaper articles; and, I've gathered information from conversations with friends and family members in the U.S. and Ireland. All these resources helped me imagine and reimagine—with a modicum of facts – life in Ireland for families facing social, religious, economic, and political challenges between 1820 and 1945 – and how women have been instrumental in the independence and peace movements despite those challenges.

I recognize, more now than when I had written the first books in this series, that the strength of Irish women is within women throughout the world. They, too, stand up right next to their male colleagues for justice and equality – inspired for the sake of their children and their children's children to reconcile differences and bring peace to their homelands. Ironically in my retirement, I have come back full-circle to speak, if possible, on behalf of women in conflict with whom I had worked in the U.S. and overseas.

I can only hope the writing in this series – which now includes Book 1, Book 2 and this Book 3 – honors their wisdom and courage as beloved reconcilers.

It is because of this hope that profits from Book 3 continue to go to the The Monreagh Ulster Scots – Scots Irish Heritage and Educational Center in Donegall, Republic of Ireland (visit monreaghulster-scotscentre.com to learn more). The work of Monreagh is a model for any peace and reconciliation effort. I hope you will agree and support it.

- Margaret Maxwell McLaughlin, Ed.D.
Forestdale, Massachusetts, 2025

Acknowledgments

This historical fiction is based on research, imagination, and literary critiques. Each resource was essential in creating factual contexts, believable plot progressions, and character attributes – factual or fictional.

For the facts, I am grateful to Irish historians, writers, playwrights, and poets who lived in or wrote about the time period described in each chapter. The writers who contributed substantively to factual contexts include, but are not limited to, Robert McKee, Carlton Younger, Desmond Ryan, Tim Pat Coogan, John Dorney, and John O'Neill. Highlighted poems were found in various anthologies including Brenden Kennelly's The Penguin Book of Irish Verse, Anne Enright's The Granta Book of The Irish Short Story, and Thomas Kinsella's The New Oxford Book of Irish Verse. Plays by Anglo-Irish playwrights were located either online or in reference books. Numerous visits to Irish museums and centers in both The Republic and Northern Ireland, as well as Scotland, helped locate facts within their relative time capsules, particularly World War 2. Of critical assistance were The Public Records Of Northern Ireland (PRONI), The Ulster Museum in Belfast, The Somme Museum in Bangor, the Tower Museum in Derry, and the Monreagh Ulster Scots-Scots Irish Heritage Center in Donegal. I would be disingenuous in not mentioning that some historical details and literary quotes came from online resources such as Wikipedia, irishfolklore.wordpress.com, and Queen's University. I have made every effort to confirm all primary sources.

Imaginary characters came solely from my own reflections on experiences with family and acquaintances in the U.S., Canada, and Ireland. The relationships and conversations between imagined and factual characters are solely products of my imagination after reading the biographies, personal writings, and public speeches of those historic figures.

Throughout the series, my Irish family members have been present in many a laugh of and tear by key characters. My Belfast cousin Carol Logier Donnelly and her husband Irving are gracious embodiments of my ancestral peace-makers. The members of their extended family (Victoria, Melissa, Stephen and Colin) resonate the same spirit. Primary among them all – and to whom this Book 3 is dedicated - is, my Aunt Kate, Kathleen Christina (Smiley) Logier. - Carol and Colin's Mum. She passed away at the age of 103 in 2024. She laughed like the swallows as an inspiration for all women.

In addition to family, I cannot thank enough new-found friends in Donegal – Una and Ian McCracken and Kieran Fegan, Brian Mitchell and Frank Galligan. Their "reality testing" perspectives and encouragement of this first generation Irish-American daring to write about Irish history remain invaluable. They are present in the personalities and values of key fictional characters who represent the best of Irish courage and honor. Frank's voice in the audio-books brings one to tears.

As for the many folks who offered literary critiques of these works, I am truly grateful for their acumen, generosity, and commitment to bear with me over eight years – and their willingness to continue with me on this journey during, not just one, but now three books – 230 chapters, week by week! First, the clutch of friends in a short story writing group that provided constructive critiques and heartfelt support. Often seated in front of a Zoom screen or around a small table in our local Cape Cod Chamber of Commerce, Barbara Berelowitz, June Calendar, Sheila Place, Ellen Nosel, and John McWilliam were constant companions on this writing journey. Poet extraordinaire Jeannie Martin was a key advisor on the art of writing and publishing. Special thanks go to a friend who believes the spirit of our ancestors is channeled through writers of history. Their presence in this series is based on many a conversation with that friend, Esq. Gail Neelon. I must also thank designer Kristen vonHentschel who made each page capture the reader's eyes and mind.

Finally, the burning questions around purpose, logic, and grammar were offered by my two life-companions – my dear friend of more than fifty years, Gayle Kelly, and my life partner of forty-one years, husband Stephen McLaughlin. Every week for the past eight years, these two have served as first-line editors and supporters, providing triage on every aspect of verbiage, character development, reality setting, and overall plot progression. Their brilliance, attention to detail, and philosophical queries have enabled this work to be what I hope the reader will find fascinating and informative, passionate and inspirational, and resonant with the spirit of equality, justice and most importantly peace-making.

Dickson Family

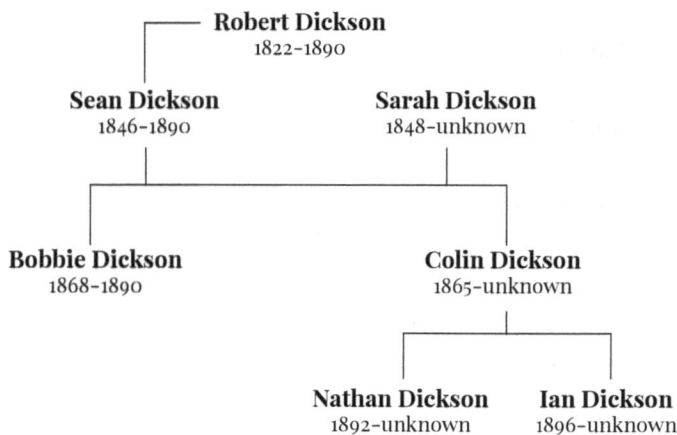

Robert Dickson
1822–1890

Sean Dickson
1846–1890

Sarah Dickson
1848–unknown

Bobbie Dickson
1868–1890

Colin Dickson
1865–unknown

Nathan Dickson
1892–unknown

Ian Dickson
1896–unknown

Gallagher Family

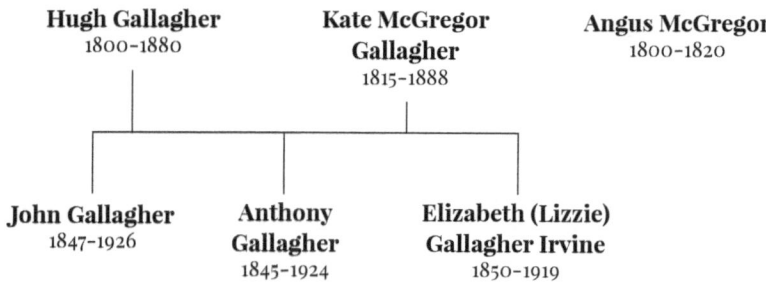

Hugh Gallagher
1800–1880

**Kate McGregor
Gallagher**
1815–1888

Angus McGregor
1800–1820

John Gallagher
1847–1926

**Anthony
Gallagher**
1845–1924

**Elizabeth (Lizzie)
Gallagher Irvine**
1850–1919

O'Leary Family

Christine O'Leary
1890–1921

Will Irvine Family

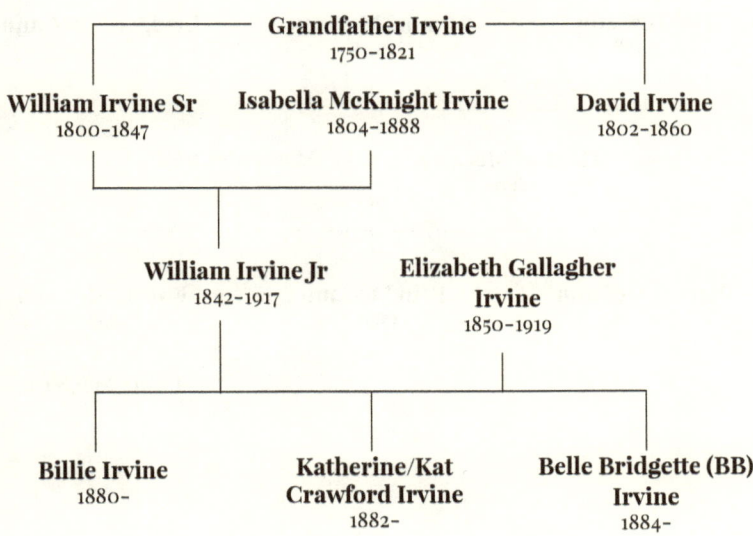

Grandfather Irvine
1750–1821

William Irvine Sr
1800–1847

Isabella McKnight Irvine
1804–1888

David Irvine
1802–1860

William Irvine Jr
1842–1917

Elizabeth Gallagher Irvine
1850–1919

Billie Irvine
1880–

Katherine/Kat Crawford Irvine
1882–

Belle Bridgette (BB) Irvine
1884–

Billie Irvine Family

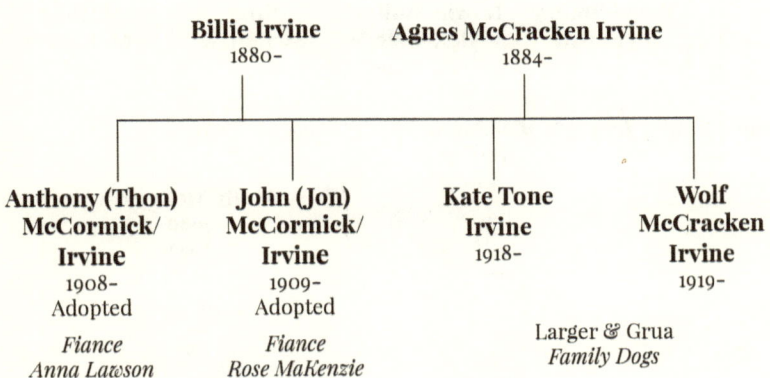

Billie Irvine
1880–

Agnes McCracken Irvine
1884–

Anthony (Thon) McCormick/ Irvine
1908–
Adopted

*Fiance
Anna Lawson*

John (Jon) McCormick/ Irvine
1909–
Adopted

*Fiance
Rose MaKenzie*

Kate Tone Irvine
1918–

Wolf McCracken Irvine
1919–

Larger & Grua
Family Dogs

McCann Family

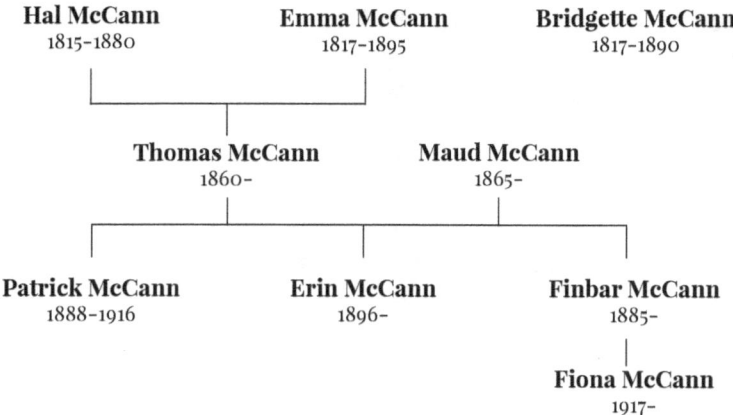

Hal McCann
1815–1880

Emma McCann
1817–1895

Bridgette McCann
1817–1890

Thomas McCann
1860–

Maud McCann
1865–

Patrick McCann
1888–1916

Erin McCann
1896–

Finbar McCann
1885–

Fiona McCann
1917–

McKenzie Family

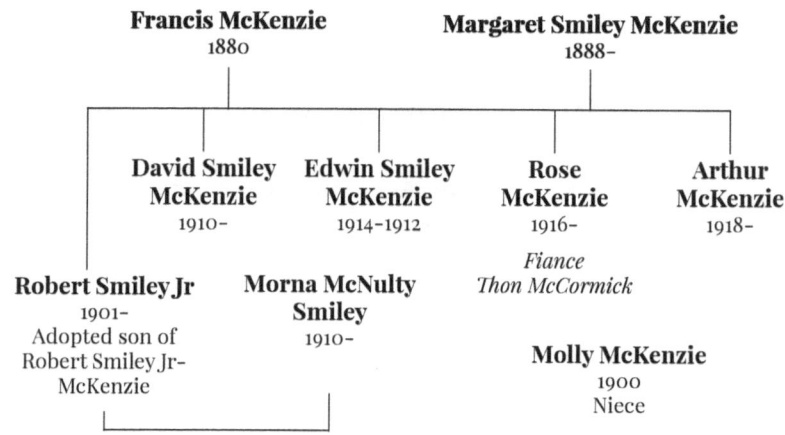

Francis McKenzie
1880

Margaret Smiley McKenzie
1888–

**David Smiley
McKenzie**
1910–

**Edwin Smiley
McKenzie**
1914–1912

**Rose
McKenzie**
1916–

*Fiance
Thon McCormick*

**Arthur
McKenzie**
1918–

Robert Smiley Jr
1901–
Adopted son of
Robert Smiley Jr–
McKenzie

**Morna McNulty
Smiley**
1910–

Molly McKenzie
1900
Niece

McCormick Family

Maud McCormack
1869–1918

Belle (BB) Irvine
1884–

Liam McCormack
1884–

Shelly McCormack
1900–

Rachel McCormack
1906–

Ryan McCormack
1885–1912

Stuart McCormack
1900–

Colin McCormack
1907–

Had sons adopted by the Irvines

Morna McNulty
1910–
Adopted

Robert Smiley Jr
1901

Maggie McGregor McCormack
1919–

Kieran Irvine McCormack
1920–
Fiance Manjula Srinavasin

Ian McNulty
1904–
Adopted

Rachel McCormick McNulty
1906–

Maude Isabella McNulty
1941–

Patrick Liam McNulty
1943–

McGregor Family

Angus McGregor
1800–1820

Kate McGregor-Gallagher
1815–1888

McCracken Family

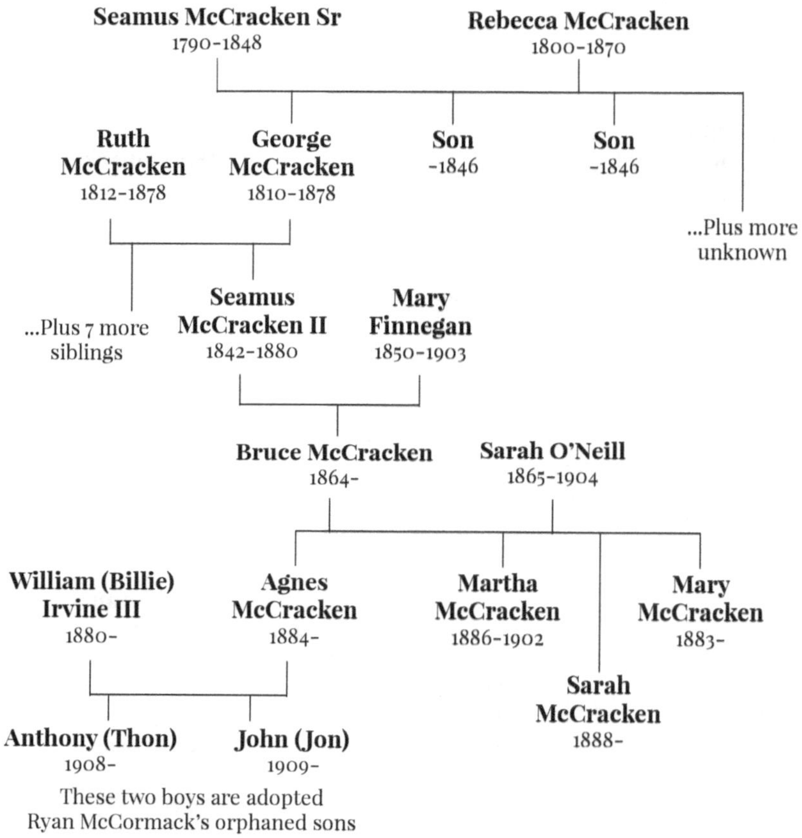

Seamus McCracken Sr
1790–1848

Rebecca McCracken
1800–1870

Ruth McCracken
1812–1878

George McCracken
1810–1878

Son
–1846

Son
–1846

...Plus more unknown

...Plus 7 more siblings

Seamus McCracken II
1842–1880

Mary Finnegan
1850–1903

Bruce McCracken
1864–

Sarah O'Neill
1865–1904

William (Billie) Irvine III
1880–

Agnes McCracken
1884–

Martha McCracken
1886–1902

Mary McCracken
1883–

Sarah McCracken
1888–

Anthony (Thon)
1908–

John (Jon)
1909–

These two boys are adopted
Ryan McCormack's orphaned sons

McKnight Family

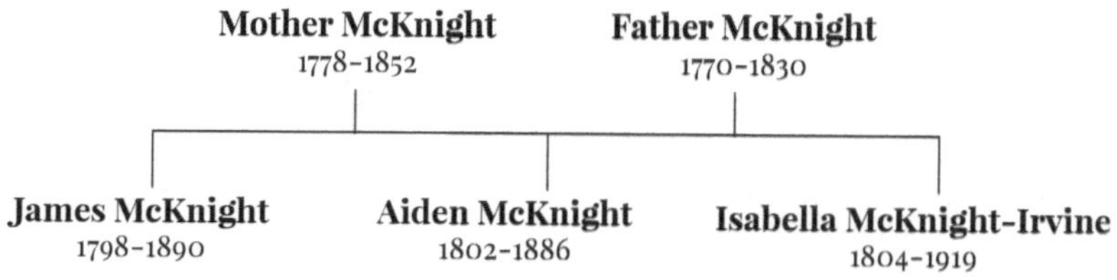

Mother McKnight
1778–1852

Father McKnight
1770–1830

James McKnight
1798–1890

Aiden McKnight
1802–1886

Isabella McKnight-Irvine
1804–1919

James Smiley Family

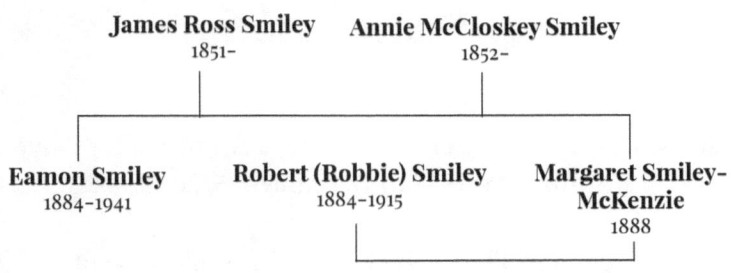

James Ross Smiley
1851–

Annie McCloskey Smiley
1852–

Eamon Smiley
1884–1941

Robert (Robbie) Smiley
1884–1915

Margaret Smiley-McKenzie
1888

Eamon Smiley Family

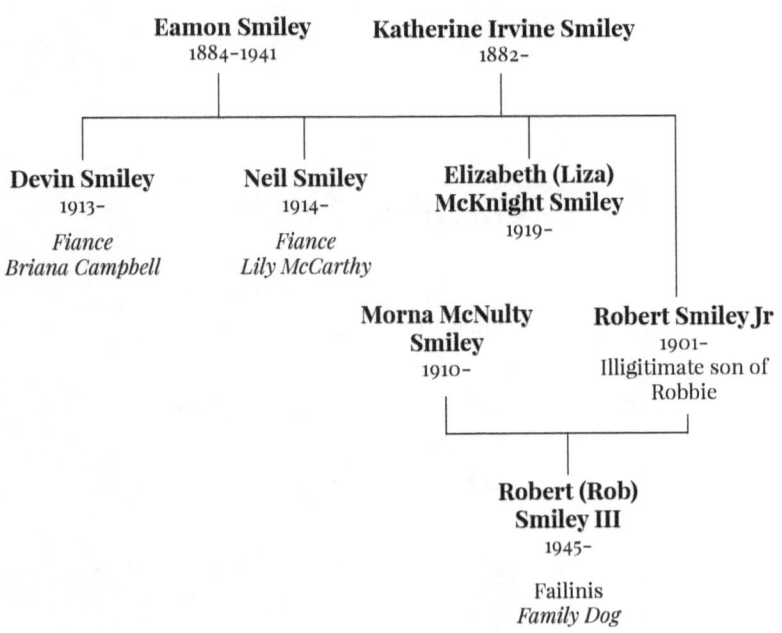

Eamon Smiley
1884–1941

Katherine Irvine Smiley
1882–

Devin Smiley
1913–

*Fiance
Briana Campbell*

Neil Smiley
1914–

*Fiance
Lily McCarthy*

**Elizabeth (Liza)
McKnight Smiley**
1919–

**Morna McNulty
Smiley**
1910–

Robert Smiley Jr
1901–
Illigitimate son of
Robbie

**Robert (Rob)
Smiley III**
1945–

Failinis
Family Dog

Dedication

To Aunt Katie
Kathleen Christina Logier – Daughter of Annie Smiley Douglas
April 24, 1921 to December 15, 2024

"They came like swallows and like swallows went,
And yet a woman's powerful character
Could keep a swallow to its first intent;"

W.B. Yeats, The Winding Stair, 1935

Opening Poem

"Yet, reading all thy mournful history,
Thy children, with a mystic faith sublime,
Turn to the future, confident that Fate,
Become at last thy friend, reserves for thee,
To be thy portion in the coming time,
They know not what – but surely something great."

- John Kells Ingram, the poem "National Presage,"
found in *Sonnets and Other Poems*, 1900

Una's Introduction to Part I

I am not of this world... well, not in the physical sense. I have been, am, and will be of many worlds.

Archaeologists would say I am an ancient vessel that holds an era's social, economic, and cultural remnants. Historians would say I am an interlocutor of fact and fiction — the witness to whoever won the war. Scientists would say I'm a genome made of three billion base pairs of DNA arranged in forty-six chromosomes. Spiritualists would say I am a ghost caught between the veil and the afterlife.

I'm not exactly sure who or what I am. Nor am I interested in finding out. What I am interested in are those with whom I have traveled over the last hundred years. They fascinate me, and, perhaps, they will fascinate you, too.

These are members of my family, an illustrious clan of Scots Irish with a smattering of Celt and Finnish genes. They are farmers, seamstresses, tanners, maids, jewelers, accountants, ministers, soldiers, doctors, engineers, nurses, and artists. They are mothers, fathers, grandmothers, grandfathers, sons, daughters, aunts and uncles. They are heroes and villains, anarchists and pacifists, novitiates and agnostics; they are saints and sinners.

Alexis de Tocqueville said, "History is a gallery of pictures in which there are few originals and many copies." Each member of my clan deserves a picture in the following gallery of stories. Because I know I will be traveling with them for another two hundred years and my current cerebral capacities are beginning to slow down, I must capture their originals before copies compromise their being.

Join me as I travel through this gallery.

And, by the way, you can call me whatever name you like. I'm most comfortable, though, with the one by which these clan members have known me — Winifred, or Una for short.

Part 1

1932

1

Rough Sailing

Sunday, January 3, 1932

Una: *Often it is said that one can win the war but lose the peace. The nine years since 1923 prove that. Looking down with sorrow and exasperation, we weep for our dear Ireland. Collins and Griffith sputter their disgust. Pearse drafts an inspiring poem but surrenders to lethargy with a sigh. Tone shakes his head. Parnell escapes to his library to write one of his illustrious missives. Bella and Lizzie furiously compose articles before whispering phrases to Kat and BB. Bridgette prays. Aiden blusters. All of us have sadly had to reexamine our attempts to sway the times. Only Bigger and Sceo appear content as they scurry across the moors after grouse.*

We admit, however, that the number of battle victims has diminished over this second decade of the 20th Century. Fewer men have been shot stepping out of tavern doors. Less women have been branded traitor after feeding orphaned, street urchins from opposing religions. Hardly any children have been silenced while playing along cross-fire lanes. But one life lost is too many. And every living being – in both The Free State and Ulster's Northern Ireland – knows how precious life is.

Despite that knowledge, the political tides of both lands have been constantly churned by swirling undercurrents. Leaders have been consistently inconsistent in sailing their respective ships to safe harbors. Lanterns in coastal lighthouses have been growing dim or have been nefariously placed on jagged rocks. Compasses have purposely been broken. Bear with me as I summarize the reasons for these calamities. First, to the South.

Formally renamed The Free State in '22, its legislating body – Dail Eireann – saw one standing party – Cumann na n'Gaedheal – govern from '22 to now with a stubborn grip on the wheel of the '21 Anglo-Irish Treaty's implementation. William Thomas (W.T.) Cosgrave, as party leader, remains today as the President of the Executive Council and Dail. His imprisonment after the 1916 Easter Uprising, his friendship with Collins and Griffith, and his political acumen serving as MP from Kilkenny since 1917 prepared him well for captaining the Free State ship.

However, gale winds from his opponent Eamon de Valera (we call him Dev) have disturbed the waves as have whirlpools spun by IRA Anti-Treatyites. Their instigated Civil War from '20 –'22 has intensified poor relationships with Great Britain across the channel and with Ulster across the island's northern partitioned border. Despite winning yearly elections since 1917 as an MP, Dev refused to sit in the Dail after 1921. He rejected taking the Treaty's required Oath of Allegiance to the British sovereign. Finally, in 1927, his new party Fianna Fail partnered with the old Sinn Fein party and IRA under an umbrella entitled Republicans. Their alliance won forty-four seats. With such growing support, Dev changed his mind and tried to register in the Dail without taking the Oath of Allegiance. He failed when the clerk of the Dail demanded compliance. Just as Dev was considering a protest, four IRA members murdered Kevin O'Higgins, vice-president of the Dail's Executive Council. The Dial's wind turned against Dev, proposing a bill to retract Fianna Fail's election results unless its new representatives took the oath. Dev compromised. On August 27, 1927, he signed the Dail's registration book but took the oath without swearing on the accompanying Bible. So began his and the Dail's manipulation of set policies.

Now, to Northern Ireland.

Belfast's Sir James Craig, current Prime Minister of Northern Ireland, also faced strong winds while captaining his political vessel during these past years. In the Northern Ireland plebiscite of 1922, a majority of citizens in six counties of Ulster voted to retain their status as part of Great Britain. The boundary between the Free State and Northern Ireland had been set in the Anglo-Irish Treaty negotiations. Despite this victory for Northern Ireland Unionists, their leaders did not want the disenfranchised Nationalists, especially Catholics, to benefit from citizenry in Great Britain.

To that end, the 1923 Craig government "Protestantized" governance policies. The number of Catholics in the civil service declined. Proportional representation in local and national elections was cancelled. Gerrymandering – as our American cousins have called it – decreased the ability of Catholics and Nationalists to represent themselves in Stormont. The predominately Protestant Ulster Volunteer Forces, now entitled the Ulster Special Constabulary, reigned havoc on Catholic minority communities with impunity from courts led by Unionist Protestants. Unemployment grew and the British Parliament was unwilling to provide welfare support. Catholics and Nationalists began to go underground in their protests. Social and economic unrest rippled across the northern lakes over which Craig tried to have control.

My family, from Dublin to Belfast and beyond to America, raised their masts, held fast to their lines, and steered as well as they could through the turbulent waves of the past nine years.

Ach...today I hear some family members gathering below in Bangor. Let us see how they are now faring.

2

The Football Match

Sunday, February 3, 1932

Sunday family dinner at the Irvine's in Dublin was not its typical gathering of like-minded souls. Another substantive win of de Valera's Fianna Fail party seemed inevitable in the national election just two weeks ahead. With it might come the Long One's succession to leadership in the 7th Dail and the ouster of Cosgrove's Cumann na n'Gaedheal (Society of the Gaels-) party, Griffith's and Collins' 1922 pro-treaty successor to Sinn Fein. Pro-Treatyites would be out and Anti-Treatyites would be in. Free Staters would be out; Republicans would be in. Collins' Stepping Stone process would be submerged by the wave of deValera's External Association. Conflicting ideas would soon manifest in conflicting actions. The family was ready first to debate ideas.

Unlike the family's historic debates restricted to elders, this evening's debate welcomed the voices of all present, particularly the young adults. They included Thon and Jon McCormick, sons of Ryan McCormick who was murdered in 1912 for having attempted the assassination of Republican Thomas Clarke. The two boys had been adopted by Billie and Agnes Irvine after their mother and paternal grandmother had abandoned them. Now, twenty-two and twenty years old respectively, they were accomplished scholars and ready to argue any political or cultural issue.

They were particularly interested in debating their biological father's quite opinionated sister, Rachel McCormick, now twenty-six. Taken away from an abusive mother, Rachel had been raised by her eldest brother Liam and his wife BB. With their support, Rachel had immersed herself in the Republican movement. Her education, with Patrick Pearse's sister Margaret at St. Ita's, focused on Irish culture and the covert world of a revolutionary.

Another young adult, Morna McNulty, now twenty-two, quietly listened. Morna and her brother Ian had also been taken in by Liam and BB after the Easter Uprising in '16. On the last night of the Uprising, Liam found Ian sobbing alongside his dog Bigger on a darkened path near Rathmines-Dublin. Ian's father had just been killed by a British soldier. Soon the story of his deceased mother and younger sister emerged. Ian never had to cry again. Both he and his sister had been embraced by the McCormick family. They had also found their life's purpose in the medical field, modeled by their adopted mother BB. Morna was currently serving as a nurse; Ian had just completed his medical studies in America.

Four teen-age children, Kate and Wolfe Irvine as well as Kieran and Maggie McCormick, were absent. They were the birth children respectively of Billie and Agnes Irvine and Liam and BB McCormick. Having been "volunteered" for an afternoon soup kitchen hosted jointly by the Catholic Immaculate Heart of Mary Church and the Abbey Presbyterian Church, their voices would have to wait to be heard.

"It's grand that our children are learning the best of both worlds-spiritual and social," said BB after the younger four had departed earlier in the day. Her words had lingered in Rachel's mind during the afternoon.

Now, as the remaining family members- adult and elder- settled after dinner in the Irvine's salon, Rachel put voice to thought and challenged BB's proclamation.

"And what exactly is the best of those two worlds?" Rachel pugnaciously asked the entire group.

A football match had begun. The first ball was thrown.

"Well," began Thon." We must be grateful that Catholics here in the south can worship as they wish without being persecuted by

Protestants."

"Aye, 'tis true." replied Rachel. "But what good is going to church on Sunday but not to a decent paying job on Monday? Emigration since 1916 has taken a quarter of a million of our citizens to lands across the sea. Ulster in the North has lured our Dublin workers to its linen mills and docks, despite most of those jobs going to Protestant Unionists around Belfast. Where are our Free State industrial jobs?"

"Hold on, now." Thon rebutted. "Ye can easily find work in the civil service, shops or on the farms in the countryside."

Jon lobbed the next football in the air.

"Ach, brother! Don't ye know that most of the civil service jobs are filled by advocates of Cosgrove's governing party – Cumann na n'Gaedheal? And city businesses are still owned by Brits overseas whose intimidated Catholic managers rarely employ their own. They don't even offer wages equal to London-based counterparts. And, when Catholic owned businesses hire, we turn on our own, like during the civil war. We ensure that a Sinn Feiner hires only a Sinn Fein brother, a Fianna Failer hires only a Fianna Failer. Once it's out that ye are one and not the other, God forbid ye keep yer job and, worse yet, yer life, especially as a judge, policeman or fireman. And mix in the power of IRA members – overt or covert. We are a Free State without the freedoms of equality and justice we deserve."

Billie Irvine relished this banter among the next generation as he heard its passion, but not the facts, daily among their elders in the Dail. No longer a member of Redmond's old IPP (Irish Parliamentary Party), he served as an TD (Teachta Dala) representing Dublin West's Cumann na n'Gaedheal.

He threw his own ball onto the field. "And, what do ye say on behalf of the farmers in our Free State? How do ye think they are faring, able now to buy their own land?"

"Ach, they are doing poorly." Rachel exclaimed. "Ye well know that the mortgages they pay to the Provisional government don't stay in our own treasury. Instead, they become annuities sent to the

British government. Those repay loans so ungraciously given us in the 20's by that British monster so that Irish tenants could buy out their British landlords. How senseless was that then as are our continued repayments today. The land has always been ours since the 1600's!" Her face was turning an apoplectic red.

"Tis true," said Thon, catching the ball in air and throwing it backward to her. "But, if deValera wins, we won't have to worry about that. He is running on the pledge that the mortgage annuities will no longer be sent to Britain but will stay in our own Dail's treasury. Thus, the funds collected from farmers will be used for national programs and taxes will be cancelled."

"Wait, wait, wait," exclaimed Liam. "Think a bit about what Dev is proposing. Isn't he saying that land payments asked of farmers would still be leveraged? And wouldn't those same farmers see their payments pay for only partisan activities, not for the entire state? Isn't that asking hens to lay eggs, give them over to the rooster and, subsequently, have the rooster give those same eggs over to his partner the fox?"

Now, Thon's face turned red. A pregnant silence fell on the gathering. The ball fell at rest.

Jon turned to his adopted father Billie and tried to pick up the ball and take it down a different field. "Father, tell us what ye think of Fianna Fail's stand on the Oath." Jon picked up his copy of the *Irish Press*, newly published and managed by none other than deValera himself. "It lays out the stands Dev will take on behalf of us Irish. No oath, no annuities, equal trade with Britain, civil service cuts at the top and expansion at the bottom, Irish language reinstated and a reduction in emigration. What say ye to these?"

Rachel could not wait for Billie's response. She intercepted the fast ball when it passed before her feet.

"Do ye really believe all that rhetoric, Jon? The Long Fellow has gone back and forth on all of these plans so many times. It would spin yer head, not just around, but off. He has already compromised on his last election by registering for the Dail while taking the Oath verbally without swearing on a Bible. Has he campaigned to eliminate the oath in a new Constitution? Nay, he has not. Ach, and where is the money sitting in American banks from the loans he solicited in '21? Ye know he lost the New York Supreme court case in '27 that ruled against him. The American judge required that the remaining $3 million dollars be returned to the shareholders – American and Irish people – who deserve their dividends. Has that happened? Nay. Instead, Dev's waiting to win the election so that donors can reinvest their money in his Finnian Fail newspaper and victorious party when he gains control of the government. Not a pound will be shared equally among all the people of The Free State. He's a swindler and manipulator of public opinion, exploiting our current social and political desires and fears."

Rachel stared at Billie and exhaled one last comment. "How we need the Big One back!" Collins smiled from the beyond.

Just as Billie was ready to respond to Rachel's tirade, there was a clamor at the door. In came the younger cousins. The football game was over for now. It would continue, however, in the next thirteen days before the most monumental of Irish elections.

The taking of sides would divide the Smiley/Irvine/McCormick family.

3

The Nurse and The Professor

February 17, 1932

"Morna? Morna McNulty?" Robert asked of the young woman seated on a bench alongside the path leading into the Botanic Gardens' Tropical Ravine.

Her dark blue cape wrapped itself around slumped shoulders. Its collar was buttoned under a Rubenesque chin below the two straight lines of pursed lips. A white cap, with the emblem of the Belfast Lying-In Hospital on Townsend Street, sat above golden curls. Hints of a grey-blue, nurse's uniform revealed sleeves under the cape that led down to worn gloves. Her skirt exposed ankles with faded white stockings tucked into smudged, brown boots.

"Aye, sir," came the hesitant reply. The gentleman's face looked familiar to Morna, but she wasn't sure why. Contrary to those whom she met in her daily rounds, he was well-dressed. A newly-starched collar secured an expensive plaid tie. His unbuttoned brown, herringbone frock-coat complimented woolen pants. His shoes were polished leather, and his eye glasses were gold rimmed. A tweed vest revealed a gilded, Albert watch chain. The clothing and demeanor obviously displayed a man of wealth.

To compliment the material status, he held tightly to the leash of a bulky mastiff that was waiting for a command.

"Professor Smiley it is, isn't it?" she asked, suddenly recalling the face more than the clothes. "And who is your companion?"

Robert nodded. "Yes, you know me after all." Pointing to the dog, he added, "This is Failinis, my uncle's new dog. His Sceo passed on several months ago."

"Ah," Morna offered. "I remember Sceo well, playing with us and his pals Bigger and Boru right here in this park." She looked away. Her voice lowered. "I was much younger then."

Quickly returning to face the two, she regained her focus. "I'm sorry for yer uncle's loss of such a fine companion, but he's chosen a new one well and given him a noble name. Did ye know that Failinis is one of most beloved Irish mythological characters – the bravest and fiercest of dogs who protects his family against the most powerful of warriors?"

"Yes, my uncle told me about the origin of the name Failinis. Fortunately, this namesake before us has yet to be tested."

A silence engulfed them. She seated; he standing; Failinis waiting.

At exactly the same moment, each said "What brings you here today?" He laughed. She smiled and again lowered her head.

The young man nodded to the dog to approach Morna. Carefully, her right hand reached out to the mastiff whose narrow and straight tail now wagged excitedly. His nose sniffed her boots and, then, stood before the two. Morna stroked the dog's forehead; he nudged her leg and sat down beside her. Neither he nor she were going to move away from each other any time soon.

Robert noticed there were tears forming in Morna's eyes and her hand crumpled a lace handkerchief. She avoided his face yet sensed his hesitation.

"You go first, Miss McNulty. Tell me what brings you here," said Robert, the ever-curious and sensitive philosopher. "May I first sit with you, though?"

She motioned a yes. He took a seat next to her on the bench, but at an appropriate distance.

Morna raised her eyes to the dog before her, not Robert, and started to smooth its long ears. "Do ye know the history of this place for our family, Professor?" Morna started.

"Which families?" asked Robert.

"Ach," Morna replied. "I forget that ye are from America and, though living here now, ye may not know that we're all family by either birth or kindness. This spot is where ashes of our Smiley, Irvine and now McCormick and McNulty elders have been spread among the ferns and gully flowers."

"Ah, yes, I've heard that told by my father's brother, but no Smiley ashes are yet here." Robert claimed.

Silence again followed.

Morna turned to Robert, hand paused above Failinis' head. The canine companion whimpered quietly.

"I must not speak of what he knows not yet," Morna reflected to herself.

Robert thought she was going to say something important, but she looked away. He waited.

She quickly turned back and continued. "Tell me why ye are here?"

As a nurse, she was quite adept at changing topics. She always refocused her women patients when they asked about her own life. Their ailments and secrets would come more quickly if she kept her questions exact and listened without judgment to their answers. Her own secrets would remain within.

Robert played into her professional role. "You may remember that I teach at Queen's College just down the street. Often I walk here with Failinis to consider my lectures or just ponder life's …." He hesitated.

"Purpose?" she queried.

"Aye," he said, looking first at her cap, then at her lovely, cherubic face.

"I do, too," she agreed. "Especially given the election tomorrow when the country and people seem so topsey- turvey on how to lead our future forward."

"But, it's not our country as we're in the North, Morna. Tomorrow's crucial election is in the Free State, not here. We have no need to worry about its outcome."

"Ach, Professor. We do!" Morna's eyes lit up and her cheeks began to flush brighter than her natural rose. "We are families despite the divide. We may not be responsible for the election results tomorrow, but we will be for their impact. Our families reside on both sides of the border – here in Belfast and in Dublin, in the six Ulster and twenty-six Free State counties. No doubt there will be trouble regardless of where we live. Be careful. Many of your students – men and women – will have opinions. Many will speak up. Ye must hear them out and learn."

Robert looked incredulous and thought, "She certainly has a mind of her own that compliments her beauty. "

Failinis sat up and stared directly at the agitated woman.

Morna clutched her handkerchief. "Why have I expressed myself so adamantly? "

"I fear I have stepped over my boundaries, Professor, in so forcefully saying what I have. I hope I haven't offended ye."

Robert turned away to look at the path beside them, returning his gaze back to Morna.

"Miss McNulty, would you join me for tea at Quinlon's? I'd like to hear more of what you are thinking."

Morna hesitated. Despite no one being behind her, she felt a gentle push upon her back.

The three stood up. Led by Failinis, they began down the path out of the garden.

As they disappeared, the branches of a silver maple tree above the bench gently shook. One leaf fell onto the ground. It seemed to curl up into a smile. Morna's mother was pleased.

4

A Second Chance Reunion

February 17, 1932

In Macroom, fifty miles away from Morna, Rachel was considering her own purpose and role in the new independence movement. She had many models to guide her. All were women.

Some were leaders in the 1916 Uprising: Margaret Pearse, Countess Constance Markievicz, and Kathleen Clarke. Others were younger activists who had betrayed Rachel: Christine O'Leary and Molly McKenzie. Within her own family, there were loved ones: Nanna Lizzie, BB, Agnes, and Kat.

Over the past sixteen years, Rachel had become disillusioned by the leaders. Margaret Pearse had become obsessed with elevating her son's leadership role in the Uprising and opposing the Anglo-Irish treaty; in 1921, she served as a Sinn Fein Teachta Dala (TD) representative from Dublin County in the Dail's Lower House. In 1919, the Countess had become the first woman in the world to serve at the Cabinet level as Minister for Labor for the Irish Dail and then Fianna Fail member of Parliament. She died in office in 1927. Kathleen Clarke had resigned from Cumman na m'Ban to help found Fianna Fail and, in 1928, became its senator to the Upper House of the Dail. Rachel was not enamored of these who had risen in the ranks of activists to, in her mind, just become politicians. She believed they had turned their backs on what would bring independence to all of Ireland. It wasn't just talk that would reject the British imposed Commonwealth status, partition from the North and economic dependence.

Rachel's rejection of politics had also been informed by its undertow of revenge and violence. She considered Christine O'Leary as a political agitator with passion and emotion rather than intellect and logic. Christine's accusations of Patrick McCann in 1916 and Ian McNulty in 1919 as traitors to the cause had, to Rachel, maligned their bravery and commitment to justice. That character flaw in Christine was coupled by Rachel's distain for Molly McKenzie. After all, Molly had framed Rachel for the 1921 murder of Father O'Hare in Macroom. And, tripling that, was the Countess' role in planning Molly's subterfuge to revenge Rachel's refusal to obey the Countess. Thus, after three betrayals by political women, no rationale for a political role nor violence would inform her role in Ireland's independence movement.

Who now were the positive role models for Rachel? What would convince her of a proper place in Ireland's future? Only her family and that mystical encounter with the figure in white outside Kilkenny ten years ago would guide her.

Rachel was considering these questions and that figure as she waited in Macroom to meet with Ian McNulty, Morna's brother. He had recently returned from a decade of medical studies and practice in New York City and was, himself, determining his role in the continuing independence movement. She was pondering hers and his when he appeared, walking quickly over Macroom's Old Footbridge.

Rachel had reflected on the few letters exchanged between Ian and her over the decade. In the first years, the norm was one page sent only three or four times. Rachel never apologized for her opinionated rejection of Ian's marriage proposal. Ian did not apologize for his surprising emigration to study long-term in New York. Instead, Ian described the studies he had undertaken and, in response, she wrote about her work with the American funded, Irish White Cross that aided children during the civil war. Soon, only Christmas cards had graced their hands and perfunctory well-wishes their minds. No messages of love were reprieved nor assumed. She was surprised at this year's Christmas card telling of his upcoming February arrival in Dublin and hope that they could meet at her convenience. She had assented.

As he approached, Macroom's 14th Century Castle behind him and the River Sullane roaring below the footbridge, she recalled an argument they had had in 1916 about Jonathan Swift's *Gulliver's Travels*. When walking home from St. Enda's, each had insisted that the other was a Lilliputian prone to petty power plays and not a Gulliver seeking to understand justice. Rachel wondered how they would see each other now.

Despite the passage of time, the two embraced upon reaching each other. A kiss on the other's cheek was rendered.

"Ah, Rachel. Ye look fine," Ian spoke.

"As do ye, Ian," she replied.

A pause in the exchange gave them time to consider which way to walk and the direction of their conversation. Toward the sentimental woods and nature or back to the practical town and commerce? As always in their youthful relationship, Rachel made the decision.

"Let's wander a bit on the path along the river."

"Lovely, " he said, taking her hand and tucking it under his own arm.

For the next hour, they shared their experiences over the past years, continuing their teenage and young adult friendship as though Rachel had never withdrawn her love from him. He regaled her with tales of the hustle and bustle of America's largest city and intrigued her with the diversity of immigrants. He held back on the sorrows and prejudice faced by his fellow Irish men and women. He did admit, however, that landlord greed and tenant poverty in both America and Ireland were similar despite their different latitudes. New York City's over crowded tenements, factories and rat infested streets were like Ireland's cramped row houses, stifling mills and polluted air. Disease and disillusionment were the same to the lower class no matter where in the world.

He added a few happier events such as accompanying the McKenzies on family outings: sparkling colored lights of Christmas trees along a large park in the center of the city, families sailing on the Hudson River under a huge bridge, fireworks above the Statue of

Liberty on the Fourth of July, summer fairs in the countryside of New Jersey and picnics at a beach on a spit of land called Long Island.

Rachel was reserved in sharing her past decade. She described attending plays written by Erin McCann, hearing poets like Oscar Wilde swoon his audiences, and dancing to fiddle playing at the tavern of Ian's grandmother in Coalisland. Rachel did mention that, after the Irish White Cross disbanded in 1928, she had become a volunteer with the reorganized Irish Republican Army, a vestige of the old Anti-Treaty faction that still disavowed the Free State/ Commonwealth status of Ireland and the partition of the North. She did not explain her role.

She fretted that, in 1931, the Cosgrave administration's Special Powers Tribunal had outlawed the IRA, as had Dev's Fianna Eirean party and Cumann na mBan.

"This is a travesty of freedom," she exclaimed, gripping his arm tightly. "That's why ye and I must vote for deValera next week, no matter what we think of him as a waffling politician. Mick would be ashamed of the strictures his and Cosgrave's old party are now strangling us with." Rachel's pace had hastened, leading Ian to increase his own to keep arm in arm.

"Ach, Rachel." He held her speed back a bit to his own. "I see ye have not changed your gift of argumentation. Although, I must admit, you speak much more logically than passionately as in our last meeting."

Ian's tug and words caused her to stop in half stride. She could feel her heart start to pound, but not because of her boisterousness and energy. Her face flushed, just as she knew those of her Aunties Agnes', Kat's and BB's did whenever their husbands gave compliments.

Ian noticed the flair and realized he just might have a chance to win her back.

"Shouldn't we continue that discussion?" he asked.

5

Playing Parts

Sunday, March 20, 1932

Erin McCann's leg stretched out to rest his foot upon the crocheted top of a footstool before him. Midnight exploits along back streets during the Uprising, across soggy bogs behind Anti-treaty encampments and inside the damp interiors of mountain caves had exacerbated his limp. Now, a crippled leg and bent back curbed his mobility. At age thirty-six, Erin's lower torso resembled an octogenarian's. His face, however, did not. The rosy cheeks, meticulously cornered moustache, and shimmering blue eyes tricked a viewer into ignoring the lower body and, instead, becoming mesmerized by his radiant countenance. After all, Erin was the consummate playwright and Thespian who could redirect his audience with the flick of a wrist or a wink of an eye.

He had refined that ability both on the stage and off through many a covert operation, supporting a role few in this current decade knew from his past – few except his peers in the McCann family and Irvine clan.

In contrast to a compromised stature, his stance on a unified Ireland had never wavered, initiated by his formative school days at St. Enda's when tutored by Patrick Pearse and Billie Irvine, embellished by his loyalty to Michael Collins during the Anglo-Irish treaty negotiations, and amplified in his decade-long theatrical career. His plays had grown audiences from Dublin's Abbey Theatre to Irish-American stages in New York City, Boston and Chicago. Now, however, he prioritized writing scripts and wearing masks for the reformed IRA's strategy of undercover actions. Erin was one of its star actors.

He had disembarked on Friday from the New York to Liverpool RMS Majestic and, then, from a Dublin steamer on Saturday. Billie and Agnes Irvine met him at the ferry dock and welcomed him to their home. After a fine meal of rabbit and cabbage, he was enjoying the Irvine family comfort before a glowing fireplace. Billie would never know that Erin had recently negotiated millions of US dollars from Irish-American whiskey investors to be transferred by J.P. Morgan and Company Vice President and family member Francis McKenzie on Monday. Francis had set up a special account for Erin in one of the bank's Dublin affiliates.

Erin would allow himself a 30 minute intermission from playing his covert role to solicit the opinions of his companions, young and old, on the current Free State government. In the February election, Dev's Fianna Fail had won 15 more seats than Cosgrave's Cumann na Gaedheal. Cosgrave did not contest Dev's succession on March 9th as the President of the Executive Council of Dail. Already speaking Dev's and his own true lines, Erin had provoked Billie by suggesting that the Dail completely cut economic ties with London. The world-wide Depression that had started in 1920 had crashed the New York Stock Exchange in '29. Diminished remittances from US, Canada and Australian emigrants back to both parts of Ireland had been devastating. The only benefit had been for the Free State to resort to its own means and build up a self-sufficiency independent from the major world powers, particularly the US and Britain. Billie, who represented Cumann na Gaelheal in the Dublin parliament, was its special envoy to London. He was currently negotiating a UK-Free State trade agreement that would include Free State relations with Ulster. On behalf of Dev, however, Erin was trying to convince Billie to be cautious.

Billie sat frowning before Erin. Agnes was amused. The Irvine teenagers, Katie and Wolfe, waited attentively for the next words.

Also, waiting was Boru. His aging torso, like Erin's, looked physically his twelve dog years times seven human. At eighty-four, the faithful guard snored louder, ate less and knew more about the Irvines than any living creature. Like Erin, he also loved them unconditionally.

"Nay, Billie. I am not proposing an all-out war with Britain nor Ulster," retorted Erin, "We've had too much of brazen bravado and bullets. I'm talking about attacking the source of partition: the fear in the brainwashed minds of common people in Ulster, be they Catholic or Protestant, politician or professor, worker or farmer. There are multiple ways to convince our allies in Ulster about our common welfare instead of our differences. That can undermine Craig and his disciples. We're all Irish after all…and we all love to banter."

"And pray, what are those ways?" Billie asked. "Given the London Parliament's Statute of Westminster allowing each of the Dominions in the Commonwealth to act as its own Sovereign nation, we have more than enough work here in our new Free State about which to raise our voices and plan development programs. Let Ulster be and care for her own while we deal with ourselves. God knows they had the chance to join us in '20 and voted against it."

Agnes looked appalled. "How can ye say that, Mr. Irvine? Ye know that the vote was taken under duress with many Catholics and Nationalists threatened if they voted at all. It wasn't a fair election."

Billie nodded defeat. "Aye, ye're right, dear Agnes. The election was a sham. But, we have much ahead of us now to prove that they should have joined us. If the policies that Dev is able to move forward actually improve our economy, it will enable our own people of different walks to live in peace. That will convince the North that they can do the same. It was Collins' dream for the future and we must fulfill it, even if we're currently being led by his nemesis."

"On that you make a good point," replied Erin. "Michael never trusted Dev. But, our economy must not rely on British benevolence during trade negotiations. While their London representatives may promise you profit sharing in ship-building, farming or whiskey production partnerships, you must uncover their ulterior motives. Rest assured, behind a curtain of cooperation is the proverbial trap door of greed. And, by the way, be careful of our own. Who is the Dail's primary lawyer reading those agreement documents with you? I bet he's a friend of a friend of a friend who is in the pocket of the House of Lords."

Billie cleared his throat, a habit that he always repeated when preparing to speak in the Dail. All three Irvines knew what would follow, even their newly acquired, second dog named Gruagach (meaning wizard) – Grua for short – was becoming just as wise as Boru.

"You speak truth, Erin. We do need to be careful in our talks, both among ourselves and with Prime Minister McDonald. But remember he grew up in Scotland and represents the Labour Party. I believe he will be quite conciliatory in respecting the rights of our Free State within the new Sovereign allowances. I....."

Just as Billie was beginning his lecture, a knock at the front door drew everyone's attention, except Erin's and Agnes'.

They exchanged knowing glances. Tonight, they were awaiting a letter from Erin's Belfast IRA contact. Knowing his mission in the US and how the funds raised would be used, Agnes like Erin would play her parts – the activist and the writer.

She quickly went to the door and returned carrying an unmarked letter and package. "Ah, Erin, here is a note and package for you from the Belfast Irish Repertory Theater. Perhaps it is a copy of your new poetry book with a congratulatory message?"

"Indeed, it must be. Let's hope the message is positive." He took both the note and package, placing them on his lap. "I'll get to them later. In the meantime, let us continue our conversation. Agnes, what do you think?"

Having already practiced subterfuge in her activist role, she now displayed her skill of changing subjects, announcing, "I think Kat, BB and I should write a fine call to question the women in Belfast and Derry in next week's Our Ireland edition. What a superb idea to gain their thoughts on this matter, don't ye think, Erin? And, actually, it's perfect timing as Katie and I are leaving next Thursday for the Easter holiday with the Smileys. BB and Maggie are joining us there."

"Now wait, wait, wait." said Billie. "This is all news to me. What is going to happen to us men left behind? Won't Thon and Jon be home for the holiday and Wolfe here off from school? What will we eat on Easter Day and the week afterwards?"

"Oh, Athair (Father in Irish Gaelic). Fear not!" exclaimed Wolfe. "Mother has already volunteered us four to serve at St. Mary's Easter luncheon plus its dinners to the needy throughout Easter week. Father O'Malley was so pleased to know we men would be there on such a special day and throughout the week. Too often he said just the nuns and older, widowed women offer to help. Don't ye think the laid-off factory workers and their families need to see us all – men included – caring for them?"

Billie stared at his young son. "Ach. How did ye get to be so wise and kind, young man? Ye are definitely ye're mother's son and ye shame me so. Of course, we'll be there. And, speaking of voices, I'll write about our time there for a speech in the Dail."

Agnes coughed. Staring first at Billie, then glancing in Wolfe's direction as the young lad scratched the ears of the new dog, Billie quickly understood the not-so-subtle reprimand. "And Wolfe. Would ye help me write the speech?" Billie offered. Wolfe smiled.

The conversation ended. Erin repositioned his foot on the stool. Agnes got up to refill the empty plate of scones. Billie unfolded the evening paper and started to read the headlines aloud. Wolfe stoked the fire, and Katie picked up her knitting. The family settled back into their expected roles. Only Boru knew that, like his own, those would be challenged sooner than each thought. He only had a short time to train his successor.

6

Larger Than Life

March 27, 1932

Following the noon mass on this Easter Sunday, the hall of St Mary's Refuge was full of Dublin's best: loquacious citizenry, culinary delights, musical instruments and hope. Father Shawn O'Malley and the Sisters of Mercy blessed all sorts of social strata, dietary preferences, creative proclivities and political perspectives. Whatever the like or dislike – God and his disciples extoled communal oneness.

The four men- TD Billie Irvine, McCormick sons Thon and Jon, and young Wolfe Irvine – joined the activities. They participated with varied attention and intent. Billie noted the faces of men fractured by years of unemployment or underemployment. Thon listened to stories of skirmishes during the War of Independence and post-battle shenanigans at local pubs. Jon was enraptured by the musicians, entertaining the attendees with fiddled rounds that erupted boisterous singing. Only Wolfe sensed the whole scene as though it were on stage at the Ulster Literary Theater.

His mother Agnes knew that Wolfe was a special child and, indeed, he was. At age seven, he had contracted a rare virus and lost his sight by age 10. Agnes had refused to accept that her second born would live a life of pity and remorse due to what others considered a handicap. He never did. Agnes, Kat and BB had joined with doctors and nurses to engender his self-esteem and independence. When called upon, the male members of the family had done the same. Only two men and a dog never needed that request.

Erin McCann was one of the three. He took the lead on Wolfe's education, ensuring the boy attended the best Catholic primary and secondary schools in Dublin. During their forays to the sea and the Munros of MacGillycuddy's Reeks in Kerry, Erin imbued in Wolfe the love of natural sounds. To master human ones, they read fables, speeches, novels, and poetry together. They acted out all of Erin's plays. Wolfe learned to decipher the literary meaning of words while imagining their sentiments. More importantly, he learned from his favorite uncle that no handicap could limit one's brilliance, nor one's motivation to serve others and country.

The second was Father Shawn O'Malley himself. Raised in the workhouses of Dublin, he had a great sensitivity to those missing a physical or emotional anchor to a stable life. His own gentleness and that of Ian McNulty had saved Shawn, as an IRB novitiate, on a night in February 1919 outside Eamon and Kat's Belfast home. That was when Christine O'Leary had killed Samuel Acheson and ordered Ian to shoot Shawn. Ian had not. Instead, he had let Shawn go. After encountering the lad months later with his dying mother at the Henry Street Clinic, both Ian and Rachel had taken Shawn under their eagle wings. He became enamored with the pacifism of the Quaker faith and had carried that belief back to his Catholic roots as a seminarian. Now a parish priest, Father O'Malley was taking Wolfe under the church's spiritual wings – both in school and in the Belfast community. Shawn knew that Wolfe would bring insight and light to others.

As Shawn approached the lad near a table full of lamb stew, onions and potato roast, he contemplated Wolfe's gentleness. "What is it about this young man who never parses out life into divisions? Why does he continuously treat members of differing circles with an integrity that is so pure and good? Surely, he is blessed."

"How are you this early afternoon, Master Wolfe?" asked the young priest of his tutee.

"Grand, Father. We're just grand," replied Wolfe, easily recognizing the priest's voice. "I am enjoying hearing everyone and smelling that savory shepherd's pie."

"I see you have brought your friend, Larger," Father O'Malley leaned down and stroked the head of Wolfe's Border Collie. "He's quite a companion, isn't he?" Wolfe nodded and placed his hand about the dog's right ear and wrapped the feathered tips around his fingers.

"Tell me again why you named him Larger?" asked the priest.

Wolfe smiled. "Ach, he was a gift from my Uncle Ian before he left for medical school in America. His own dog Bigger had just passed away so a new one had to be found. Uncle Ian and I went to the McNulty farm in Coalisland and found a farmer whose bitch had just laid a litter. The smallest one came over to me and licked my hand. Bigger had been named in the hope that he would grow, but never did. I said to Uncle Ian that perhaps this one would be larger than Bigger. The name seemed just right. At least, now, he's larger than any smaller dog, don't you agree?"

"Aye, and so he is. You've also trained him well to accompany you wherever you go. He certainly is giving you a larger life than many of us have!" The priest noticed Larger pressing against Wolfe's leg.

"Yes, now I have six feet, four ears and two noses. I just wish his two eyes could read all the books I want to learn from. I feel like such a burden to Uncle Erin, my sister Katie and fellow classmates." Wolfe's sigh was audible to the priest.

"Nay, Wolfe," retorted Father O'Malley. "Think of it this way. Every time they read with you, you are reinforcing their own memory of the words. And, because you all talk about what you understand, I hear from your classmate Rory O'Donald that you have caused them to check their own understanding of such luminaries as Aristotle and James Joyce. By far, you are the better teacher and conversant than I."

Wolfe smiled. "If that were only true, Father. How I would love to keep learning and teach someday."

"You will, dear lad. You will. Come," said Shawn, "let's learn from our companions today."

As the two plus Larger ambled the center aisle of the dining hall,

Wolfe heard the numerous voices and sounds – the chatter, laughter, and anticipation of a full meal. He felt the energy around him- the distress of the men, the desperation of wives, the anxiety of children. But he also perceived their determination, their hopes, and their gratitude. He sensed it all.

Father O'Malley offered a prayer. Food was served. The music began and hope reigned larger than life.

7

The Women's New Circle

March 30, 1932

The seven figures followed the Bangor Lough path to the Beastie King Tavern, still managed by Maud McCann, mother of Erin and Finbar. Now sixty-seven, Maud had proven that it was she who supplied the pub with food, drink and restoration for the weary. Her husband Thomas had supplied the IRA informants with their instructions. Since his passing five years prior, Thomas' spirit still inhabited the bar. Regulars often commented that they heard his laughter and felt his foot tap in rhythm to theirs on the bar rail. Particular IRA members swore they heard his whispered messages. Others heard several women chiding him to behave. Maud was sure one was her aunt Sister Bridgette, the McCann member who had devoted her life to the spiritual side of the independence movement. Today, Maud would remember her husband's and aunt's banter when guiding the next generation's gathering at the tavern.

Agnes and Kate Irvine, with BB and Maggie McCormick, were arriving along with Rachel McCormick and Kat and Liza Smiley to determine their roles in galvanizing women from both The Free State and Northern Ireland. The Inde Pen newspaper had published Kat and BB's call for action just this past Easter Sunday. Already, numerous commitments by script and speech had been conveyed to the two. Maud had offered to be the conduit between these volunteers and her dear Aunt Bridgette's family that had been formed "in accord" with Uncle Aiden McKnight. Family was family, after all, with or without a church blessing. Maud had closed the Beastie

King to hear the current generation's decisions on nation building. She would listen carefully to the women and girls to charter their courses with them.

Maud knew she had to lead them to safe harbors, particularly Rachel and Agnes. Intrigues against them were already rumored, initiated by newly elected Fianna Failer TDs and various IRA members including the nefarious Molly McKenzie. While retaliation for these intrigues by certain members of Maud's family was unpredictable, the impact was certain. Maud knew of Agnes' capacity for subterfuge when she had exposed Nathan Dickson to Rory O'Connor during the Four Courts siege in '22. Maud also recognized Rachel's passion for action before considering its effect. Though Maud had no control over either woman, she was as wise in business negotiations with market women and serving maids as she was with estate manager wives and their wealthy patrons. She had anticipated the imminent conversation and laughed to herself: "Thomas, stop ye're blustering about how I advise our friends today. I'll fare far better than ye when I listen first and then speak." She could hear her deceased husband's "Humph" and her Aunt Bridgette's "Carry on, good lass."

As the door opened to the tavern, Maud noted the mixed bustle of laughter and chatter. First to enter was Rachel, speaking adamantly to Agnes.

"How can ye believe what any newspaper or bulletin is saying these days? Will we Irish never know or tell the truth?" queried Rachel.

Agnes answered while placing her shawl on one of eight chairs neatly arranged by Maud around a table in the tavern's main room.

"Ye're right, dear Rachel. The battle of words between Dev's newly circulated paper *The Irish Press* and the Murphy family's *Irish Independent* proves that our countrymen choose to read stories that only serve their partisan views. After his win last month, Dev wants the policies of Fianna Fail in his *Press* to garner support and those of Cumann na n'Gaedheal to be diminished, if not disparaged. The

Independent is just as biased against Dev's Presidency as it is biased for Cumann nan'Gaedheal."

Maud joined the two. "'Tis true. The battle is about who gets to hear which side. Just this morning, I went to Mrs. Gordon's for the morning goods and paper. Wouldn't ye know, she no longer carries the *Independent*. She said her son, a new recruit to the local IRA, told her not to sell it or she'd be sorry. The only paper she had was the *Press*. What are we coming to when a son threatens his own Mum?"

The remaining six women considered this last remark as they somberly placed their parcels of eggs, bread, tea and milk on the tavern counter before settling wraps on their respective chairs. Each, in turn, kissed the forehead of the elder Maud. She, in turn, kissed them back.

"Let me help ye with the tea, Auntie," offered Liza. The youngest of this august group at age thirteen, she was practicing the Smiley graces inherited from her Gran Lizzie after whom she was named. "Don't decide anything until we return," she pleaded. "I want to be part of whatever we do." In that assertion, she sounded like her Great Gran Bella McKnight Irvine or was it Bella's brother Uncle Aiden McKnight?

"Never fear," stated her Aunt BB. "We want to hear what yer thoughts are along with the ideas of the rest of us. God and our fellow women need ye."

Rachel frowned at this reference to God needing anything, especially from such a young girl as Liza. Forgetting her own voice at that age, Rachel thought: *"I'll surely need to speak up strongly with this group of idealists."*

After the tea had been set and grubbery partially consumed, the conversation had moved rapidly from topic to topic, action to action, and finally to decisions.

Maud, as the matriarch and close ally to multiple leaders within the newly reformed IRA, emerging political parties and affiliated organizations, summarized the agreements.

"My dear ones. Let me attempt to capture our rich discussion and proposed decisions. I hear that we will continue to contribute to *Our Ireland* paper through the Inde Pen letters. In order to offer the background to these letters, we will research and write articles as well. Those will be based on our talking with women throughout the Free State, hearing their needs and their thoughts about addressing those needs. We will seek financial support from the women in the suffragette movement as well as sympathetic business women and wives of company owners. We will represent the voices of all women – poor, rich; home makers, professionals; Catholic, Protestant; Finnian Fail, Cumann na n'Gaedheal, Labour, Independents, and Farmers' Party. We will be a sounding board for truths spoken by any of our sisters – young, middle-aged, or old."

"Have I heard ye well?" asked Maud.

The women nodded in agreement – some more energetically than others. They, then, went on to identify the roles each would take to carry out these decisions.

BB and Kat would continue to be lead writers for Inde Pen in *Our Ireland*. Maud, Rachel and Agnes would quietly engage the women with whom they worked and volunteered to hear their concerns and solutions. They would reach out, particularly, to Morna whose work took her into workhouses and prisons. (Today, she had been unable to join them since she was attending a clinic for women and their children in the Crumlin Road Gaol.) Kate and Liza would listen to their schoolmates and various youth club members recounting their daily lives. Writing their own articles, Kate and Liza's works would be featured in Our Ireland under the name of Young Inde Pens.

Roles had been chosen and fixed among the eight. But not all were singular nor exclusive. Rachel and Agnes knew they had other roles to play – those that would be kept secret from the family. Kat and BB would increase their travels to the various clinics their mother had established. Conversations with patients and staff there would confirm factual information and give life to their writings as well as to inform their husband's activities – whatever Eamon and Liam choose to undertake politically. Kate and Liza's roles would expand their virtues as they transformed from listeners to activists. For now, the eight would commit to their part in this family effort.

After they departed, Maud reflected on the day. She swore she felt a kiss on her forehead and heard Aunt Bridgette's voice saying again "Carry on, dear lass." Maud nodded and said to herself "Aye. We shall."

8

Many Windows

April 30, 1932

Morna looked out her 2' by 2' window in the tiny room she rented from Mrs. Henderson on the Shankill Road in Belfast. The four panes of glass within the square frame gave her four views of the neighborhood: children playing with sticks pushing discarded cans on the road; men slumped over in doorways of grey stucco, row houses; women leaning out of windows to shake the dust and fleas from worn blankets; and empty flower baskets with chipped green, painted edges. Four views of Belfast's crowded neighborhoods – four views of the city's economic woes from the '29 Wall Street Crash and its subsequent Depression still plaguing the city. Morna could not see above these four quarters, but assumed the sky was grey and a storm pending. She could feel the darkness and dampness increase.

"I hope those children come inside quickly enough to get warm once the pellets begin," she worried.

As a nurse in Belfast's Public Health Department, she was a practiced observer of medical conditions, particularly those related to sanitation and the welfare of children. She had been encouraged to enter the field of health education by letters from her brother Ian when he was studying medicine in New York City. He had described an internship in the slums where specialized doctors and nurses cared for the indigent. Morna, already a licensed nurse at the Lying In Hospital, had been deeply moved by her brother's compassion and insights. She decided to follow, not in but alongside, his footsteps in Belfast.

The city's medical statistics were worrying: 45,000 (1/4th to 1/3rd of the formerly working male population) were unemployed; the infant mortality rate was 97 out of 1,000; and 20% of all children received no medical or dental assistance. There was much work to do. Fortunately, she was recruited during a recent visit to the Lying In Hospital by Dr. T.F.S. Fulton, Chief of the Belfast Education Committee's school medical service. She jumped at the chance to join his staff. Now, with a small group of outreach professionals, she inspected neighborhood homes, schools, factories and, of course, local workhouses. On her own, she volunteered in the women's section of the Crumlin Road Gaol. Morna had opened the window of her heart and skills to a worthy calling.

Today, as she collected her sack with basic medical supplies and an observation notebook, she thought of another window she had recently opened – or had it been opened by the man with whom she was now confiding, Robert Smiley? Their talks began first at Quinlon's and continued every weekend since then during walks in Botanic Gardens and along the Bangor coastline near the Smiley's home. They learned that each had lost parents early in their lives – his by tuberculosis and desertion; hers by childbirth and murder. Each had been given the greatest gift of loving families who had adopted them – he the McKenzies, she the McCormicks. Each had been able to study and secure careers that were respected: he a professor, she a nurse.

More important than these family similarities, however, was their growing ability to share their most personal fears and hopes. Never before had Morna been able to do that – not with her brother Ian, her adopted parents the McCormicks nor her adopted siblings – Rachel, Thon or Jon. She had kept all her pain and dreams to herself. Now, she realized she did not need to do that. Here was a man who seemed to listen to every word she said and to always have a shamrock-embroidered handkerchief ready for her tears. And, likewise, she listened to him. Instead of a handkerchief, she offered him an open ear and heart which he seemed to dearly appreciate. They also were able to laugh together, a welcome habit she was beginning to cultivate.

"Ah, I wonder what lies ahead for Robert and me," she pondered as she opened her door, closed it and started down the stairs toward the street.

Entering Shankill Road, she opened her umbrella as the skies had also opened with torrents of rain. She could almost hear the protests of the gods above in the rumble of thunder...or was that the sound of workers protesting? She wasn't sure.

9

Years Need Not Part Family

May 15, 1932

Eamon and his nephew Robert left the grounds of Queen's University together without saying a word. Robert had just completed his philosophy lecture on the aspects of a just life according to Socrates and Plato. Like his uncle who offered the same lesson in 1919, Robert gave an assignment to his students: Define what is meant by a just life according to one of the philosophers we have studied this session. Then, propose your own in contrast or agreement with that philosophy.

Robert was a more pragmatic professor than Eamon, consistently asking his students to relate philosophy to their current lives. Thus, the last piece of this assignment was to answer the question: How can you act justly to address the current unemployment in Northern Ireland?

Eamon had been in the last row of the theater hall listening to his nephew's lecture.

"Ach," the aging professor reflected. "I'm sitting in the exact spot where Michael Collins sat that day thirteen years ago when I asked my students to define a just life. How I wish he were with us here today to answer that question again."

Now, as uncle and nephew left the university grounds and turned onto Stranmillis Road, their thoughts appeared at first blush to be years apart. Eamon was thinking of his final conversation in '22 with Michael just before the nation lost its finest leader. Robert was thinking of his conversation the day before with Morna.

"Ye cannot believe the conditions on Falls Road at the work-house, Robert." Morna had said. "Children are breathing in the toxic dust of flax. I see them in my clinic and weep, for I know the devil tuberculosis is not far ahead of them, waiting to take them hostage. Their mothers and fathers, especially Catholics, feel hopeless when factories lay them off and they are underpaid in the work relief programs. Where are they to earn a living such that their children can go to school, not to work? What can our politicians do to right this wrong?"

"It's true what you say, Morna." Robert responded. "Working conditions are pitiful today and unemployment has risen drastically in the last three years. Married men have two choices – "indoor relief" whereby their families enter the workhouses and exchange work for accommodation and sustenance. Or they can live outside the work-house and work on "outdoor relief" schemes such as constructing roads and government structures. Look at who is building the new Stormont Parliament on Dundonald Road in Belfast."

Robert shook his head. "I agree with the government that men should be working when on relief, but their payment must be a fair wage in cash, not in food or chits for services. Also, hiring should be equally apportioned between Catholic and Protestant. Finally, it should not be required that the man be married to secure relief as many single men are suffering, too." He was almost out of breath at the end of this assertion.

Morna, while impressed by Robert's newspaper knowledge, sought direction from her personal experiences. The two young people seemed to represent two sides of the perception coin: one informed by ideas, the other by circumstances; one by lofty thoughts, the other by grounded reality.

"Oh, Robert." Morna began. "I heard last week that in Glasgow, a married man gets 35 shillings a week for such work; here he receives only 12. Are we still being punished for being Irish? And while more Protestants are being hired than Catholics, it appears that both groups are uniting to object to their common conditions. It's shameful. It just isn't fair. What can we do?"

Robert faced her. "We'll do what is morally right. Socrates believed that a just man is wise and good so he should act in an intelligent and fair manner. I strongly believe that. We must help folks become wise by helping them understand how they can change their lives. They must also disavow violent actions to retain a moral high ground. If not, they will contribute to the oppressors who relish criticizing anyone who is being destructive. The elite need not have the upper hand legally. I would submit that addressing demands peacefully is what any fair and just person would honor today."

Morna turned her head away from Robert. She was learning more and more about this man. She did not yet feel comfortable disagreeing openly with him on what she considered a naïve strategy for a peaceful reconciliation among the Northern Ireland people or between the North and South. She had seen too much unjust subjugation of workers by factory and mill owners. Now, she sensed a festering agitation among the exploited. Strikes and protests were being planned, particularly within the Belfast Trades Council. She knew frustration would explode in anger sooner rather than later. Robert needed to hear that and so he had the previous evening. Now, he pondered its content.

Eamon, likewise, was remembering a conversation, one that had moved him deeply. After his philosophy class in 1919, he and Michael Collins had talked at length about the meaning of a just life. Several students had prompted both men to consider three lenses through which such a life could be viewed: political, cultural and economic. Eamon cherished the writings submitted for this assignment.

The one he cherished the most, however, was contained in a letter from Michael sent a month after the class. Surprising Eamon, Collins had actually completed the class assignment as though he were Eamon's student. Later in 1922 under the Hungry Tree in Dublin, they had returned to it during their last conversation, a month before

Collins was assassinated. The consummate historian, Collins had reconfirmed his views.

Now, those views were memorialized in the former leader's own handwriting, phrases of which had been woven into many of his speeches – repeated now after his death. Eamon kept Collins' letter in a Bible by his and Kat's bed. In times of turmoil, he would reread it. Now, in his mind as he walked next to his nephew, he reflected on some of its most memorable phrases.

> *The pertinacity of Irish civilization was due to the democratic basis of its economic system, and the aristocracy of its culture…It was the reverse of Roman civilization in which the State was held together by a central authority…*
>
> *Gaelic civilization was quite different. The people of the whole nation were united, not by material forces, but by spiritual ones. Their unity was not of any military solidarity. It came from sharing the same traditions. It came from honouring the same heroes, from inheriting the same literature, from willing obedience to the same law, the law which was their own law and reverenced by them.*
>
> *This democratic social polity, with the exaltation of the things of the mind and character, are the essence of ancient Irish civilization, and must provide the keynote for the new.*

Tonight, Eamon would share the entirety of Michael's letter with Robert. Perhaps, the years between uncle and nephew would not separate them, but rather bind them to each other. And, perhaps, it would give Robert direction for his own just life.

10

Beyond the Cackling Goose and Brawling Bull

May 30, 1932

"Ye're a cackling goose, Rachel" exclaimed Thon.

"And ye're a brawling bull," she responded.

The two McCormick family members – related as nephew and aunt – were continuing a rousing argument that had started on their way home from Thon's football match in Newtonards, Northern Ireland. Their debate was now in its third, "hand-passed" back, walking toward Bangor along the Belfast Lough path.

Thon raised his voice over the blustering, Spring wind. "Ach! Ye're just as Ian constantly describes ye when yer opinions of disagreement are loudly voiced. How he has managed ye over the last months since his return from America only the blessed Lord knows," Thon stated emphatically.

"Listen to me, young man. No one manages me, not Ian nor the blessed Lord. I can take good care of meself, thank ye, and my opinions arm me against men as adamant and ignorant as ye." Rachel's face was turning a fiery red.

"And" she continued, "I am not a cackling goose. Geese don't cackle; they honk. And I certainly don't honk ," she retorted.

Thon, started to laugh. "And, dear Aunt Rachel, if we are now at the ending kick of our conversation, I can say back to ye that I'm not – nor was Ian – a brawling bull. Bulls don't brawl. They grunt and snort."

Rachel's demeanor changed in an instant. Ever since he was little, her nephew always made her laugh. He calmed her as she started to grin.

"See how more logical we have become over the last fourteen years since ye last called Ian a cackling goose. What year did that teasing start when everyone in our family began to use that term for him, including ye? 1918, wasn't it?" he asked.

"Aye," she said. "It was then when Ian and I were just youngins', I a mature twelve and Ian fourteen. Ye were only ten and yer little brother Jon was nine." Rachel sighed. "So much time, so many losses and so many gains since then. And yet here we are: you at twenty-four, I at twenty-six, and half of this island still arguing about the meaning of terms – Nationalists, Unionists, Socialists, Communists." She paused for a moment, having lost the stream of her verbal momentum.

"Let's sit for a while," Thon suggested as they rounded Wilson Point with a view of the Lough before them and Bangor to their east. He knew he only had a momentary chance to win a three point goal in the rational that would be in play during their argument.

"Aye," she said. "Ye need to explain again why ye are running off to a job across the Channel. Of all places, Thon, couldn't ye choose Glasgow in Scotland or Aberystwyth in Wales? Why London, the den of our adversaries?"

He took his stance on the debate playing field. "First, Rachel. They are not our adversaries. My fellow footballers on the Bangor Football Club team are good lads. Ye know Tommy and Jim Lawson. Both have been good friends to me since I met them at Foyle College in Derry. Their family invited me many times for outings at their Portrush home. We've had so many discussions – not debates – about Unionist versus Nationalist views, similarities between Catholics and Protestants, desires of workers and bosses. Their da is a kind person who convinced me of the economic benefits aligning with Great Britain. He's a Protestant like my father – your brother Ryan – and Uncle Eamon. Have ye, as a McCormick, forgotten yer roots in that faith?" Thon stopped to assess if Rachel had grasped the basis of his argument.

Rachel was pensive, considering the direction Thon's logic was taking. In an uncharacteristic move, she questioned it rather than attacked it. Perhaps this was the influence of her tempered and gentle Ian with whom she was continuously renewing her admiration. She would not confront Thon's assumption that she was religiously inclined. She definitely was not. She would, instead, focus on his economic ideas.

"So, ye believe that meeting three kind Protestant Unionists is enough for ye to abandon yer motherland just for a job?"

"Hear my second point." Thon continued. "I need to find a position that will support me coming back home fully self-sufficient. Tommy and Jim are going to London to work in their father's company there. I can apprentice with them as an engineer for at least a few years before securing enough funds to return. Ye know the difficulties finding a position here, Rachel. Unemployment is catastrophic, and protests are bound to undermine any financial stability. I can't dally around playing football and drinking at Dublin or Belfast pubs before being independent from father Billie and Uncle Liam in Dublin as well as Uncle Eamon here. While those three have supported my education, it's time I strike out on me own." Thon took Rachel's hand as their eyes followed the direction of a sailboat tacking back and forth among the waves before them.

"And for my third point: I will never abandon my Ireland, but, like that wee vessel, I must raise my own sails and exploit the winds to reach my own shore of loyalty. Of all people in our family, ye should understand that the most," he finished.

"Aye. Ye're right. Ye must do what ye must, Thon. I just don't want ye to forget us – our family and our dear land. Perhaps, like Ian and Robert, ye'll adventure out, find yer-self and return home to build our land for the future. At least for ye, the North Channel is not as wide as the Atlantic. Ye can visit us at holidays for yer mother Agnes' scones and soda bread instead of those manufactured, British foods like Kellogg's Cornflakes and Kit Kats."

The two chuckled.

Rachel could not hold herself back, however, from having the last say. "But promise me, ye won't get involved in any Unionist group in London and come back with all their nefarious ideas about keeping Northern Ireland forever anchored to Westminster."

Thon held her hand tight. "I promise, Rachel. And to prove that, I've already told Tommy and Jim that I won't be joining them on any London football team that competes with our stars here in Bangor."

Rachel released her hand from his and nudged him gently on the shoulder. "Oh, Thon, ye are definitely a brawling bull and, as our great-Uncle Anthony named ye after the Irish King Thon, yer The King of the Beyond."

11

Following the Workers

June 15, 1932

Unlike his brother Thon who was independent in his thinking and actions, Jon was a dependent follower. Like their deceased father Ryan McCormick, Jon sought acceptance in whatever group might value him. Little did he realize that his value was often exploited more than respected. He was shy and highly vulnerable to ideas he found difficult to verbalize in his own terms. Little did he even air his ideas as he had been a stutterer for most of his life, probably due to his traumatic early years hearing his mother be criticized – and, worse, beaten – by his drunken father. Whatever the momentary and situational trend in current political and social fashion, he kept his opinions to himself and participated only by joining in silence.

Agnes had tried often during Jon's early childhood and teen years to build up his self-confidence, speaking and critical thinking skills. She had taken him to many a meeting of the Cumann na m'Ban Youth and Na Fianna Eireann (the Irish National Boy Scouts) founded by the Countess Markievicz to support Republican and Catholic policies. Agnes had hoped Jon would learn to accommodate for what he labeled himself as his "goat-like" speech patterns. She prayed he would increase his self-esteem, seek his own individuality within a group and secure his own beliefs and values. Instead, he seemed to acquiesce to the beliefs of others by listening, not questioning – and, for sure, not sharing his own thoughts. At twenty-three, he was a passive actor in developing his identity and societal interactions.

"So, good sir," Agnes began as she and Jon sat in the garden behind the Dublin home Billie and she had provided the two McCormick lads since 1912. She loved all of her children – the adopted McCormack boys Thon and Jon and her own biological Wolfe and Katie. But Agnes felt a special compassion and concern for Jon. Perhaps it was because she had a sister Martha who also stammered and went silent after she had been threatened and abandoned when becoming pregnant by the abuser Nathan Dickson. Agnes would always tuck Jon in at night telling him he had the voice of an angel, quiet yet full of wisdom and grace. Sometimes he believed her and sometimes not. He always loved her, nonetheless, for those words.

She and Billie had guided Jon to become a journalist. After all, thought Agnes, journalists just report on events and, as objective observers, don't need to take part in or advocate for positions. That might just fit Jon's passive character. Billie's colleague and friend, Joseph Devlin, a Westminster MP from the Irish Parliamentary Party and representative of the Nationalist Party in Stormont with Eamon, had spoken to Jon many a time about journalism. "Wee Joe" Devlin was a journalist himself as well as a model orator and negotiator who advocated logic and compromise to peacefully address the labor issues facing Northern Ireland. Billie and Agnes had taken Jon to Devlin's popular children's activities each summer and had seen Jon's face light up. They thought Jon might be influenced by Devlin to consider a position at the Irish News where Devlin was chair.

And Jon was. Fortunately, when studying literature at Trinity College in Dublin, he came to adore writing poetry and reading others' literary works. He soon saw journalism as an occupation that valued the skills in which he succeeded. Just a year ago, he had been offered an apprenticeship at the Irish News.

Today, the sun was warming the afternoon as well as Agnes' determination to learn about Jon's newly shared plans. His sister Katie, having inherited the inquisitive and determined behavior of her aunt and namesake Kat, had been insistent the night before that Jon tell her where he was going in such a rush after dinner. He so rarely left the house after 9 PM. To recapture his solace and quickly extract himself from her questions, he had told her. Katie, again like her vociferous aunt, had immediately told her mother Agnes.

Now, Jon sat across from this beloved guardian whom he had followed to church, clinics, social events and protests. He had shied away from Billie and his brother Thon whose personalities always commandeered the dinner conversations. He rarely got the chance to speak, nor did he want to. Agnes alone drew him out and listened to whatever he was eventually able to express.

"Now, my darling, Jon. Tell me how your evening was last night. I heard from Katie that you were out with friends at an RWG (Revolutionary Workers Group) meeting?"

In typical fashion, it took a few minutes for him to respond to Agnes' question. He looked away from her, saying "Yes. Some friends from the paper invited me to go with them to the meeting."

Agnes waited for an extension of this comment. None came.

She gently probed for one. "What were the RWG leaders talking about?"

Jon took out his small, leather bound notebook and opened to one of its lined pages. "The leader Tommy Graham spoke about the working conditions in the North, in Belfast, particularly," he offered.

"And what did he say those conditions were?" She again prodded.

"Oh, it's the inequity of relief payments."

"And what else?"

"The hiring of Protestants, rather than Catholics, in civil service."

"And?" Agnes, as patient as she could be, was beginning – as she sometimes, but not always, did with Jon- to feel more frustrated than inquisitive.

"Not much more," he finished.

Agnes considered her options. She could accept what Jon had said and move on to another topic or she could finally present her own fears. She knew the RWG was a growing movement ready to, like its companion groups in the US, Germany, Spain and Italy, espouse

Communist rhetoric and support protests that often led to violence followed by a repressive reaction from government, or worse, vigilante groups. She worried that he might be drawn into the movement just by hearing the words of Tommy Graham. Yes, as a journalist, Jon was already an accomplished listener, but he was still learning to be analytical and objective after listening. Agnes knew he wasn't quite yet skilled nor gifted enough to draw a direct line between propaganda and truth.

"Are ye going to write an article about last night for The Irish News?" she queried.

"Aye, but I'll need to go to Belfast and several other Northern towns to hear about the actual impact of the relief programs." He lowered his head and looked at his notes.

Agnes knew he had returned to his quiet world of the written, not spoken, word.

"Will ye be safe, Jon? I hear from Robert and Morna that there may be street protests in Belfast soon." She leaned closer to him to lessen the space – and time – he had to feel her concern and respond. He looked up.

"Ye need not worry, Mum. I'll stay with Uncle Eamon and Aunt Kat each night. They'll feed me well and, like you, Uncle Eamon will listen to me." He frowned. "I'm not so sure Aunt Kat will as she'll be all into questioning me."

"Ach, Jon," cautioned, Agnes. "That's her way of caring for ye. She wants to know all ye are doing so she can be sure ye are safe."

"True, I know that, but, ye must admit. Once she gets the answers she wants out of me, watch out. She'll write my article for me." Jon started to relax and laugh.

Agnes, too, relaxed. 'Tis true. Knowing ye, though, I don't think ye'll let that happen. She won't have any idea what approach ye'll take in writing it as ye won't let her – nor anyone – know the words until they're on the page and street. That's how ye use your brilliance, Jon, and stay loyal to the truth ye perceive."

Agnes took his hand in hers. "I love ye for that. Ye're coming into your own by listening so well to others and being truthful about what ye hear. I'm so proud of ye."

Jon closed his notebook, stood and kissed Agnes on the head.

"I'll see ye in a week or two, Mum. Please don't worry about me."

12

Reality Returns

June 19, 1932

Robert, Morna and Jon approached the corner of Shankill Road and Riverview just south of Queens College. The early summer day was providing a few hours of relief from the damp and grey brush of factory haze that usually painted the streets and store fronts by noon. Morning sun was emanating from above, and the three basked in it.

"It is good to see you, Jon, on such a delightful morning" said Robert offering his hand to the young man walking toward them.

"And ye, Robert and Morna," replied Jon, taking Robert's hand and placing his other under Morna's elbow.

Morna thought to herself how well these two had bonded over the past decade. Robert in his professorship at Queens had encouraged his student Jon. The elder, though only thirty-two, had carefully read and commented on Jon's essays related to the great philosophers. Jon, in turn, had provided Robert with an Irish historical context for his lectures by describing the impact of colonialism on Dublin and Belfast poor. The two men had undertaken many a discussion about the opposing – or were they complimentary – perspectives of idealism versus realism. Robert thought they were two sides of the same coin. Jon thought they were two different coins.

Morna cherished the fact that the men she loved as family could, at least, listen to each other and, miraculously, hold a civil conversation. If only they could speak at government and worker meetings to calm the thoughts and actions of our leaders, she wished. Perhaps, then, the inevitable violence soon to erupt at upcoming marches could be avoided. Robert could remind folks of their ideals and Jon of their impact.

As Morna was contemplating the possible, Robert stated the necessary. "Let's sit for a while at Quinlon's and catch up on our respective news. It has been too long since we have shared our comings and goings among just the three of us."

"Aye," Jon nodded his head. "Coincidently, that's exactly where I am heading to meet someone in an hour."

Morna's curiosity was piqued by this last comment. Was Jon finding a lass of Belfast to lure him from his work and solitude? Morna and Agnes had shared many a fanciful scenario of Jon meeting a Queen Bridgid. Hoping that his shyness could be lessened by a sympathetic and romantic partner, Morna had even arranged spontaneous engagements with several of her fellow nurses as possible candidates. None had borne fruit.

"Is this a new friend whom ye're meeting or someone whom ye're interviewing for The Irish News?" asked Morna, masquerading her match-making with an interest in his new position at the paper.

"I've an appointment with a member of the RWG who contacted me last week. My colleagues thought she might be an excellent source of information." Jon replied.

Robert frowned. "Ah. It's a new day when radical groups use the national press to spread their propaganda rather than the press seeking them for objective information. I hope you'll be able to differentiate rhetoric from fact."

"Now, come," said Morna. "Let's not get too confrontational before we have had a cuppa and scone."

And so they proceeded to Quinlon's, each thinking about what they might learn in the next hour.

And learn they did.

Sitting at a table set for three next to a beveled window, half opened to let in the early summer breeze, the three exchanged their most recent activities. Robert told about the new philosophy book he was writing: *The Practice of Moral Thinking.* He was particularly focused on how philosophies of ancient times could be applied practically to the current economic and social plights facing Northern Ireland. He wanted Jon's opinions.

Morna was busy at her various clinics and neighborhood schools, ensuring they were meeting the hygienic standards recently set by the Public Health Department. She asked Jon to spend a day with her to see the conditions surrounding the unemployed and working poor. She specifically asked him to join her at the Gaol.

Jon was his typical quiet self who needed multiple queries to provide personal information.

Fortunately, Morna, like Agnes, was an excellent questioner and listener. A few looks from her to Robert reminded him to be the same. By the end of the hour, Jon had shared his plan to travel around the rural areas of Northern Ireland interviewing folks from all backgrounds about their needs. He summarized his short recitation saying, "I want to know what they think, not what our leaders believe they think."

Morna and Robert were impressed by this approach.

"You mean you're going to write an article on the people's stories about their lives, not what the government believes those lives are or should be?" asked an incredulous Robert.

"Aye," said Jon directing his eyes to his mentor's. "And it's not stories. Don't ye think it's time for our people to share their lives through facts, not just poetry, songs and story-telling? Sometimes, I think we lose the ability to face our challenges if we're constantly describing them in dramatic terms and, more so, in myths of the past."

Morna was taken aback by Jon's insight and intent. How well Jon has developed, she thought to herself, into such a thoughtful and imaginative soul. Agnes should be so proud of him. And yet, I understand her fear that he might be exploited. Time will tell. Time will tell.

And in the short term, time did tell or, at least, posed some questions. Right at the hour, the individual whom Jon was going to interview entered the tea-house and caught his attention. She had indicated he could identify her by gold, wired-rimmed glasses, a broad-brimmed navy-blue hat, and a bluebell corsage she had pinned to her left lapel.

Jon rose, said good-bye to his companions, and walked toward the stately, middle-aged woman.

As Robert's eyes followed Jon's figure toward the women's face, Robert gasped.

"Good Lord," he whispered to Morna. "It's my cousin Molly McKenzie."

13

Touché

June 19, 1932

Jon reached out his hand to greet the woman before him. She did not offer hers.

"Sit thee down, Mr. McCormick. Or do I call ye Mr. Irvine?" came a gruff request that Jon immediately perceived as a command and the question as an inquisition.

Surprised, but refusing to express that visually, Jon quickly rethought the interchange he had planned for this interview: he asking the questions, she answering them. He was going to have to listen, remember, and listen again.

A sparring match had begun. He would make the first move, however, by being polite.

"May I invite ye to take yer place before I sit meself down, ma'm?" he said, capturing a few minutes to reframe and redirect. He graciously pulled a wooden chair out from the small table before which she stood. He motioned her to sit.

The woman's face colored, not from embarrassment nor pleasure, but from disdain.

She made the next move by being obstinate.

"I need no lad to position me, young man."

She remained standing.

Jon bowed his head.

"Ah, then," he replied. "I beg yer forgiveness for my assumption." He gestured to the table. "Please choose yer own seat." He looked up at her and smiled a coy Thespian grin.

The woman humphed, walked around Jon to the other side of the table, pulled out a chair opposite the one he had held for her, and sat down. She faced Quinlon's front door.

Jon walked clockwise around the table and sat in the chair to her right.

Corners had been taken.

"Ye may call me Jon McCormick, if ye like. And what may I call ye?"

"Mrs. O'Connor. But my name is not important." She placed her blue, embroidered, silk bag on the table before him. He noticed an unusual bulge within it, unlike any normal cosmetic or everyday essential.

He had not prepared for a verbal sparring that might become a physical confrontation.

He had to repartee carefully.

"Do ye know my family, Mrs. O'Connor?" he asked, trying to give his journalistic footwork and personal courage time to adjust.

"No need to ask me that," she gruffly responded, winning the first point of their duel. "I only need to know ye are who ye are or I won't continue with ye." She noticed his eyes on her bag and slowly withdrew it from the table-top, placing it on her lap.

"Well, I am who I am. And I believe ye already knew that." Jon replied, taking out his small notebook and pencil. "Now. Pray can ye tell me who ye are and what organization ye are representing in this interview?"

The woman frowned. "This will not be an interview," securing her second point.

She continued: "I will tell ye what I have to say and that is it. Ye may ask me whatever ye want, but if I don't like the question, I won't answer it. And what group I represent is not a group; it is the true people of this nation. We have no specific name."

Jon knew this woman did represent a certain group and that, indeed, it had a name. The individual who had contacted The Irish

News to arrange Jon's meeting with her had given Jon a thorough background of the Irish Republican Army's Northern Ireland structure, despite the IRA being illegal as of '31 in both the Free State and NI. Jon knew this woman was a leader of the outlawed Belfast faction, headquartered within the Catholic community of Queen Street.

After partition between Northern Ireland and The Republic, it was easy for the southern IRA to mobilize Northern Catholic and Nationalist minorities against the discriminatory religious, economic and social policies taken by Prime Minister Craig's Stormont government and London. The Belfast IRA was already carrying out numerous nefarious actions against the Unionists. Opposing those actions was the government's Royal Ulster Constabulary (RUC) and the voluntary Ulster B-Specials. While Jon did not trust the name this woman had given him, he did her reputation.

Now, planning his countermove in their verbal duel, Jon resumed his cordial and patient stance. He would mitigate her arrogance by his typical quietude: listening, clarifying, and affirming what he had heard. He was certain that would lead her to reveal more than she had intended.

"What are ye wanting to tell me?" he tactfully asked, looking directly at her and raising his pencil like a sword in mid-air.

He won, for the woman described the Northern IRA goals and demands for over a half an hour. She finished with a lengthy tirade about the threats that would occur if others, particularly the Protestant populations in both voluntary and government forces, did not "behave". Throughout her diatribe, Jon encouraged elaborations by asking questions such as "And ....what do you mean by protecting laborers....and what is your relationship with Sinn Fein, the Irish Parliamentary Party and the Nationalist Party....and what do you mean by respecting Irish culture....fair housing....land rights.... equal education....strikes....boycotts...and, finally, what do you mean by behave?"

Jon thoroughly enjoyed the conversation as it took on this new jousting. The duel had become a conversation of questions and answers. He was becoming very comfortable with its back and forth when she abruptly stopped.

A male voice behind her had interrupted her.

"Molly? Molly McKenzie?" Robert approached the woman's back.

She stood, turned around and quickly drew in her breath. Her face turned a smoldering red, brows pointed like cross swords above two flared nostrils.

Not a word was said. Clutching her bag, she brushed Jon aside who had also risen from his seat. All he saw of her as she hastened toward Quinlon's entrance was a dark feather, bobbing from her navy colored hat above a bent head and crouched shoulders. She vanished out the front door.

"Good grief, " said Jon. "What caused that?" He looked at Robert, waiting for a response.

"Sit down, Jon. We need to talk about an incident that happened years ago. You must be forewarned about this woman."

14

Who is an Activist?

June 27, 1932

"I need to tell ye some news, Rachel." Ian guided her away from the cabinette door of the Belfast to Cork train from which she had just descended.

The diminishing evening light was camouflaging her face as was a black veil lingering from ear to ear under her low brimmed hat. How beautifully mysterious she looks, Ian said to himself as he felt his heart beat in time with the train's wheels now sounding out their onward journey. Will I ever cease from loving her more each time we're together? Nay. Knowing how the heart works physically, I am still in awe of how it works emotionally.

He stopped his pondering as she took his arm and teased. "And what news do ye have that I haven't heard already?" Handing him her traveling sack and a bag of edibles from BB, he knew his immediate task was not to cater to her safety but to her whims. And yet, that safety was critical.

The two were now a formal couple. Their engagement had been announced to the family – Irvines, McCormicks, and Smileys. Ever since the Uprising in '16, Ian's sister Morna had sensed that Rachel would eventually be her sister-in-law. Morna also knew it would take more than a decade for Rachel to sense it, too.

Slowly but surely, Ian had listened to Rachel, understood her values and purpose, and guided her to recognize that neither could be practiced without love. She, in turn, had convinced him that his love of humankind, particularly his fellow countrymen, women and children, could not be practiced without values and purpose. Thus, his medical profession had become a key contributor to the welfare of Ireland's poor. Whether he knew it or not, it was also a perfect cover for her to contribute to the IRA. He would heal the bodies; she would feed the minds. At ages twenty-six and twenty-eight respectively, Rachel and Ian had become a perfect pair of the next generation to deliver justice to the unemployed, unhoused and uneducated. They would follow their similar goals but through different means.

Tonight, Rachel would deliver a message to Macroom IRA battalion leader Amos McDuffy about the upcoming workers' protests in Belfast. Dublin-based IRA incursions into the North had fallen sharply due to the Free State's ban on the IRA and a lack of funds for IRA representation within the dying Sinn Fein party. A small pro-Republican contingency within this diminished IRA still partnered with allies in Belfast – not as a political entity but as a defensive, para-military group. They needed to protect Northern Irish Nationalists and Catholics against the Royal Ulster Constabulary (RUC) attacks condoned by the Unionist-led Stormont government. IRA activists within the working and unemployed populations were mobilizing.

Ian would deliver a message to Rachel that IRA member Molly McKenzie, alive and active in Northern Ireland, was planning to come to Macroom. He worried that Rachel would hear that news from others willing to exploit, not calm, Rachel's memory of Molly. He knew Rachel abhorred Molly for implicating Rachel in the '22 murder of Father O'Hare. To this day, based on the enduring rumor, several Macroom colleagues were leery of Rachel's passionate nature. Nor, did Ian believe Molly had forgiven Rachel for exposing the lie to Collins before his death. She had disappeared for over a decade with tales of her traveling intermittently with IRA leaders Peadar O'Donnell and Sean Hayes to Brussels and Berlin. They were exploring financial support and arms from fellow Communists there. Now, Molly had returned and Ian was extremely worried for his fiancée. All these years later, both women held fast to their respective grudges. How they would resolve them put him on high alert.

"Let's go to Finbar's so you can unpack before meeting McDuffy and his companions. Erin and I have alerted Finbar that ye are coming, and his daughter Fiona is very excited about your stay. She is a shy lass, ye know. Since her Mum died, she lacks a confidante and model like ye." Ian switched physical sides and subjects with Rachel as he shifted the travel bag to his other hand.

"Ach, Rachel. What do ye have in this bag? It weighs many a stone." The minute he asked the question, he wished he had not. She could go on and on about how she needed to read more books than he as she had not been able to attend college as he had. And, of course, that's exactly what she said about the content of the sack. He knew, however, that was just partially true.

"Ye have had all the luck of the Irish going to yer fancy college and medical school in New York City. I have only read the books provided by St. Enda's and listened to stories told from the streets." She was about to continue with her typical tirade when Ian stopped her abruptly.

"I have a surprise for ye regarding just that argument. Francis and Margaret McKenzie are sending a locker of books from New York City for our new Macroom library. The shipment should arrive in just ten days. Ye'll have many more books to read than ye'll have time to prepare for our upcoming celebration." He squeezed her arm.

"Aye, ye goose. I already knew about it so don't think yer surprising me." She laughed.

Ian stopped abruptly on the path. "Oh, no. Don't tell me there are more than books in the locker as well as in this sack?" He frowned. In the increasing dark, Rachel knew he was not pleased.

"Ian, my love." She stopped in mid-stride, turned to face him and placed her hand upon his cheek. "There are only books and clothes in my sack. And, please do not be angry about the forthcoming shipment. I promise that ye will know what is being sent by our Irish

American brothers and sisters. It's all for the good of our island. As a matter of fact, along with the books are medical supplies and medication. Our friends across the Atlantic are not without concern for our health along with our safety." Rachel did not feel any remorse in relating a half-truth about the content.

Ian held the sack of edibles closer to his waist. He placed her sack on the ground between them. He was, indeed, not pleased by the insinuation of her statements. Arms such as revolvers and rifles were often shipped from the US, Australia and Canada to IRA battalions in The Republic. The weapons would then be smuggled over the border to Northern Ireland and, eventually, to IRA allies in Great Britain. Never were they used only for the purpose of defense.

Rachel rarely told Ian about this activity for which she was a messenger. However, as their wedding day approached, she recognized that he would need to know as much as she could tell him without putting him in danger. With the Northern Irish spies traveling about The Republic, and informants living in Macroom, the less Ian knew the more he would be protected.

Ian, on the other hand, felt the more he told Rachel the more she would be protected. Morna had sent a message to him with one of her Shankhill Road medical team visiting family in Macroom. Ian would share Robert and Morna's sighting of Molly at Quinlon's and Jon's summary of his interview with her as 'Mrs. O'Connor'. According to Morna, Molly had been a tad too braggadocio in telling Jon she was traveling to Cork for a special assignment. When Jon had probed, Mrs. O'Connor had only smirked, saying she was going to avenge a long time offense.

Both Morna and Robert were worried for Rachel. Now, Ian was as well.

No IRA radicals ever forgot an offense nor failed to seek revenge.

15

Jon's Compass Editorial

June 27, 1932

"Ho! Ho! I am totally gob smacked! Look at what the lad has done!" exclaimed the garrulous and bulbous Uncle Aiden. Upon entering the great beyond, his voice had not lost its exuberance nor his body weight its excess. BB had tried valiantly to calm his nerves and lower his blood pressure but, as he was already among the ancestors, it really didn't matter. His spirit would live on no matter how many pints drunk, mutton legs chomped or diatribes blustered.

She sighed. "Ach, dear Aiden. What is exciting ye now?"

"I'm just reading an editorial from today's Irish News *written by none other than our Jon McCormick-Irvine. He's definitely following in Bella's and Lizzie's footsteps. Listen to this title: 'Where is Ireland's Compass Leading Us?'"*

Aiden put the newspaper down on his lap. "Mary, Joseph and Jesus! Like us, he is asking that same old question. Why can't we ever answer it?" Aiden's voice rose and his sputtering increased.

"Calm thyself, me love. Let's hear his answer," implored BB, putting down her embroidery and moving her seat closer to her beloved partner. Hearing loss was not an issue in the beyond. Nonetheless, she always asked Aiden to repeat himself. Ever since they had met over a century ago, she never quite caught his first rushed words. He had to say them twice. She, in turn, had to repeat them twice to ensure she heard them correctly. "Thank

the Lord," BB reflected. "I was trained as a contemplative nun,
then, as a nurse." Her listening skills – to God and humans –
were stellar.

Aiden stopped his complaining and turned to Bridgette.

"Having just finished a tour around the entire island, Jon
describes our present turmoil as ...well, let me read it to ye."

Aiden began reciting aloud.

'The Free State elections in February and the
current protests in Northern Ireland beg us to consider where our island's compass is directing us. It
may seem particularly confusing to us mortals how
the conflicting policies of so many opposing political
parties have set the needle of that compass spinning.
The magnetic forces in both the Free State and north
are pulling in all directions. Where is the balanced
compass we need to guide us?

During recent conversations I have had in pubs
and hearths from Cork to Dublin and Belfast to Derry,
I have heard our fellow countrymen and women say
that we are dearly challenged by opposing policy
writs and, dare I say, rumor waggings. From east to
west and north to south, the brisk winds off the Irish
Sea are carrying too many conflicting voices across
the Morne Mountain and MacGillycuddy Reeks into
the lowlands.

Perhaps if we hear those voices, we can better
understand their magnetic pulls.

Let's start with the voice of *Sinn Fein*. We all know
that Arthur Griffith founded 'We Ourselves' in 1905
as an Anglo-Irish dual monarchy party but that, after
the Easter Rising in 1916, it transformed into an Irish
party supporting the Republic ideal. Even though

Sinn Fein played no leadership role in the '16 rebellion, many members participated in the fighting, representing the old Irish Republican Brotherhood and, eventually, forming the Irish Volunteers. Britain claimed that Sinn Fein had actually led the Uprising. That misinformation campaign backfired on the Brits and mobilized more and more men and women to join Sinn Fein. As a result, you may recall that in the 1918 general election just before partition, Sinn Fein won 73 of the 105 island-wide seats in Parliament.

But did Sinn Fein stay Sinn Fein? No, indeed, it did not. After the deaths of Griffith and Collins in 1922, Sinn Fein leader W.T. Cosgrave knew he had to distance the party from the pro and anti-treaty crisis that had torn our island apart in the Civil War. Thus, in 1923, Cumann na N'Gaedheal (Society of the Gaels) was born as an off-shoot of Sinn Fein, winning Free State elections in '24 and '27. Over nine years of leadership, Cumann na N'Gaedheal again transformed – this time from a locally focused, transitional government to an administrative and economic system reflecting too much British influence. You could say it had returned to its 1905 original Sinn Fein roots. As a result, the party lost its citizen support.

So, good people of the Free State, where did that support go? It went to another party: *Fianna Fail (Warriors of Destiny)*. And why? Let us recall who walked out of the Second Dail in '22 and formed this new party in '26. None other than Eamon deValera and the Countess Markievicz! For six years, they had launched their writs and wags upon the winds throughout the land. They rejected British influence and promoted Republican ideals of economic self-sufficiency, religious equality (Christian), equitable land distribution and the resurrection of Irish culture and language. Obviously, our citizenry agreed with them. That's why Fianna Fail has just won 72 seats over Cumann na n'Gaedheal's 57. Is it not surprising that Dev now holds leadership in our Fourth Dail? Indeed, it is not!

So, here, in our Free State, we now have two major magnetic forces pulling our compass in opposite directions.

But dear reader, don't stop here. Let us look at the forces north of us.

We know that the Ulster Unionist Party (UUP) walks hand in hand with London. Having emerged from the 1891 Irish Conservative Party and the 1905 Irish Unionist Alliance, it has been consistently loyal to the monarchy. Aligned with the historic Protestant Orange Order, it attracted signatories for the anti-Home Rule writ of the 1921 Ulster Covenant. Its members have joined the Ulster Volunteers to confront Catholics. After partition, Sir James Craig (Viscount Craigavon), an Orangeman and signatory of the Covenant, became the first UUP Prime Minister in Stormont and remains in power today. Claiming self-defense, the Ulster Volunteers now carry out the 1922 N.I. Parliament Special Powers Act primarily against Catholics and Nationalists.

Uncle Aiden put down the paper. His cheeks turned a bright red and his breath belabored. "That is a wag! I see all too well the offensive, not defensive, actions taken by the Ulster Volunteers and their Royal Irish Constabulary collaborators. That damned Special Powers Act we know as the "Flogging Act" promotes such despicable behavior!"

BB rose from her chair and quickly poured him a second cup of tea.

"Ach, what's this?' he sputtered. "I need a pint, instead, as I'm getting all riled up!"

"Nay, ye do not need a pint. That's exactly the wrong elixir for right now. Hush a second and take a sip," she cajoled. "We both need ye're clear mind to understand Jon's intentions in writing this piece."

BB had taken control of this giant's obsession of the nectar's delight, convincing him that she was his only joy instead. While he agreed, he couldn't refrain from reminding her of the sacrifice he had made, thirty years ago, after she had thrown away what she thought was his last amber bottle. With the good Lord on her side, he knew his appeals were futile. With Sucellus, the Celtic God of agriculture, forests and alcohol, on his side, he knew he could continue hiding replacement bottles.

Reluctantly, he took the tea cup and drank. "Ach, ye'er a good lass, BB. Always taking care of me." She smiled sweetly, but noted his feigned sincerity.

"Continue, me love." She resolved, sitting back in her chair and, again, taking up her embroidery.

Looking at her over the besmirched, wirerimmed glasses resting precariously on the bridge of his nose, he lowered his voice. "Ye know BB, that I have nightly conversations with Wee Joe Devlin during his dreams. What a principled and brilliant MP he is, leading the Nationalist Party both in Stormont and London. Despite complaints from his Free State allies, I encouraged him to remain in the North working on behalf of Irish workers and to not be distracted by invitations to move south. But let me not praise myself for what he is doing."

"Hear now what Jon says about the Nationalist Party."

As for the opposition party to the UUP, the

Nationalist Party (NP) is gaining strength. An 1891 out-growth of Redmond's Irish Parliamentary Party (IPP), the NP has stood for religious and political equality which led it to oppose partition. Since then, fear of attacks by the Royal Ulster Constabulary and Ulster Volunteers has deterred many NP members from voting. But that disenfranchisement is changing due to the eloquence and commitment of its leader Joe Devlin. The party now holds 11 out of the 52 Stormont seats.

Uncle Aiden's voice rose and his fisted-up hands shook the newspaper's pages. "The NP should have more than 11 seats! Where are the socialists who make workers stand up to the UUP and vote with Joe? He needs more support!!"

BB took a final stich, placed her work again on her lap, and quietly suggested. "Perhaps we should call Bigger in to calm ye, Aiden." BB opened the door, whistled and in came the shining eyes and wagging tail of their dearest, canine companion. He had been waiting outside since, as he always did, he had sensed that one of his beloved family members was in stress. Sitting before the elder, he offered his attentive ears. Stroking them, Aiden could feel his heartbeat slow.

"Ach, another good listener by the hearth. Thank ye, BB. Now, I can continue on those last two forces about which Jon has written: Sinn Fein and the IRA."

Current membership rolls indicate that *Sinn Fein's* popularity in Belfast and throughout Northern Ireland has petered out quite a bit. As with the Nationalists, potential recruits fear threats from the Ulster Volunteers and Royal Ulster Constabulary. Also, funds from the Free State have dried up. Thus, Sinn Fein's Northern Ireland goal for an island-wide republic has been temporarily deferred so that

Nationalists and Catholics may remain as safe as possible. Nonetheless, the wag is that Sinn Fein is planning to reorganize in the north and will soon contest upcoming elections.

Uncle Aiden puffed his cheeks and pouted: "Ach! Damn the "Flogging Act" and the RUC! We need the IRA in Northern Ireland."

"And what does Jon say about the IRA?" asked BB. Aiden resumed his reading.

Based on the writs and wags I have heard in my travels, *The Irish Republican Army's (IRA's)* role in Belfast and Derry, as well as in the small towns and rural villages of NI, raises a critical question: Is the IRA a political entity with a paramilitary arm or a paramilitary entity with a political arm?

Many IRA members living in the North have been caught up in the leadership battles of the Free State's IRA when responding to that question. No answer currently exists from IRA voices on either side of the border.

The only voices clearly heard are those of Northern Ireland Protestants. They consider the IRA as a paramilitary entity, no matter what relationship its leaders have with Free State or local politicians. Stormont has banned the IRA, implemented the writs of the Special Powers Act and mustered the Royal Ulster Constabulary to expose IRA violations – actual or contrived. Unapproved meetings, unlicensed arms, inflammatory writings, and suspicious trainings are targets for arrests, imprisonment and potential executions. Any actions in support of worker protests, strikes, boycotts, marches, military drills, treasonous literature, etc. are labeled as IRA organized and, therefore, illegal.

The wag, however, is that many citizens in the North, particularly Catholic and Nationalist, are disinterested in defining the IRA as political or para-military. They only focus on its goal to save Ireland financially, socially and culturally from the throes of colonial-based capitalism and imperialism. As such, they agree with its strategy of armed aggression, but not with all of its tactics. IRA bombings of Brit-ish-owned factories or RUC headquarters are qui-etly condoned. But when innocent by-standers – no matter Catholic or Protestant – are killed or targeted assassinations are conducted, neither is accepted. Any IRA opinion, however, is whispered behind closed doors and windows. After all, might an RUC or Ulster Volunteer collaborator be listening?

Alas, dear readers, we must finish this long edi-torial. I thank you for your patience in reading it through to its end.

Let me close by saying that the writs described are documented policies proposed by various parties – political and paramilitary. The wags reflect opinions offered over a wee pint with fathers who, like you, may be businessmen, farmers, factory workers and, offered over brick and dirt doorsteps with mothers who, also like you, may be housekeepers, teachers and nurses.

I hope you can envision more clearly the oppos-ing magnetic pulls on our island's compass and how those forces are spinning its needle round and round.

If so, perhaps you can answer this question: Where is Ireland's compass directing you?

Aiden and BB looked at each other in silence. Bigger placed a paw on Aiden's knee.

"Ach, dear boy. Ye're right as always," said Aiden. "We need to call a family gathering to answer Jon's question. After all, we have much to share with those below."

16

Today's Gallery

June 28, 1932

Una: How I cherish my gallery of few originals and many copies. As I told you in 1820, Alexis de Tocqueville would agree that my family is a mix of the original McKnights and McGregors from Scotland and their current Irish copies: the Irvines, Smileys and McCormicks. Over the past one hundred and twelve years, our clan has added more dearly beloveds— the McCanns, McKenzies and McCrackens. Those who have yet to join us here are still needed below to reconcile our homeland's conflicts. Today's afternoon gathering would determine which of our roles might help them accomplish that task.

Last night, Aiden distributed his copy of Jon's Irish Times *editorial to us all. And by us, I mean family and friends – the Irvines, Smileys, McCormicks, McCanns, Dixons, O'Learys. and – yes, even Bigger's canine companions Sceo and Boru. Being the keen readers and thinkers we are, it didn't take long to ingest the article's main content and consider its intent. Aiden knew he didn't have to worry about sharing the paper with our political champions Tone, Parnell, Griffith, Collins, Pearse and the Countess. They had their own communication lines between earth and our beyond. Most probably, well before us, they had already read and discussed it among themselves.*

The garden in which we all had sat this afternoon was crowded. And, like most natural settings here, it was perfect for our deliberations. The Horse Chestnut trees surrounding three of its borders offset the radiant sapphire, ruby and diamond colors of summer flowers we so loved- not just for their beauty but for their meanings. Blue Irises representing faith, wisdom and valor nestled against tree trunks. Fronting the Irises were Red Poppies, signifying the dreams and eternal sleep which honor those lost in battle. Reaching out from the Poppies to the grassy lawn cover were white Lilies of the Valley, reminding us of purity and humility. All these flowers were protected from winds and storms by the boughs of the Horse Chestnuts. Their sturdy arms embraced us as symbols of independence and justice. We had chosen this site well for the afternoon deliberations.

Dear Collins opened our meeting, proposing a format by which we could respectfully share our opinions and feelings. He reminded us of a tale he had told ten years before to the children of Kat, BB and Billie in their Dublin living room.

"Ach, Mick." said Lizzie. "I loved you telling us how the animals of the forest came together to live peacefully. Guided by the lion Lester and the lamb Louisa, the animals formed a symphony despite being different and self-centered. Each animal learned to play his or her part in harmony with the others and contribute to the common welfare of all. We need that reminder more than ever now. "

"Aye." Mick smiled. "Sadly, as I told Liam that very night, no human would listen to that message. And, in '22, no one did. But, we can, right now, as we guide those we love below."

How wonderful it was to see everyone nod his or her head in agreement — some more ardently than others, however.

For about two hours, each of us offered an opinion. Bella suggested: "We can talk to BB and Kat about their Inde Pen articles in Our Ireland. *Those two magnificent writers could highlight what their clinic women say about party members working together for the betterment of both the North and The Free State." Lizzie agreed adding, "Young Katie and Maggie can*

add the perspectives of their school and sports chums. Good-
ness, the four could start a mother-daughter column." All of our
women clapped.

The men just nodded their heads. I must admit we in the
beyond have as much to do to enlighten ourselves on gender
equality as we do to enlighten those below!

Patrick McCann commented next: "I give Cosgrave another
year, and he'll settle into a reconciliatory mode with Dev. In
advance, though, let me visit with brother Erin. He knows Cos-
grave well. Perhaps Erin could write a new play that subtly – or
perhaps more transparently – reminds folks about reconciling
differences." Padraig Pearse looked up from his reading a poetry
book and smiled. "Hear, hear," he said. "The arts are always the
mirrors of truth."

Will had been pacing along the back of the garden. In his
typical analytic and diplomatic way, he had been pondering
and rethinking, thinking and repondering. He proposed: "I
need to have a strategic conversation with Billie. In his role as
a Cumman na N'Gaedheal TD for Dublin, he could suggest to
Dev, without alienating the Tall One, cross-party negotiations
with Cosgrave. Dev must represent all of the Free State citizens
whether they were for or against the treaty. And he definitely
needs to be more clear about his relationship with the IRA."

"And what shall we do about the North?" asked Mick.

Dixon stepped up, feeling over the years that he now would
be listened to by his former adversaries. He warned: "There's no
way that Carson nor Craig will reconcile with the Nationalists
and Catholics. Beware of old wounds and prejudices."

Uncle Aiden puffed up his cheeks and pouted, in response:
"Ach! Damn the UUP and its lackies in the RUC and Ulster Vol-
unteers! Raise up the workers and fight back!"

"Now, now, Aiden," said Parnell. "We must always start off
peacefully before taking on an oppositional stance. Let's see if

we can get Eamon to meet with Craig. I hear they attend the same church in Belfast. In addition, we could ask Robert and Morna to use their teaching and nursing skills to practice Lester and Louisa's creation of harmony. Educating the minds and strengthening the health of all our people will go a long way in building community and unifying Ireland again."

Christine O'Leary snorted and sputtered. "Ye must be daft, Parnell. Religion, highbrow philosophy and inequitable health care have only muddied our waters over centuries. I think I should talk to Rachel again and see if she can take charge of an IRA battalion in Derry. That might bring those indecisive IRA men to their senses and to take concrete actions."

"Nay, nay, nay, Christine," spoke up Patrick. Even though the former lovers had reignited an amorous relationship after their fateful Easter Rising separation, Patrick could not condone Christine's passion for revenge. "Ye must leave Rachel alone. She's moving on to another path."

I stepped in to quell the growing tension between the two lovers, reminding Christine that we were promoting among our descendants a future well beyond violence. I also took note that Bridgette and I would need to mentor her a bit more in the next months.

As the meeting came to a close, we identified who among us would visit whom below and what our individual messages would be. Each of us picked a flower from the garden to carry with us during our interventions. The Irvines chose the Iris for their belief in wisdom; the Smileys chose the Poppy to honor eternity; the McCanns and McCormicks picked a Lilly of the Valley to remember purity of thought. Dixon chose the same to practice humility. Will, Parnell and Mick choose the pinky-white flowers of the Horse Chestnut plus its prickly conkers. The men knew independence and justice entailed both beauty and danger. Only Christine did not choose a flower. Instead, she dug into the green grass cover and pulled up a shamrock – a four leaf one at that. Was she thinking of luck alone to guide our next generation? I'm not sure.

Pearse had been quiet during our meeting except for his comments about Erin's possible play. I knew he was thinking, pondering an action that would, as in 1916, be captured for him in words, but alas, not in practice. When I asked him to share those words, he agreed, opening the book he had been perusing.

Sweetly, he read parts of George Russell's poem entitled On Behalf of Some Irishmen Not Followers of Tradition.

> *We are less children of this clime*
> *Than of a nation yet unborn*
> *Or empire in the womb of time.*
> *We hold the Ireland in the heart*
> *More than the land our eyes have seen,*
> *And love the goal for which we start*
> *More than the tale of that has been.*
> *The generations as they rise*
> *May live the life men lived before,*
> *Still hold the thought once held as wise,*
> *Go in and out by the same door.*
> *We leave the easy peace it brings:*
> *The few we are shall still unite*
> *In fealty to unseen kings*
> *Or unimaginable light.*

I felt the collective sigh of our family and friends. Surely, with our help, the next generation could, not just through words, but actions, reach an unimaginable light.

17

A Poppy and A Prayer

Sunday, July 17, 1932

Eamon sat in the third row of Bangor's Prospect Presbyterian Church on Castle Street facing Ward Park. The Sunday service had yet to begin although the contemplative atmosphere was being set by an organ prelude of Johann Sebastian Bach's exquisite *O Mensch, Bewine dein Sunde Gros (BWV 622)*. Like Bach, Eamon had suffered from the loss of both parents at an early age and the estrangement of a brother. Both were committed to enhancing the cultures of their times: Bach through music that elevated listeners' souls; Eamon through philosophical lectures that elevated students' minds. This morning, Eamon would draw on both music and words to give him the eloquence and wisdom to engage the individual assigned to him by his Nationalist Party friend Joe Devlin and a local IRA battalion contact, yet to be openly named.

James Craig, the current Northern Ireland Prime Minister (PM), was to give the sermon at Prospect today. Based on their populist and Republican views, none of the Smiley nor Irvine family members chose to call the PM by his title of First Viscount Craigavon, granted by King George V in 1927. Second after his ally, Edward Carson, Craig had signed the 1912 Ulster Covenant and organized its paramilitary Ulster Volunteers. Subsequently, as a staunch Unionist, he had successfully advocated for the retention of six Ulster counties within Great Britain during the 1921 Anglo-Irish treaty negotiations, securing the partition of the Free State and Northern Ireland. His adamant pro-Protestant and British Empire stance led him to say upon taking the leadership in 1921 of the Ulster Unionist Party (UUP) in Stormont and, thus, the premiership, that he was an "Orangeman for an Orange country leading a Protestant government for a Protestant people."

Eamon was to persuade Craig to rise above his partisan ways and seek reconciliation between his constituents and Catholics. Choosing a church service followed by an intimate luncheon at the home of the resident minister Rev. Chandler, Eamon hoped to convince Craig that their common military experiences – Eamon in WWI and Craig in the Boar War and WWI – would enable them to agree on the futility of violence. More so, Eamon hoped that their common Christian faith would lead them to agree on God's message of peace.

Eamon was fearful, however, of accomplishing his task. He, Joe and the IRA viewed Craig as the nemesis of those attempting to reconcile partisan groups – be they politically, religiously or economically motivated. For over twelve years, Craig, as leader of the Stormont government, had been no friend to democratic policies. He had abolished proportional representation of Catholics and Protestants in parliamentary contests. Catholic employment in civil service jobs had greatly decreased. Favoring Protestant over Catholic recipients for trade and economic development opportunities, the gap between those who had hope for self-sufficiency and those who did not had widened. Irish cultural education had been ignored in British-centric curricula. Nonetheless, as a scholar of philosophy and a budding practitioner of realism thanks to his younger scholars Robert and Jon, Eamon knew he had first to understand Craig's rationale for his oppositional views. He had also dreamed that Will Irvine had spoken to him about the act of listening. Only following that guidance could Eamon engage Craig respectfully on the necessity for change. The current and future peace of Northern Ireland depended upon reconciliation, not alienation.

Listening to the last celestial-like chords of the prelude, Eamon reached for his 1789 Prayer Book for additional inspiration. Since his days recuperating at the Craigmaddie Hospital in Scotland, he had followed a tradition of randomly opening the worn cover to any page, letting whatever spiritual power intervene. Doing so and looking down at today's selection, he noticed a pressed flower stuck in the page's stitched binding. He smiled knowing that Kat had placed it there in 1916 on behalf of her father Will. Eamon was first to smell it, and, then, to read the designated reference for comfort.

It was a dried poppy, formerly red and now faded to a gentle pink. The words to which it pointed were from Psalm 56. Miserere mei, Deus.

> *Yea, in God have I put my trust; I will not be afraid what man can do unto me. Unto thee, O God, will I pay my vows; unto thee will I give thanks. For thou hast delivered my soul from death, and my feet from falling, that I may walk before God in the light of the living.*

As the organ began the processional hymn, Eamon replaced his prayer book with a hymnal. He turned to page eighty-eight. Clearing his throat, he began a rousing baritone rendition of "God Is Working His Purpose Out".

God is working his purpose out as year succeeds to year:
God is working his purpose out, and the time is drawing near;
Nearer and nearer draws the time that shall surely be,
When the earth shall be filled with the glory of God
As the waters cover the sea.

What can we do to work God's work, to prosper and increase
the brotherhood of all mankind, the reign of the Prince of Peace?
What can we do to hasten the time, the time that shall surely be,
when the earth shall be filled with the glory of God
as the waters cover the sea?

Eamon would listen carefully to Craig's sermon. Then, meeting him for lunch, Eamon would continue to listen. Hopefully, God would stand guard while Eamon convinced Craig that the brotherhood of all mankind was God's purpose. If not God standing by, Eamon knew his long-departed, father-in law, Will would be there, poppy in hand.

18

Horse Chestnuts in View

Sunday, July 17, 1932

The Chandler's dining room was spacious in size but simple in decoration – an earthly reflection of conservative, Presbyterian beliefs. One wall hosted three, beveled windows that enabled a guest to view the church tower flanked by high branches of the Horse Chestnut trees reaching upwards toward the expansive sky and, symbolically, heaven. The morning rain had ceased, leaving the tower to glisten in the emerging sunlight. On the opposing wall of the room hung numerous family portraits of somber-looking pastors and politicians, all male garbed in somber liturgical or ceremonial robes. Below them was a long oak credenza with several silver platters of meat and potato remnants garnished with thyme and parsley. A large crystal pitcher of lemonade with floating mint leaves perched at one end. At the other end was a tall vase of flowers beside which rested a porcelain plate of Irish toffee. The third wall was empty except for a large mirror, framed by intricately scalloped, wooden edges. The fourth wall did not formally exist as it was, instead, a wide opening into the hallway which, when crossed, led to the salon. Its opening was bordered, left to right, by twin doors that could be opened or closed upon request by an easy touch of the hand, usually performed by Mrs. Chandler upon her husband's instruction.

She had just been summoned to close them as the meal was over. The three remaining men were positioned to talk. Rev. Chandler placed his linen napkin on the table and unbuttoned his formal waist coat. James Craig and Eamon Smiley followed suit, settling themselves in their respective chairs opposite each other. Eamon faced the windows; Craig the portraits.

"I am so sorry," Rev. Chandler said "that we must remain here for a little while until Mrs. Chandler holds her women's charity meeting in the salon. We know there are rumors of imminent protests against the Outdoor Relief program so she has called an emergency meeting of our Prospect Women's Auxiliary. As soon as they finish, we can move across the hall."

"No need to apologize, " said Craig. "It is good for our women to be engaged in such welfare work. They help greatly in teaching morality and abstinence to Catholic families."

Eamon frowned and counted to ten, then another ten. He deeply resented the assumption by Craig that Catholics were in need of such lessons. Fortunately, he also knew from Kat's and BB's work that there were Protestant and Catholic women who also resented that assertion. Craig's bias was just that, arrogance born out of ignorance and hubris to justify partisan beliefs. During the morning's sermon, Craig had used words that were clearly meant to excite, if not anger, the parishioners about the role Catholicism was playing in Northern Ireland. He cited the recent, June Eucharistic Congress held in Dublin. It had been attended by several Catholic Aldermen of the Belfast Corporation who had been ostracized by Protestant officials for traveling to the Congress in their NI ceremonial robes. Craig had also ranted resentment at the 100,000 NI Catholics who had crossed the border to reach the Congress despite clashes with Protestant groups. His Bible quote justifying such anger was from Psalm 7: Verse 11 "God is a righteous judge, and a God who feels indignation every day."

Eamon had been appalled at the verse and dearly wanted to start their conversation this afternoon with a retort from another Biblical reference: Proverbs 22:24 " Make no friendships with a man given to anger, nor go with a wrathful man." Instead, he relied on his better angels (or was it on his sister-in-law BB?) and chose an alternate verse to guide him: Psalm 86:15 : "But you, Oh Lord, are a God merciful and gracious. Slow to anger and abounding in steadfast love and faithfulness." Eamon knew that he had to understand the basis of Craig's resentments and try to offer alternative views. He counted a third ten before beginning the conversation.

"Good sir, " Eamon started. "I was interested in your sermon this morning, particularly referring to God's indignation. You seemed to be indignant, too. Am I correct in that assumption?"

Craig looked across the table at Eamon. "Of course I am indignant. Half of our Northern Ireland population profess every Sunday – if not daily – that the Pope and his representatives should be obeyed first and then the King. No one like that should hold office in our government nor should any citizen benefit from the prosperity of our nation unless they pledge loyalty to country over Pope – and certainly not to the IRA which is full of murderous heathens." Craig started to sputter such that Chandler got up and refilled Craig's empty glass with lemonade, putting his hand on Craig's shoulder to calm the politician.

Eamon counted a fourth ten before commenting. "I understand your reason to resent certain people. May I ask, though, if you think all Catholics consider their loyalty to the Pope and the IRA more important than their loyalty to their families and homeland? Might there be a certain percentage who, still faithful to the Catholic Church, are also faithful to the economic and social welfare of Northern Ireland? You have had many a discussion I know with Joe Devlin in which you both have agreed on the ways by which Stormont and Parliament can support farmers, mill laborers and dock workers. After all, aren't most of them Catholics? And don't they provide the backbone upon which our wealth stands up?"

Craig took a long gulp of his lemonade. He paused and, with his finger, swirled the mint leaf bouncing in his glass, attempting to capture it. He had to capture his next thoughts as well.

"Aye," Craig responded. "Ye are correct. Both Protestant and Catholic workers are the backbone of this nation. However, the latter need to speak up more against the IRA and recognize that their managers and government officials like myself know what's best for them. And, if they don't like that, then they can leave for The Free State or the US, Canada or Australia. May God bless them elsewhere."

Eamon sighed. "It sounds as though you are resigned to their always being second-class citizens as opposed to reconciling with Joe that they have a place in this country's future as equals to any man, including you, or woman, including your wife?"

A bustle outside the closed door caught Craig's attention. He coughed and frowned. "Rev. Chandler, I believe your wife has just dismissed her Auxiliary meeting. Perhaps I should leave as well. "

Craig rose from the table. Eamon was deflated. He had failed to gain Craig's interest, let alone trust in reconciliation.

"Professor," Craig said, reaching his hand across to Eamon. "I would like to attend one of your lectures. It seems I may learn more from you than what you have just shared today."

Eamon was surprised at this conciliatory proposal. He stood and took Craig's hand. "I would welcome that. My summer, evening classes are every Monday and Wednesday from 7-9 in Lanyon Hall. And, please call me Eamon."

Craig smiled. "Good. Very good. I will see you this Wednesday evening. And, please call me James."

As Craig left, Eamon looked out the windows and saw the Horse Chestnut trees branches waving at him. "How amazing," he said to himself.

19

Time On Their Sides

Sunday, July 17, 1932

Eamon was relieved, albeit temporarily, as he entered his Bangor home. Having expected the worst in meeting with Craig, he had been surprised at the Prime Minister's receptivity to hearing his ideas. Or, at least, Eamon assumed it was receptivity. Knowing a bit about the political vagaries in the Free State from Billie and his own position in the N.I. Stormont government as TD from Bangor, Eamon was leery about the governing strategy by which the end justified the means. He wondered exactly why Craig had offered to attend one of Eamon's philosophy classes. Was it to learn or was it to have another audience in which to preach a partisan sermon? Would Craig use Eamon's class to soap-box partisan rhetoric or to listen to students' ideas?

As he opened the front door at Park Avenue, he didn't have the chance to consider possible answers. Instead, he knew immediately that other confounding questions were before him.

"Ye're not going to stop me," came a full-throated exclamation from the kitchen.

"Aye, I will do everything I can to do so. Ye're crazy to go!" rose an equally passionate response.

Eamon knew his two sons, Devin and Neil, were at it again.

For over a week, each had been arguing about the other's immediate plans to either leave or stay in Belfast. Devin, at age nineteen, had just graduated from Belfast Royal Academy, a private school with an excellent academic reputation, despite promoting a Protestant evangelical curriculum. That along with his membership in the Fisherwick Presbyterian Boys Brigade had shaped Devin's view of himself as a citizen of Great Britain first, then of partitioned Ireland. Despite, or perhaps because of, his mother's Catholicism and pro-Republican stance, Devin had rebelled early in his political and religious allegiances. As an incredulous Kat had often complained to Eamon, "Your son has joined the Cromwellians."

Neil, on the other hand, had spent his eighteen years, skipping merrily along his mother's path. He had not attended the Academy; rather, he had been taught by the Catholic Sisters of Mercy at St. Francis' primary and secondary schools. For the last four years, he had been tutored in Irish Gaelic and assisted his Aunt Morna during her Saturday home visits to Catholics on Falls Road and Protestants on Shankill Road.

The only place the two young men were equals was on the soccer field; but even there, they were on opposite teams with their respective schools. Eamon sighed as he knew the current competition in the kitchen was not going to be without injuries. In addition, there would be no referee. Both Eamon and Kat had decided to let the lads solve their own conflicts, as difficult as that might be. A tie or truce would be the only resolution. However, more often than not recently, there had only been half-times.

As Eamon entered the kitchen, he was uncertain if any end to their match could be reached.

"I will do whatever I want, and if it means going to London, I will. There's nothing in this backward, heathen country to keep me." Devin faced his brother across the wide kitchen table that had so often brought them together for meals and amicable conversations. With Neil standing firm on the other side, the table seemed to secure their being on opposing sides of the pitch – different teams, different goal posts.

"And what does that mean – heathen?" asked Neil. "Are ye saying Mum and I are heathens because we are Catholic? Are ye saying that half of our Northern Ireland population is heathen?"

"Aye, ye are! Ye follow a Pope far away when yer King is right across the Channel. And he's a benevolent King bringing jobs to us and protecting us from those murderers in yer Irish Republican Army." Devin's naturally ruddish cheeks were flaming hotter and his closed hands curled into fists.

"That's not true, Devin. And ye know it." Neil leaned over the table toward his brother. "How can ye say that when ye know what Mum is doing in her newspaper, Dah is doing in Stormont and Aunt Morna and Uncle Ian are doing in their clinics? None of them want the violence of the IRA nor do they care about what religion their friends, students, readers, clinic patients and fellows on the streets follow. We're just human beings trying to get along as best we can, Devin. Can't ye see that?"

"Nay, ye're all wrong, wrong, wrong. If ye got rid of the disease, there would be no illness. And the disease is blind faith to a pompous, Papal leader. Craig is right, this is a Protestant country for a Protestant people. Grow up, Neil, and stop being so idealistic. There is no way Catholics and Protestants can get along unless Catholics like you give up your blindness."

"Ach. There is no way unless Protestants like you give up your deafness," retorted Neil.

Eamon could not restrain himself, hearing his two, dear sons argue by rejection of each other.

"Boys, please stop this arguing. Is there no way ye can hear and see each other as equals rather than adversaries? Come, sit with me and use your brilliant minds to understand each other."

Devin turned to his father and softened his tone. "Dah, I'm sorry to say that yer reasoning and hope for that are useless. I've already decided to leave for London. Yesterday, I received my acceptance at Oxford's Merton College with a full scholarship. Ye must agree that I can't give that up."

Eamon stared intently at Devin, then shook his head. "Ach, lad. What can I say? Indeed, ye must take advantage of whatever opportunity comes yer way. I…I…I am so proud of ye." He reached for his son, took his shoulders and pulled him into a fatherly embrace.

Neil stood in shock. His argumentative, hot air balloon had just been pierced. "Devin. Why didn't ye tell me this news?"

Released by his father, Devin turned to his brother and rounded the table. "I was about to, but ye took up the stance of adversarial stubbornness too quickly before I could. Ye are just like Mum in that respect."

Neil bowed his head in agreement and humility. Then, he reached out to his brother. Like Eamon, Neil pulled Devin into a brotherly embrace.

"Don't tell Mum I said that," begged Devin.

The three laughed. Eamon saw the resolution. There was neither tie nor truce about his sons' political stances. The current game was over. Now, there was a new playing field upon which a new game would be contested.

"Which of these boys will be the next champion of a united Ireland?" Eamon asked himself.

Eamon heard a quiet voice behind him whisper, "Perhaps both."

20

Finally, the Wedding

August 13, 1932

Robert had been surprised at her willingness to marry Ian. Watching Rachel in 1922 as she dreamed across the aisle from him on the train ride from Dublin to Macroom, she had fascinated him. Taking in her beauty as they waited for Michael Collins in the moonlight on that March night of the dancing fairies behind the rocks and low bushes of the Grange Stone Circle in County Limerick, she had enraptured him. As an American-born's first love of an Irish-born lass, Rachel offered Robert the most exuberant experience of cross-cultural infatuation. It was, however, short-lived.

It took Robert only six months to discard that first blush of emotion and to reimagine spending his life with her. He was quickly convinced she was not the right gal with whom to settle down. Her rebellious nature, her extreme passion for justice, and, he had to admit, her volatile temper were too much for him.

Good luck to Ian, he said to himself as he stood next to the groom this year of '32 at the back of the Belfast Botanic Garden's Palm House. "I'm so content with my dear, dear Morna, who, if she has me, will soon stand with me here. This is a grand day for a wedding, but, thank Mary and Joseph, it's not mine with Rachel!" He chuckled to himself.

Ian stood next to him. "What are 'ye chuckling at?" Ian asked, trying to calm himself by turning attention to his best man.

"Ah, dear Ian. I'm just contemplating how blessed you are being a doctor. No other man would have the patience and wherewithal to navigate life's decisions with the soon to be Mrs. McNulty. After all, Morna tells me you can conduct surgery without anesthesia or electricity and, thus, should fare well when managing your wife. Forgive me for comparing a demanding medical procedure in difficult circumstances to what it must be like having your way with Rachel."

Ian laughed as the two watched various family members and friends enter the front of Palm House to take their seats in the rows of white folding chairs facing them as they stood under the rose covered arbor.

"Ah, Robert," whispered Ian. "Most Irishmen know that there is no way ye can have yer way with any lovely – or unlovely – Irish lass. Ye have to accept that she is much smarter than ye and that she knows it. But, trust us. She will rarely tell ye...unless ye deserve to hear it. Never underestimate how such a gifted lass helps ye know what's best for ye and the family. My Great Aunty Eve who owned The Hawk Tavern in Coalisland taught me that."

Robert leaned into Ian, asking. "How so?"

"After my Mum died, Grand Aunty used to say 'Never forget that the most intelligent and kind men learn the best lessons of life from their Mums. Who else carries you through yer creation for nine months and brings you safely into this world? Not yer Dah!' Rachel is definitely a strong lass, Robert, but she reminds me of what's best in me. I always know she'll make me a better person tomorrow than I was yesterday and am today."

Bagpipe music began to harken the wedding procession. Robert paused his thoughts, thinking about his own birth-father, mother and two step-mothers. Ian was right. He turned away from Ian and sighed, deciding – let me focus on this day, not on the past.

Robert looked toward the two young girls approaching down the center aisle. Dressed in flowing lace dresses bowed around the waist by pink silk ribbons, eleven year old Maggie McCormick and thirteen year old Liza Smiley walked in step to the resonant notes of the bag pipes. From their respective wicker baskets, each girl was dropping sprigs of lavender and rose petals on the grass aisle before them. Robert caught his breath as his Morna followed them, her face aglow looking at him with the most angelic smile. Her golden curls were lifted up by a bright green ribbon into a halo-like embrace. "My beauty," he said to himself. "Soon you will be all mine." He felt a tug at his collar, but ignored it.

He wanted her to know, right then and there, that he would not be like his father. He would learn to treasure her wisdom more than his own. He would wait to tell her that. Perhaps then she would agree to marry him. But, reminding himself, this was Ian and Rachel's time to declare their eternal love for each other. His time would come soon.

Robert could hear Ian catch his breath as the bride appeared behind Morna. A radiant Rachel wore a simple, floor-length white-linen dress and crown of wild-flowers circling her auburn tresses. She held onto her brother Liam's arm with her right hand. The oldest brother and youngest sister were a natural fit walking together. Over twenty-six years, they had done so regardless of their differences-sometimes he walking ahead of her, sometimes behind. He had carried her first as an infant in his arms along Harriet Street and, then, as a child leaving their chaotic home forever. She had comforted him when he had lost his dearest friend Collins and had challenged his doubts that BB would ever accept his marriage proposal. Clutched in her left hand was a wild-flower bouquet of lilies of the valley. Liam had chosen it for her.

Robert noticed it shaking. "Good grief," he mused. "Is Rachel finally nervous?"

He thought again of Ian's words – or was it a voice speaking to him? "Never, ever underestimate the courage of an Irish lass, especially this one and, more so, the other lass whom ye're lucky to know loves ye!" Robert felt a second tug on his collar. What is this? he said to himself, adjusting his bow tie.

Standing now before Ian, Liam released Rachel for the final time as her greatest guide and comforter. She reached for Ian and greeted him, whispering into his ear. "Grand Aunty Eve is here, but I don't think she is talking to either of us."

Ian winked. "She no longer needs to guide me, my love, since she knows ye will so well. I think she's moved on to teach another man."

Rachel smiled. Robert was dumbfounded by a third tug.

21

No! No! No!

October 5, 1932

"Ye must be careful, Morna," warned Ian. The crowds are becoming too large for the RUC to manage without using batons. And, we know what terrible injuries those can muster. Please watch yerself."

Ian and Morna were outside St. Mary's Hall in Belfast, the strike headquarters of the Belfast Trades Council. The devastating Wall Street crash and its rippling impact on the world's economy were taking their material and human toll in both the Free State and Northern Ireland.

During numerous protests over the past four months, the two McNultys had offered their medical compassion and skills to the dissenting public – Protestant and Catholic, Unionist and Nationalist, IRA and RUC. As their Hippocratic oath declared:

...Into whatsoever houses I enter, I will enter to help the sick... and shall minimize suffering whenever a cure cannot be obtained, understanding that a dignified death is an important goal in everyone's life.

And, as their father had declared to Ian in his last words during the Rising, "Do not be a lesser person than those whom you have seen kill. Run your own race for righteous justice." The siblings had honored their father's words by choosing to be a doctor and nurse respectively, serving all people. For them, righteous justice started in helping anyone, no matter what background or belief, live healthy lives – free of physical and mental afflictions.

Today, they would honor those declarations when providing aid to victims injured while protesting the Outdoor Relief policies. Since August, more and more citizens, employed and unemployed, had unified to march in solidarity with the homeless and workhouse poor. Their primary complaint was the inequity and humiliation of Board of Guardian policies among which single men and women were denied benefits. Working wages were less than union rates, and local compensation was half that provided to the poor in Great Britain. On Monday, October 3rd, over 60,000 people had marched in Belfast. Today, it was estimated, there would be more. Undoubtedly, injuries would increase as the IRA was now forging its covert stand against the overt actions of the RUC.

Morna replied quietly, holding the hand of her brother. "Ah, dear Ian, worry not. I have no fear of adversaries as the women with whom I work daily know me well. They will protect me if I need help. And of course, I have God. How can I be harmed when I know He is watching over me?"

Ian smiled. "In addition to the Good Lord, better ye have our ancestors Sister Bridgette and Nanna Lizzie. They seem to have protected our family through equally trying times for more years than we can imagine."

"True." said Morna, repositioning her sack full of medical supplies upon her hip. "But, today, I may ask for additional guidance from Bigger and Sceo. Those two surely knew how to avoid dangerous back allies as well as to comfort injured on the spot. And comfort will definitely be needed today."

Ian shook his head in agreement. "Shall I see ye and Robert for dinner tonight with Rachel and me? He mentioned ye might have special news for us. Might this be a celebratory evening for ye two?"

Morna blushed. "If so, I haven't a clue to what ye are referring. I have not been forewarned of any extraordinary news or, as ye may be teasing, a significant announcement."

Ian laughed. "We'll wait and see." He kissed her forehead as they departed in different directions; Ian to Shankill Road, Morna to Falls Road.

Within less than an hour, each had treated over fifty injured, many from baton beatings by the RUC. It was later in the day that more deadly means were used.

Just as evening shadows were falling, Morna started up the steps of St. Peter's Cathedral off Falls Road which had been receiving the injured all day long. Both physically and mentally weary, she was focused on the placement of her feet rather than on her back.

"And where do ye think ye are going, little lady?" came a gruff voice behind her.

She turned to the face of an elderly man in an RUC uniform. He carried a bloody baton in one hand and pistol in the other. She could smell whiskey on his breath and the pungent sweat of his fetid shirt.

"I'm a nurse, good sir, going to help the injured in the Cathedral." She knew to calm an adversary by gentility, not confrontation.

"Nay, ye ain't. They need no help. Let me see what ye rally have in yer sack here." He reached toward her bag.

She pulled it closer to her chest.

"Sir, there are only medicine and bandages here. Trust me. There are no weapons to hurt anyone." She placed one hand on his approaching arm.

He grabbed her hand and squeezed it tightly. "Are ye threatening me?" he slurred, now lunging at her face with baton raised.

Morna felt the blow and saw a flash of light.

"No! No! No!" she cried, as she fell to the pavement.

22

Well Saved

October 5, 1932

The sky erupted into a brilliant yellow. A rush of air suctioned Morna upward toward an opening framed by sparkling diamonds and gems. She could feel her body, seemingly weightless, lift up vertically at a speed faster than any train in which she had traveled. She sensed a strange, magnetic force pulling her higher and higher. Suddenly, she was through the opening.

Immediately, she was upright, seeking balance on a rippling carpet underneath her. Before her was a garden basking in sunshine. Bordered by Horse Chestnuts overlooking an assembly of glorious colors: blues, reds, and whites emanating from blossoms of Irises, Poppies and Lilies of the Valley.

"Where am I?" asked Morna, feeling the throb in her head subside and her heart calm.

"Ye are with us," came a soft Irish brogue with a hint of Scottish mirth.

"Who is speaking? I can't see ye." Morna squinted and slowly turned around in a circle, taking in the colors and sweet scents of the flowers. She felt a light breeze brushing her left cheek; then, a gentle kiss upon her forehead.

"Aye, child. Ye can't see for now. Listen instead." The breeze became warmer. What seemed like a translucent shawl slipped around Morna's shoulders. She let it embrace her, moving her hands through whiffs of air to capture the braided ends upon her chest.

"Can you at least tell me how ye know my name and if I am in another world?" she asked, feeling the shamrock-covered path settle underneath her between two parallel rows of poppies.

The voice started to fade.

"Aye, I can, but move a bit along the path before ye, up toward the Blue Irises. There ye'll hear yer answers more clearly. And, as well, there is someone who wants to greet ye."

A nip at Morna's heels pushed her ahead as a second voice beckoned. Morna obeyed and strode up the path, leaving the red Poppies behind.

Approaching the Blue Irises, she felt her heart beat faster. The nudging at her feet ceased. She stopped. There was a presence reaching around her torso that felt so familiar, so reminiscent of another, yet foreign, touch.

"Morna, my dear," came a Coalisland lilt, quiet and gentle like a morning mist kissing the lavender.

Tears began to fill Morna's eyes.

"Mother? Is that ye?" Morna asked.

"Aye, my darling. It is I." The shawl suddenly turned into clouds of filigreed lace enveloping Morna's entire body. "How I have longed to hold ye close again."

"Ah, Mother. How I have longed to be held by ye." Morna's tears tumbled down her cheeks. She watched them expand into droplets that fell onto the irises below her. She saw that, with each tear, a new bud blossomed.

Morna was amazed at the sight.

"Is this heaven, Mum?" she asked, trying to grasp the lace, but it eluded each touch of her fingers. "Am I going to stay with ye?"

"Nay, my child. It is not yer time to rest here. Ye and yer brother have much more to do. Our nation needs ye to offer healing and compassion for whomever is in need. Yer father and I are so proud of ye both."

Morna heard a whimper at her feet. The tugging began again.

Her mother's voice became quiet, fading into a whisper.

"Go back, dearest Morna. Give our love to yer brother. Know yer Da and I will always be with ye both. And, take care of that special beau who is waiting for ye. Go, now. Ye are well saved."

Morna felt a pressure in her head return but less intense, more like an inexplicable lightness. She grabbed at an iris before falling.

"Mother! Mother! Mother!" Morna cried.

She opened her eyes to see three faces before her. She was alive, lying in a hospital bed.

"My darling, darling, Morna," came a voice from the first face. Sitting beside her, Robert pressed her hand to his lips. He was almost, but not yet, in tears. Ian and BB were standing behind him. Ian expressed relief by sighing loudly. BB expressed gratitude by reciting a silent prayer.

Morna raised her eyes to her brother. "Ian. I saw Mother. Truly, I did. She was with Bigger in a garden of Horse Chestnuts and beautiful flowers – Poppies and Blue Irises and Lilies of the Valley."

Morna saw the incredulity on his face. She tried to sit up. Her brother gently pushed her back, nestling her head upon the pillow.

"Morna. Rest. Ye are so lucky to be alive. Ye have had a nasty head wound and have lost a lot of blood. If it weren't for a stray dog breaking the impact of yer fall on the concrete steps of the cathedral, I fear ye'd be permanently with Mum."

Morna settled back, closed her eyes and saw a vision of her mother and Bigger. They were beaming radiantly from the garden before disappearing completely. "Thank you, Mother, and thank you, dear Bigger," she whispered.

She reopened her eyes and looked at Robert. With one hand, he wiped the tears that had started to fall from his own eyes. With the other, he offered her a bouquet of Blue Irises – in full bloom.

23

The Sack and Bonnet

November 5, 1932

Rachel gathered up her pamphlets from the table in the Women's Auxiliary Hall of St. Patrick's Cathedral in Armagh, forty miles southwest of Belfast. She could have left a few but wanted to make one more stop this evening at which they were also needed. Her task of helping Ian and Morna's medical clinic services by speaking to and sharing literature with widowed and unemployed mothers throughout Northern Ireland was becoming more and more fulfilling. It also allowed her to balance her marital obligations with her covert IRA role. She shared life-saving messages of hygiene, inoculations, and child care while getting to know the needs of local women. The latter, along with some detailed intelligence about Royal Ulster Constabulary locations and activities, she would share with her IRA Belfast Brigade Commanders.

She clutched her sack with the remaining fliers and turned to cross the meeting room and reach the exit door. Head down, she was contemplating the Smiley family dinner she and Ian would attend the next night. She mused; Robert and Morna might finally announce their engagement now that Morna had recuperated so well from her attack. Rachel heard the exit door open. Thinking it was Ian who was to go with her to the next engagement, she looked up. Stunned, she stopped.

A figure she had long despised was crossing the room, too – inching slowly toward her.

"'Tis ye," Rachel asserted, trying to cover her alarm.

"Aye, 'tis I," came a raised, yet raspy, response.

The woman approaching was middle-aged, stout and round shouldered. Her bulk was neither Rubenesque nor matronly. Rather, it was heavy and dour above swollen feet shrouded in an ankle length brown skirt topped by a ragged, short jacket. A rust-colored blouse with a high neck collar rose up to a bulbous chin. Tilted left upon the woman's grey hair was a black felt bonnet, indicative of the previous century's fashion, far from contemporary. Over her shoulder was a bulky sack, paisley in design but plain in intent. Rachel shivered at what might be inside.

"It has been too long since I have seen ye," said Rachel, slowing her pace as the features of a scowling face came into focus.

"Aye, eleven and a half years exactly since that April '22," said Molly McKenzie, known by Rachel from Robert's warning as Mrs. O'Connor.

That space in time was shortened by each adversary's tentative step towards the other.

"Much has passed around and between us in those years, Molly," offered Rachel, taking a deep breath. She beckoned Ian and BB's advice for her next words. The three had often discussed the possible encounters Rachel might have with adversaries, particularly this woman whom the Countess had recruited to frame Rachel for the murder of Father O'Hare and whom, subsequently, Rachel had exposed to Michael Collins.

Rather than leading right into an action that would definitely not be favorable to either of them, Rachel relied on her family's wisdom to question and listen first. Instead of asking "What do ye want to do?" she asked "What are ye thinking, Molly?"

"What do ye think I'm thinking?" sneered Molly. "Ye turned me in to the enemy such that I have been traveling ever since my release from prison last year – homeless and family-less- sleeping in unfamiliar beds with unfamiliar people for over a decade, relying on the directives and desires of faded heroes."

Rachel heard hesitancy in the last phrase, tempered by halted breathing. Was there a realization of guilt, a tinge of regret, a sadness of sorts? Or was there something else affecting this woman?

Rachel took a step closer to her.

Noticing dark circles under swollen eyes and the sour whiff of soiled clothing and body, she pondered. "Is this really the same woman Jon interviewed just months ago? If so, she is not well," Rachel thought.

Finally recognizing the debilitating onset of either heart or kidney disease that was so apparent in her clinic attendees, she leaned forward.

"I'm sorry for ye, Molly."

Molly jerked back. "Nay, ye need not feel sorry for me. I have accomplished much in honor of my Ireland – much more than ye," she growled. "I have recently followed yer travels around the island convincing women of their rights and sharing information to help them and their families. What good is that if their men are still without jobs and considered less than rats by an oppressive tyrant?"

"Ye are right, Molly." Rachel nodded. "Men must have the same rights and opportunities as their women to live healthy and productive lives. I just don't believe that violence and hatred bring such ends to fruition. Rather, I think they keep us at terrible odds with each other, just like ye and I have been for years. To what end has our estrangement been: ye on the run and I in hatred? Should our brothers and sisters live the same way?"

Rachel saw Molly's shoulders begin to sag. The sack slipped off the left one. Its content sprawled onto the floor – soiled undergarments and moldy pieces of bread. Molly herself followed them, collapsing onto the concrete.

Rachel quickly reached Molly's prostrate body, placing an arm under her head. The aged bonnet rolled away.

As Ian came through the open door and raced across the room, Rachel cried out.

"Molly! Molly! Stay with me. Stay with me."

Molly did not.

24

Colorful

December 31, 1932

"Let us raise our glasses to our dear Ireland!" said the Irvine elder, Billie.

"To our dear Ireland" came a resounding response accompanied by right arms, lifting half-filled or empty, amber colored goblets. "To Ireland! To Ireland!"

After the last tribute, Billie continued. "Now, as we do each December 31, let us declare the item for which we give special thanks during this year of our Lord, 1932. Remember, ye can say it, sing it or act it out. If ye do the last, however, we must guess within three tries or we'll be here until well after mid-night." The family laughed, knowing full well that, no matter how skillfully they tried to restrain their loquacious members, the earliest to bed would surely be when the master hall clock chimed two times.

Among the four lineages present (Irvine, Smiley, McCormick and McNulty), seventeen representatives settled around the salon of the Irvine Dublin, row house. A red velvet sofa hosted four members -the newly-married couples Ian and Rachel next to Robert and Morna. In the two wing chairs next to each of the sofa's arms were Eamon to the right and Billie to the left. Kat stood next to Eamon; Agnes next to Billie. Both women were ready to refresh empty glasses of beer, cups of tea and plates of delicacies from Lemon's Confectionary – mint humbug and yellow man rocks. Fortunately, both husbands knew to alternate the tasks and seats with their better-halves.

Liam sat with BB in the love seat reserved for them across from the sofa and wing chairs. "What is it about Uncle Liam and Auntie BB that allows them to have that place each year?" a curious, eight year old Neil Smiley had asked one New Year's Eve a decade before. "Ach," replied Rachel. "Those two have been love birds before they were individually carried to this earth by the snow geese. They deserve to nest wherever they like." And so, since 1919, the oldest McCormicks had taken up their hallowed spot each December 31st.

Seated on straight-backed wicker or wooden folding chairs to complete the clan's figurative and literal circle were the remaining seven youth: Neil and Liza Smiley; Kieran and Maggie McCormick; Jon, Katie and Wolfe Irvine. Devin Smiley and Thon McCormick were spending the holidays across the channel. Devin had decided to stay in Oxford at Merton College claiming he needed to study. His sister Liza, triumphant in her inimitable curiosity, had learned he had met a lovely, Scottish lass in his Gaelic mythology class. Liza doubted Devin's written rationale. Thon was with the Lawson family in their seaside estate outside Brighton. Kat and BB had commiserated about their absences from home; Eamon and Liam had commiserated about their absences from the homeland.

The circle would not be complete without the newest generation of loyal canines: Larger, Failinis, and Grua. They were settled under the circular table in the middle of the gathering, paws over paws and tails curled around petals woven into the rug's flowers. Familial devotion was growing by the months in this, their first, year of companionship. During a June family outing, Jon said he was beginning to believe in reincarnation because the three pets were exactly like Bigger, Boru and Sceo in temperament. Upon hearing Jon's comment, the dogs had cocked their heads to the right – surprisingly in simultaneous motion. Blind Wolfe felt the movement in Larger while stroking his head; Jon, the journalist, noted the coincidence by observation and related it to Wolfe. After that, the two cousins would forever share a common intrigue in and an unspoken reverence for the three dogs' unusually similar habits.

All was now in place for the beginning of the festive tradition.

Billie began: "Round One calls on the senior adults – ladies first." As precedence had dictated, they went in alphabetical order. Agnes thanked her Billie for his understanding of her actions during the Four Courts siege. BB thanked the Lord for keeping everyone safe, referring particularly to Morna's thorough recuperation. Kat thanked Robert for formally joining their family. She was followed by Billy, Eamon, and Liam who praised their respective wives for understanding their various, personality traits that often were seen as curmudgeonly oppositional. Being the gender they were, no husband would publicly admit what he would later say in private – his thanks for being loved unconditionally. Each man would keep that for when the clock struck three times. Then, he would be wrapped in the arms of his shamrock, as Eamon still called Kat. Liam and Billie had come to choose their own endearments.

Round Two included the junior adults. The newlyweds shared their thanks for each other: Robert and Ian for the "yes" finally offered by Morna and Rachel respectively; Morna for the offer she had hoped would be coming but wasn't sure; Rachel for the offer she was sure she had lost. Jon turned to Billie and Agnes and held up a copy of The Irish Times, saying "Without your encouragement, I would not be speaking on behalf of our nation." The family members chorused in syncopated time: "Hear! Hear!"

As for the youngest members in Round Three, they led a lengthy series of charades. Neil pushed a virtual set of eyeglasses up his nose and opened his hands flat before him to indicate his father's newly published book on Descartes. In one hand, Liza held up a fictional monocle to her eye; the fingers of her other hand mimicked holding a song book. She hummed the ballad of the Tain Bo Cuailnge. On Liza's birthday, Kat had given Liza Gran'mother Bella's 1870 version translated by Bryan O'Looney. Much laughter occurred when Kieran, Maggie and Kate performed a short skit with Kieran playing on a ghost fiddle in thanks for his music lessons, Maggie stepping an improvised sean-nos dance in gratitude for her ballet classes, and Katie singing silently, acknowledging her private voice lessons. Guesses were quick and accurate.

When it came to Wolfe, the family waited. He was often last. Being blind, he was either overseen or seen over by others. Agnes always saw him, though, as the brilliant intellect he was. Proving the superlative listener, he had laughed during the charades although he could not see the actions. Tonight his mother would not let others forget his abilities and presence.

"Come, Wolfe. For what are ye thankful this year?" She asked.

He stood up from his chair and looked around the circle of faces. He had captured each one in memory from when he was sighted during his first ten years. These relatives were envisioned in stone, descriptions he would remind them of when future decades greyed their hair and diminished their own cognitive powers.

"I have a poem of thanks," he said, his own Round Four.

The room went silent. Fingers that had been busy holding glasses or pastries now set the items down. Hands reached for the ones next to them. A figurative Christmas wreath formed, interlacing tender boughs, lace ribbons and decorative berries. Wolfe was the red velvet bow at the top.

Larger rose and stood by Wolfe's side. Wolfe placed his hand on the dog's head and started with the poem's title: *A Colorful Life*, emphasizing the separation of the word color from full. He went on.

"Do ye ever wonder
why the sea is rippled blue,
the clouds on a hazy day pale coconut,
the sand a speckled tan,
yer child's eyes
a shimmering hazel?

Do ye ever wonder why
the shamrock is a verdant green,

the furze a flaming orange,
the lavender an indigo purple,
freckles on yer brother's face
burnished a chocolate brown?

Do ye ever wonder why
the fox is a brilliant rust,
the hare a dotted grey,
the mole a dusty ash,
the finch a golden hue,
the braid of yer lover's hair auburn?

Do ye ever wonder
why the sun is a radiant yellow,
the moon a translucent white,
the stars a field of diamonds sparkling light,
yer mother's kiss a velvet red?

What mysterious Artist took out a palette
and filled in the blank spaces of our existence?
How blessed are we by His gift."

He stopped, looked up at the family, and finished: "I give thanks for the gift of our color-full family."

A hush was followed by the clapping of hands and stomping of feet, a roar of praise.

The clock chimed twice. For an instant, the twelve numbers on the dial faded away and were replaced by misty visages of smiling family members from the beyond. In unison, Larger, Failinis, and Grua simultaneously cocked their heads toward the clock's sound and sight. Tails began to wag.

25

Beyond Proclamations

December 31, 1932

Una's Epilogue

There wasn't a dry eye among us, here in the beyond, at the end of Wolfe's recitation. I noticed that even his name sake, Theobald Wolfe Tone, unfolded a one hundred and thirty-four year old wool, pocket square to wipe his nose. He declared, "That's me lad." Bella, of course, held Lizzie's hand tight to reassure her that nothing Lizzie had contracted and spread during Agnes' pregnancy had eventually caused Wolfe's blindness. Michael reminded us that those who have the greatest insight are often those who use their senses first to subsequently inform their thoughts.

Thomas McCann agreed. He shared his inimitable farming wisdom: "Ye can't plow a field just thinkin' about it! Ye first have to touch the dirt, smell the air, feel the wind, and hear the raven's call. That boy has the gift of sensing his surroundings before offering the best judgement." We nodded when Thomas ended his remarks, saying "He may see differently than most of us; but, by God, he clearly sees."

"We are certainly happy," said the loquacious Aiden, "that our loved ones below offer thanks after the facts for the blessings in '32. But, they have no idea of our influence in creating those endowments and diminishing many the year's possible misfortunes.

"Come. Let us now begin our traditional, end-of-year fete to predict next year's affairs and plan our roles in them."

Several of us rolled our eyes knowing he would take up the remaining hours of '32 sharing his own prophesies for '33, inevitably '34, '35, '36, and perhaps the entire decade. The spirits of modesty had not yet imbued themselves into his soul. But, since we are timeless here, there are no clocks. And, since we are forgiving, we indulge him.

Let me summarize our eventual predictions and those family members assigned to guide their decendents' earthly passages.

First, on the political side, we believed that the Free State of Ireland would become The Republic of Ireland. Patrick Pearse was quick to predict that its declaration would include the exact words he had written in 1916. None of us saw the same future for Northern Ireland. It would, sadly, remain a colony of Great Britain. deValera would become the President of the Republic; Sir James Craig would remain the President of the Stormont government. The IRA of Belfast would grow covertly with no political allegiance; the Royal Ulster Constabulary and Ulster Special Constabulary Volunteers would grow overtly, relying on British backing. deValera would negotiate the strictures of the Anglo-Irish Agreement and attempt to deny the British occupation of Free State Irish seaports.

Michael, Griffith and Will Irvine declared their willingness to intervene on these proposed events. All three recognized the global turmoil roiling on the Eastern European horizon that would sorely impact the entire island and the whole world.

Secondly, we predicted more conflict economically between the Free State and Britain on trade, led by deValera's government and local labor unions. Tariffs would be increased on respective items – British taxes on The Free State's sale of cattle; Irish taxes on British sale of coal. De Valera's government would continue its refusal to pay land annuities to the descendants of the British ascendancy. Unemployment in both the south and north would continue to force many young Irish to emigrate. Young girls would continue to leave their rural homes to seek income as maids or factory workers in urban areas or overseas in North America, Australia or Great Britain. Many would become indentured slaves, particularly by our own Catholic Church.

Thomas McCann and Jonathan Gallagher committed to ensuring the creation of a modern agricultural and engineering workforce. The Countess, Sarah and Mary McCracken and, surprisingly, Christine O'Leary voiced their support of women's rights for universal voting, child support and employment of female teachers after marriage. Molly McKenzie joined them. Uncle Aiden blustered about his role with unions. Considerable humphs and grins on our part accompanied his commitment to that!

Patrick McCann and Anthony Gallagher claimed the cultural predictions. Their hope to require Irish language in schools and the study of philosophy motivated both men and, with little debate, we all agreed. Of course, Patrick Pearse raised his hand in approval of these predications, quickly writing a poem. We foresee that one of our youth below will pick it up – perhaps Erin McCann in a new play or Jon McCormick in an editorial.

Interestingly, we debated the viability of our social proclamations. Catholics and Protestants in both the South and the North would continue to separate their housing, schools, churches, hospitals and social activities. Nonetheless, we determined that some families and community groups would serve as models of reconciliation and earn respect from even the most partisan of groups.

Christine and the Countess objected to this prediction saying it was hopeless. Bella, Lizzie and Sister Bridgette adamantly disagreed and pledged to ensure their fruition. Lizzie was passionate about those related to health care.

As the family's matriarch, I, of course, was given the duty of proclamations about the fate of familial ties, those loosened by differing opinions and loyalties and those tightened by common persuasions and beliefs. Weaving the rug of my family's tapestry is a hefty chore. None of our members here in the beyond wanted to take it on.

The determination of destiny's warp and free will's woof was, thus, assigned to me.

Come with me into our next years to learn how well I and my dear family members will weave our respective knots and rows.

Part 2

1940

26

Looking Ahead

Sunday, January 1, 1932

Una's Introduction

How do we forsee, among the unpredictable, the impact of time's passage over the next eight years, 96 months, 416 weeks, 2,557 days...dare I go on with hours and minutes? So many beliefs shared and hidden. So many actions planned and conducted. So many actions planned and delayed. So many lives born and lost; so many loves steeled and unrequited. The only constant is the need for peace.

Were any of those who lived and loved during these years listening to the wisdom of their ancestors? Those who came to us in the beyond, after less than a year of life or after many years, included women and men; soldiers, nurses, teachers and farmers; heroes and villains; politicians – Republicans, Unionists, Nationalists, Fascists and Communists; Protestants and Catholics. Each had a soul. Each had a voice from the infant's first cry, to the child's laughter, the tenor's song, the prisoner's curse, the soldier's last breath, the widow's sob, and, finally, to the elder's prayer. Each lived through a time and world needing reconciliation between great joy and great sorrow.

We welcomed them all – forgave and praised them, comforted and consoled them, offered them unconditional love. But that was not always an easy task. We had journeyed with them while they were on earth, offering advice and warnings. Most did not heed our guidance.

For some, their free will turned them away from us. As Uncle Aiden said when he oriented a recent newcomer who had ignored our counsel, the result of which had brought much grief to his or her world, "What the blazes were ye thinkin'?"

How I wish we greeted more who had taken our directions. To those who had, our dear Bella recited her welcome: the poignant funeral ode by Edward Hazen Parker.

"Life's race well run,
Life's work well done,
Life's victory won,
Now cometh rest."

As you travel with me now into these next years, I hope you will bear witness to those who stray and those whose victories will be won. May you learn from both.

27

Red Poppies

January 19, 1940

The telegram to 7 Parkview Street, Bangor, has been short on content but massive in weight.

> *Neil in St. Thomas Hospital. Stop. Come quickly. Stop. Don't tell Mother. Stop. Devin.   5 AM, 1/17/40*

Eamon Smiley's hand had trembled. Failinis had quickly gone to his side.

Monday, January 19, Eamon was more settled.

"On this I don't think he was involved, Father."

"Ach, Devin. I wouldn't be so sure." Eamon clutched his overnight satchel as he sought to secure his thoughts regarding Neil, Eamon's youngest son and Devin's brother.

The two men hurried through London's Westminster Road Bridge train station amidst the mass of uniformed soldiers and civilian workers – the former ready for battle overseas, the latter ready for battle in Parliament. Eamon and Devin had no idea if their own battle would be for Neil's life or for his conscience.

"Tell me what ye know, Devin," asked Eamon.

Devin began. "Neil and I had supper together this past Thursday. He seemed uncharacteristically quiet. I noticed his eyes averting mine – again, uncharacteristically. I must admit going on and on, at first, about my upcoming deployment with the First Royal Irish Fusiliers to France. As you can imagine, my Scots lass Briana is quite proud of me, yet I sense she is also quite upset. I decided Neil could guide me in fashioning my parting conversations with her, using his uniquely pragmatic yet passionate words inherited from Mother. Quickly, however, I saw he was not listening to me.

I asked him what was distracting him.

He was hesitant at first; then, he spoke evasively. 'What do you think of these Irish bombings on London soil?'

I asked him a second question in reply. 'Do you mean those conducted by the IRA after its declaration of war on Britain a year ago this month?'

'Aye.' he responded, now looking me eye-to-eye.

I told him I thought they were useless and cruel, causing the IRA to lose trust at home. Why hurt the arms factories and mills supplying our own boys and those of Scotland and Britain to fight the real enemy Germany? I also reminded him that too many innocent people here in London had been killed or injured.

He became quite heated, saying 'But isn't this the best time to undermine our own greatest enemy, the British empire? How can you fight on its side when for centuries it hasn't fought on ours?'

I could not argue with him on that point. He was logically correct and, yet, his thinking was not based on foresight, rather only on the past and present. And he avoided accounting for the loss of life and devastating burns the IRA attacks caused on the innocents. How I wished you had been with us to temper the roots of his emotions by reminding him of the branches that will eventually protect us in the future."

Eamon paused as the two approached the front doors of St. Thomas Hospital, the former glass replaced by poster-board.

Turning to Devin, he placed his hand on his son's shoulder. "Ye did the best ye could, good lad. Now, we must hear about your brother's condition and, God willing, his reckoning with the circum-stances that have brought him to this time and place."

By the hospital's entrance door stood an older woman, draped in a paisley shawl. Her translucent face was circled by grey hair peeking out from under a felt, bucket cloche hat. On her left breast was a British Red Cross pin and in her hand was a basket of red poppies. Not noticing her, Eamon passed through the doorway.

Devin, however, paused beside her.

"Good sir, may I give you these?" she beckoned, handing Devin three individual lace dollies, each bundling several red-blushing buds.

"Thank you, my lady" said Devin, taking them from her with a bow. When he looked up to compensate her, she was gone.

"How strange," he thought.

28
Fate or Coincidence?

January 19, 1940

Walking the center aisle of St. Thomas Hospital's second floor, Eamon and Devin had the opportunity to reflect before they reached Neil's bedside. Eamon remembered his days at Craigmaddie Estate where he had convalesced from his devastating wounds – physical and mental – acquired thirty years before in the WWI trenches of Loos. Devin thought about what might soon face him in the same countryside of France, battles only imagined. The rows of metal cots, white sheets and Chatham wool blankets enveloped bodies that few could recognize as human; faces bandaged across eyes, ears or mouths offered only hints of shape and shade underneath.

Despite the low moans of pain, there was a sense of peace as Red Cross nurses seemed to float from row to row, figure to figure. Other women sat by the prostrate, reading softly from pages of scented stationary, leather-backed books or worn Bibles. The mummer of healing and grace camouflaged troubled breathing.

Eamon and Devin counted down to the twentieth row and turned left. There was Neil, lying on his back with two thickly bandaged hands resting upon an outer blanket covering his chest and legs. His face was turned left away from them.

"Neil, my lad," called Eamon quietly. The lips did not reply. "Neil, my son. It's Da."

Slowly the head turned. Eamon and Devin muffled their gasps. The entire left side of Neil's face was burned, one eye closed, the cheek seemingly melted into the chin. No recognition of him was forthcoming if one focused on that half of his face, nor could he recognize his family from there either. The right eye opened; a tear began to form.

"Neil. Neil. Neil," whispered Eamon as he leaned over his son and kissed the only part of his beloved son that was unwrapped – the top of the lad's curly-haired head. "Ye are alive, me boy."

A muffled voice replied. "Father." The tear dropped.

"Hush. Ye need not talk. We are here now and will be for as long as it takes to bring ye back home."

Another tear formed and flowed, followed by another and another. Father mirrored son. Eamon's grief – or was it relief – cried silently for his son. From his vest pocket, he pulled the linen hand-kerchief Kat had embroidered with a shamrock as his Christmas gift. He wrapped it around one of his son's bandaged hands.

Eamon pulled up a wicker chair positioned beside the small table next to his son's cot. He looked at the accompanying medicinal tray set so carefully with necessary supplies. How familiar it looked, all these decades later. Eamon reached for what he assumed was a san-itized bandage, opened a closed bottle of petroleum, and carefully wiped the tears from his son's right cheek. Three deep blue eyes met. Both men attempted to smile visually; Eamon more successfully than Neil. Neil closed his eye and settled his head flat on the pillow. From his son's settled breathing, Eamon could tell Neil had fallen into a drug-induced sleep.

Devin stood behind his father. Quietly, he said, "My God, Father, what has happened to him?"

Before either could speak came a calming, voice with a Scots-Irish lilt. "I can tell ye both if ye would like." A young nurse stood at the foot of Neil's bed. She had flaming red hair tucked under her nurse's cap, but a flurry of strands had escaped their enclosure. It seemed that her curls embraced rather than fled from cheeks that were flushed and round, as in a Reubens' painting. "I have been car-ing for him, and he has told me a bit of what has brought him here."

Eamon rose from his chair as Devin turned toward her. Both men walked to the end of the bed. Forming a trio, the three stood guard over their ward in the long, central aisle perpendicular to the rows.

"I'm Lily McCarthy, his day nurse. Neil suffered greatly upon his arrival here three days ago, but is making great progress physically. We could have lost him if it were not for the quick thinking of those who found him on the curb outside Euston Station's post office. At first, based on his burns, the police thought he was part of the IRA band that had set the mailbag bombs to explode, but an older lady – quite distinguished looking – recognized him as the nephew of TD Irvine from Dublin's Dail and rushed Neil here. We thought she would return to visit him, but she has yet to come. He probably will tell you about her when he can. For now, though, he must rest."

"We thank ye for the good care ye are obviously giving him, Miss McCarthy," said Eamon, looking intently at her face. "We will sit here until he awakes so please tell us what we can do that will assist him and ye."

Quickly yet thoroughly, she gave them instructions on curative tasks family members were allowed to take. She finished with another that resonated with Eamon: "Listen, listen and listen more," she offered.

Eamon sensed she was wise beyond her years, and for some other reason, was uniquely familiar in looks and demeanor.

"May I take yere poppies and put them in a vase," she asked, "so Neil can see them when he awakes? I'm sure they will comfort him."

As Devin handed her the three bouquets, Eamon asked: "Tell me. Where are ye from in Scotland?"

"Ah, ye have a good ear," she said. "My family is from Paisley. Do ye know it?"

Eamon stared at her again. "Yes, indeed I do. My wife's family is from there." He hesitated and then asked: "Ye're not related to the former Governess of Holloway Prison, Mistress Fanny McCarthy, are ye?"

Lily's eyes widened in surprise. She quickly responded. "Aye, indeed I am. She's my gran."

29

St. Thomas' Staircase

January 19, 1940

Eamon, Devin and Lily descended to the hospital lobby on the first floor. Eamon's limp ensured he was the last in their journey down the circular, marble staircase.

How agile they seem, he thought as he followed the two young people. May that benefit them as they travel through this decade.

In the first months of a second world war, the six-hundredth year of an Irish revolution, and a future replete with doubts, Eamon knew his sons and their peers needed to garner all the wisdom and strength their ancestors and living family elders could offer. "But will they listen to us?" he pondered. The times are so full of our mistakes, why would they?

Arriving at the bottom of the staircase, he stepped onto the lobby floor and followed their lead. "Let me take Nurse Murphy's advice for Neil and just listen to him and them as well."

Lily led the two men into a small sitting room to the right of the stairs and left of the blackened, glass doors leading to Westminster Bridge Road. The three took seats around a rectangular, coffee table upon which were placed various brochures about the hospital services next to a King James Bible. On the wall before Eamon and Devin was a recruitment poster for the British army – an armed soldier heroically standing on a dirt mound surrounded by anti-aircraft tanks. He was gazing up at explosions depicted as successful bursts of power against an air-born enemy. A second poster offered the somber face of another soldier whose helmet warned "Keep it under your hat." On the opposite wall was a poster seeking Women Army Corps members (WACS) above another highlighting a woman farmer, hoe in hand, in the Women's Land Army. Lily faced that wall; Eamon and Devin the other.

"Please tell us more of what Neil told you, Lily," asked Devin. "We don't want to exhaust him with our questions, but need to know what to say to our mother. She has just telegrammed that she is on her way here. God only knows how she so quickly learned about his plight."

Eamon chuckled, looking at Lily with a smile. "Knowing the reputation of your Gran and her relationship with the women in our own family, I have no doubt that she relayed whatever she knew to them as soon as she could."

Lily hesitated, frowned and, then, smiled. "Ach, Master Smiley. If my gran spoke to your wife, it was from the beyond as she passed away just last month. Truly, though, I have no doubt she was capable of communicating from there. She is the most spiritual person I have known. Notice how I say 'is' as I feel her presence daily."

Eamon and Devin looked at each other. Mother Kat and Aunt BB had often spoken about their Grandmother Bella's spirit embracing them in precarious or celebratory situations. Was it the Scots Irvine/ McGregor mysticism in their blood? Devin scoffed off Lily's comment; Eamon knew he would ask Kat how she so quickly knew to come to London. Whatever he said, he would believe.

"Let's get back to the truth in this present situation, Lily," insisted Devin. "Tell us what my brother has said."

Lily elaborated on what Neil had shared about the circumstances of his injuries. She cautioned them in believing Neil's words for he had been in a fever, tempered by much medication. He had often been lucid, then confused, and then garbled.

"Nonetheless," she continued, "this is what he related just before you arrived. He had entered the Euston Station at about 6 pm on Friday. There he met two acquaintances. He did not tell me who they were. He just said they had invited him to attend an Irish play. He did not relate the play's title nor who the performers were. He became quite flustered and kept repeating: 'I told them not to do it. I told them not to do it.' Breathless, he then seemed to go into a trance.

"After a few minutes, he opened his eye and looked directly at me with such a desperate expression, whispering, 'Tell my family, I didn't do it. I didn't do it. Promise me you'll tell them I have lived a just life.' Before I could reassure him, he fell back into the sleep from which you just woke him."

The three fell mute. Lily placed her hands on her lap, left over right. Devin's were knotted on his knees, at the end of thighs now perpendicular to his straight backed torso. Eamon's were clasped in prayer.

Several seconds passed, counted only by the measured ticks of a grandfather clock whose decorative orange, half sun looked out at the three. Eamon rose and bowed his head toward Lily. "Thank ye, Nurse Murphy, for yer kind and thorough telling. I suggest we go back upstairs. Neil may be awake now to share whatever he can and wants."

The three re-entered the lobby.

"Oh," exclaimed Lily suddenly. "There is the lady who brought Neil to us."

The three looked at the back of a matronly figure ascending the staircase. She was dressed in an ankle-length, white woolen coat trimmed at the neck by a single pelt collar of brown sable mink. Clipped to two paws, its head and beaded black eyes faced directly backwards at the trio. An old-fashioned wide brimmed, hat – well out of fashion – covered her head.

"My lady. My lady" Lily cried out.

The woman did not stop. Instead, she reached the top step and, turning right, entered the patients' ward.

The three hurried up the stairs. They also turned right, certain they would catch up to her. However, as they entered the hall, she was nowhere to be seen.

Eamon knew he had much to tell and to ask his dear Kat.

30

Flashes

January 19, 1940

Taking advantage of Eamon's decision to surprise Devin and Neil in London with a visit, Kat had just finished writing her Our Ireland segment. Now she began opening the mail that had arrived earlier in the day. Her mind had been so focused on relating the tales of the women whom she and BB visited each week in the various clinics scattered around the six Ulster counties that she had not noticed the special, air mail envelope from the US.

Ah, dear Margaret. I wonder what her American news is. So much is happening there to engage the boys – and girls – from over the pond in our fight against Hitler. I pray Roosevelt can convince the pacifists that this is no time to live in the clouds when the earth is erupting below.

Kat quickly opened the envelope and thought more to herself.

"Perhaps she has some insight gained from Francis' close connection to FDR. Discussion on a possible Lend Lease program by which America will offer us its ships and food supplies in exchange for bases in the Caribbean and Newfoundland seems to have been a priority in their chats.

But, of course, Margaret only hears this via what she calls her 'pillow talk' each night with Francis, just before he nods off and begins his nightly sonorous growls."

As Margaret used Eamon's silver-plated letter opener, awarded to him after thirty-years of teaching at Queens University, she thought of how gifted both Eamon and his sister-in-law were.

Margaret is so savvy when sharing her insider tidbits. Whatever sensitive information she learns is hidden in her Women's Aide Society newsletter on page three – the weekly schedule of events. Her Fifth Avenue Garden Club meeting represents the food initiative being discussed by none other than Eleanor Roosevelt, FDR's farsighted wife – a friend, of course, of Margaret's. Her weekly Flushing Book Club confab conveys the title of the book and number of pages to be read. That number actually indicates the representatives of Congress who are beginning to side with FDR on preparing for an all-out war declaration against Germany, if not Japan. Her work with the Manhattan Red Cross Office needs no cover. It indicates the actual number of New York nurses now volunteering overseas in France and Great Britain- as well as the number of local boys who have volunteered to fight. It's so sad that they have had to lose their US citizenship before the US condones conscription. I pray they get that status back if – or should I be more positive – when the US formally enters the war.

Let us see what Margaret has to say today. Kate pondered as she unfolded the inserted letter.

Ach. Only one page. I wonder why?

January 5, 1940 9 AM
My dearest Kat,

I have such little time to convey my news as Francis is rushing out to a meeting and will hand-carry this to the post for the quickest air mail delivery to you. Let me be brief and concise...two traits quite foreign to me as you know.

News flash #1 – Our dear Rose is coming your way within the week. She has decided to volunteer for the Red Cross in London. I know that Devin and Neil are bunking together there. Might she stay with them for a while until she gets her own place? Having graduated as an English major from Notre Dame College in Staten Island, she was seeking an alternative to teaching while volunteering with me at our Red Cross Office. Her summers with you, BB and Agnes – along with cousins Liza, Kate and Maggie – convinced her that her place was overseas. Like you, she can't just wait for the US to decide its actions. She must take her own.

News flash #2 – My Smiley boys, David and Edwin, have followed the physical path of their father, Robbie. Fortunately, not his moral path. Both have joined the Royal Canadian Airforce. While I am proud of them, I am also fearful. You understand, of course, so I won't belabor that similarity in this letter. Please know I am praying for Devin along with my two...and now Rose. What has Neil decided?

Again, I apologize for the brevity of this letter and its self-centeredness. More on my Women's Aide Society schedule next time.

Please tell me all that is going on with you.

All my love,
Margaret

Kat folded the letter back into its envelop and pressed it to her chest. She closed her eyes and held Margaret and the eight children named in the letter – now adults – close to her heart.

For a moment she dozed off into what she recollected later as a beautiful garden. Approaching her on its pathway bordered by poppies and lilies was her mother, Lizzie, arm in arm with a stately looking Scottish matron. As Kat and her mother embraced, Kat heard the following words whispered in her left ear: "Go to London. Neil needs ye." The matronly lady nodded in agreement.

Kat jerked awake, her heart now pounding. She rose, looked at the photo of her mother on the mantle place. Next to it was that of Fanny McCarthy. Kat knew what she had been called to do, but not why. She called to her daughter.

"Liza. Liza. Come pack a bag for me."

Kat flashed into action.

31

Lilies for Lily

January 21, 1940

Kat had arrived at St. Thomas Hospital with satchel in hand, a bag of various items dear to Neil, and a recently purchased bouquet of day lilies. She knew he had been injured but did not know to what extent.

Only when she had closed her eyes and dozed during the previous day's ferry ride from Larne to Liverpool had she sensed the seriousness of his condition. She had dreamed of a blind infant calling to her and unable to hear her voice. She tried holding him in her arms and rocking him, but he would not rest. Strangely, she had placed him in the arms of a young girl. That girl had sung to him, and he had finally settled into a deep sleep. Kat had, too.

When she awoke, a copy of the Wednesday, January 20th, Belfast Times had been placed on her lap, she knew not how. Its headline awakened not only her rest, but also her fears. The usually smooth hairs on her pale white arms stood upright like warrior pikes along the front line of the Scots' Battle at Bannockburn.

The headline read as follows:

BOMB BLAST AT EUSTICE STATION KILLS TWO-INJURES FOUR: IRA IMPLICATED
Story by James Forrester

"What has my sweet lad done?" she asked herself.
She quickly read the text.
Two Irish gentlemen were found dead on Friday, January 16,

outside the post office of Euston Train Station. Another was seri-
ously wounded and is a patient at St. Thomas Hospital on West-
minster Bridge Street. Witnesses say that a loud explosion was
heard and debris scattered within the station's entrance and street
before it. Four local residents passing by – two women, a man and
a child – were slightly injured; none, fortunately, seriously. Train
service was not disrupted.

An elderly female witness told this Times reporter who was, as
you can imagine, soon on the scene, that the third Irishman was the
young son of Belfast MP Professor Eamon Smiley and his wife, the
women's charity leader Katherine Irvine Smiley. She is the sister of
the Eire's Dial TD William Irvine. The older brother of the injured
is about to deploy to France with the First Royal Irish Fusiliers. The
younger brother's presence at the site had been initially questioned
by the British police but was quickly corroborated as coincidental
by the elderly witness.

This is the fourth attack on British soil by the IRA over the last
year in its attempt to undermine the war effort. Sadly, no one is safe
from the group's savage activities – not even one of its own culture.

The Times sends its condolences to our four injured citizens
and hope for a full recovery by young Mr. Smiley.

When Kat finally reached the hospital's front door, she had
calmed herself, knowing she must be a source of the same to her
son. She remembered all too well the instructions of Dr. Chatwick at
Craigmaiddie Hospital over three decades earlier. He had advised her
to listen to and humor with love the victims of wartime trauma. After
applying the perceptive doctor's guidance to Eamon, she now applied
it with BB at the women's clinics. Kat had surprisingly perfected it
and amused herself as she hastened up the hospital's staircase.

Mother would be proud of how far I have come in truly listening
before I speak or shed an emotional tear. Some women actually say I
am the most loving and cheery of souls. Today, I'll be the same for my

dear lad and his father and brother.

And that is exactly how she acted upon greeting the latter two standing at the foot of Neil's bed. They turned immediately toward her upon hearing a light-hearted brogue approach them.

"And what is with these droopy faces? Have ye lost yere fishing rods and spinners along with the biggest salmon catch of the day along the River Maine? And look who is reposing along its banks when he should be up walking the Weir Hill countryside? Have my men become the stones of Newgrange?"

Kat embraced her Eamon, then Devin, before approaching the head of the bed. She leaned over the bandaged side of her son's head to kiss his uncovered forehead.

"Come, me lad. How are ye faring?" she asked.

Neil's one eye looked directly at his mother. At first, he was astonished at her demeanor. For the past two days, he had been surrounded by the somber faces of his male family members. Only Lily had cheered him up with her smiles and laughs. She had sung him many a Scottish song with which his Grandmothers Lizzie and Kate had enlivened him as a child. Now, how comforting it was to have his Mum double that young woman's efforts.

"Ach, Mum. How grand to see ye….at least with one eye…and hear yere voice…at least with one ear," he said.

Kat listened to his spirit regain itself.

"Me lad. Are ye saying I'm only half my size and half my wit of wisdom? Sounds to me ye're ready to get out of this bed, turn in a circle by 180 degrees and start grabbing your world back. Where is that young Scottish nurse that's been singing to ye? She and I will get ye up and goin' in no time."

Eamon and Devin frowned. "How can ye know about Nurse Murphy?" Devin asked. "We just met her ourselves two days ago."

"Silly boys," Kat teased. "I've known Lily longer than ye can possibly imagine. For sure, she's her Gran in spirit and presence. Here, find a vase to put these lilies in before she gets here. We need to thank her."

32

Sunday's Well Poisoned

February 18, 1940

The three sat in the last row of the Dean's Chapel in Saint Fin Barre's, Neo-Gothic, Anglican Cathedral in Cork. The stained glass windows above them to their left allowed streams of colored rainbows to brighten the grey slate flooring and highlight the small altar before them. BB and Maggie McCormick prayed in their respective ways for guidance; Rachel McCormick McNulty folded her hands and waited. The women were blessed by familial ties that enabled each to rise above ecclesiastical differences and act on a higher moral plane when undertaking collaborative tasks. Today, they had attended a memorial service for a distant McCracken family member. Now, they would consider the living.

"It is unbelievable," whispered BB, tightly clenching her revised, 1940 Anglican Book of Common Prayer. It was a gift from the women of her ecumenical Bible group formed to support the clinics she and Kat visited monthly. Few, fifty-eight year-olds traveled around Eire (the newly constituted name of the Free State) and Northern Ireland as much as the two sisters. Few were rewarded across so many religious and partisan lines as they. Inside the first three pages of BB's prayer book were signatures from over fifty women of all walks of life whose names she felt blessed to remember and honor in her prayers today. She had just prayed for those who were yet to be entered.

"I know, Mum," replied Maggie. "But ye must believe me." BB 's twenty-one year old daughter raised her voice. "We must do something about these atrocities. I know ye and Father are preoccupied with all that is going on with the Dail regarding trade negotiations with Great Britain as it prepares for war. But the needs of women right here in Cork's Sunday's Well and elsewhere around our country must not be hidden under the cover of a habit or robe. If we are to be a nation of laws and compassion, what's happening in and by our churches with impunity must be brought to light just like these streams of yellow, red and blue illuminate the grey stones before us."

Maggie was about to continue her impassioned speech when Rachel interrupted her.

"My dearest Maggie. I understand yere concern and have heard the rumors ye have just cited as well. We must have facts, however, in order to go to the authorities and have them investigate. I fear they will just mock ye if ye don't have the evidence warranted to question, let alone arrest, whomever ye suggest are at fault.

Rachel continued. "Believe me, my years now have shown me that two stories do not a fact make; ye must have more and they can't just be stories. The women about whom ye are speaking must come forward themselves and state explicitly what has happened to them. Is that possible?"

"Ah, Auntie Rachel." Maggie replied despondently. "I doubt any one of them will come forward. If they do, their families will be shamed and they will be banned back to the dungeons – literal or figurative – from which they just came. What might ye suggest we do?"

BB opened her prayer book, scrolled down the names on the third page of signatures and smiled. "I know exactly what we can do. We'll meet with Teachta Dala (TD) Maureen McCarthy, our Dail representative. Her mind is an encyclopedia of ways to get around the hierarchy of the church and reach its most moral of leaders. Her brother is Thomas Carney, Cardinal in the North, who was with us during the '16 Uprising. He opposed partition with Michael Collins and is now protesting the war conscription of our Northern Ireland lads, including our dear Kieran. Joseph will listen to his sister and your facts. He'll advise us on what we can do."

Rachel frowned. "Auntie BB, ye are always the idealist. What Maggie has told us and ye are suggesting confound all logic. Why would any religious leaders believe that their own are complicit in such crimes. Would Carney really invite evidence that exposes behavior contrary to the vows of his nuns and priests? I truly doubt it. And never forget the business contracts set up between the church and our Dail to employ these slave laborers – seamstresses, lace-makers and launderers. Trust me; money speaks louder than the ten commandments."

Maggie turned to Rachel. Taking out sheets of handwritten papers from her satchel, she first shook them and, then, began to read:

" I, Maud Sullivan, swear that I was beaten with a stick and cross."

"I, Mary Flynn, swear I was forced to lie on the ground and kiss the dirty floor because I spoke a word."

"I, Grace McCarthy, swear I was placed in confinement after I begged to keep my baby son. I never saw him again for the rest of my life."

"I, Siobhan O'Connor, swear I have crippled hands and burning lungs from years of scrubbing clerical robes and habits with lye and hot water."

Maggie held up the pages and shook them before Rachel's face. "These are only four of the fifty-five women I have interviewed who were able to leave their humiliating, slave labor at Sunday's Well right here in Cork," continued Maggie. "The Sisters of St. Mary's Good Shephard Laundry is just one coterie of the many others that supervised exploitative laundries and abusive institutions around this island. Together, they created the Magdalene community of cruelty. Ye, of all my family members, must know that we can't just sit by and do nothing."

Rachel blushed, not from anger but from embarrassment. How right Maggie was. Why am I so hesitant to stand up for these women? She placed her hand on her lap and caressed the growing bulge below. Perhaps it was because she now had another priority closer to home.

But, for herself and the child yet to be born, she took Maggie's hand.

"Ye're right, Maggie. I should be more understanding. And ye are a saint to remind me. Come, let us return to Dublin and meet with TD Maureen. I also think ye, yere Mum and Aunt Kat should write an Our Ireland article about these women, quoting them anonymously, of course. Once the church aristocracy see such trauma displayed in the public arena, the Devil will be unleashed unless its leaders admit their sin and ask for forgiveness."

The three rose, walked down the nave and left the church just as the bells from the newly reframed tower above them began to chime. At the end of seven rings, BB stopped and remembered the Irish myth about bells communicating with saints. "A new saint has just been recognized among us," she stated whimsically. "I wonder if it's our lovely Maggie here?"

The three laughed and proceeded down the cathedral stone steps, arm in arm together. Little did they know that only they could hear the bells, rung by their ancestors Bella, Bridgette and Lizzie.

33

The Halo

March 24, 1940

In his eight years as a budding journalist at The Irish Times, Jon McCormick-Irvine had done more than bud. He had blossomed. His writing topics had ranged from the most controversial, e.g. the passage in 1937 of deValera's revised Constitution changing the title of The Free State to Ireland/Eire to the less controversial, e.g. the first female winner of a sheep herding contest in the north town of Dunfin.

Initially, his stories about local citizens in both parts of the island had garnered a small, but enthusiastic, readership. The publishers, however, had been more interested in deValera's policies with the British, the fading IRA and the war rumors and actions of Germany, Italy and now America. Jon had forged ahead, however, with the blessing of Joseph Devlin, to raise the voices of rural and urban folk, those exploited and those benefitting from the exploitation. Jon constantly felt that another voice from beyond was suggesting every word he wrote. He had learned so much about his family's Uncle Aiden that Jon often heard the elder's voice. Slurred as it may have been from time to time, the elder's bidding was decipherable and always ended with "That's me boy. Go for the truth!" By 1940, Jon's commitment to the common person's truth had garnered more than a small chamber of followers. He now had a full orchestra.

Today, Jon was ready to listen again as he waited on the train platform for the new, extended family member, Rose McKenzie. She had been in London staying with their cousin Devin while he helped his brother Neil recuperate from a bombing incident. It became quite evident to Rose, however, that once Devin was off to France and Neil well cared for by his day nurse and constant companion Lily, she Rose was no longer needed by her cousins. Advised by her mother and Aunt Kat, Rose decided to pursue her original intent to become a Red Cross volunteer. Not in London, however, but in her mother's native town of Belfast. Like her step-brother Robert, Rose was drawn to the Irish side of the Atlantic and the Channel.

Jon was assigned by Aunt Kat to meet Rose and accompany her to the Smiley's Sunday gathering at the formerly named Beastie King Inn in Helen's Bay, just west of Bangor.

Maud and Thomas McCann's ownership had passed, along with them, into the next generation's imagination and reality. The renamed Lester and Louisa's Tavern had not lost its covert guise from the days of partition negotiations in '21 but was currently known as high-lighting Irish Gaelic traditions. Erin McCann and his brother Finbar had inherited it from their parents and transformed it into a center for all things Irish: plays, ceilis, poetry readings, and, of course, all foods Irish – at least those that were not currently limited by war time restrictions. Fiona, daughter of Finbar, had been recruited from Macroom to take over the establishment's management and menus; Erin the cultural festivities. It was only appropriate that Rose should be introduced to her Irish roots this Sunday by the living descendants of her ancestral family.

Jon was not concentrating on her as he read a letter from his cousin Maggie – daughter of his father's brother Liam. Instead, Jon was absorbed in Maggie's interviews with formerly interred women in various Magdalene institutions. "How can this be?" he said to himself. "How have I missed hearing about this travesty during my travels around the island, both in the North and Eire? What evil has shut the mouths of those victimized and those colluding with the persecutors. Ach, we fight a war against the greatest, political tyrant of them all in Germany, and we don't even hear about the religious tyrants in our own land."

His head burrowed deeper into Maggie's letter. His shoulders shrugged up to his ears covered by the woolen scarf his mother had knit him for Christmas. He hardly noticed nor heard the Belfast to Bangor train arrive at the Helen's Bay platform until a voice brought him back to the day's obligation.

"I guess you're Jon McCormick-Irvine?" a young women stated loudly before him.

Jon looked up to see the owner of the voice. He blinked. The winter's afternoon sun had set a halo around the head of a Rubenesque figure such that he could not make out her face. What he could capture in those first minutes of engagement was a fur wrap flowing from neck to knee and black leather boots pointing directly at his own, worn brown. He rose and, with the halo receding down her back, he blinked again. Before him was the face of a true Irish lass – full cheeked and rosy, surrounded by an abundance of shimmering, black curls nestled on each of the coat's lapels. Her sparkling blue eyes locked his gaze.

He fumbled. "Ach, how did ye guess who I was?"

"Guess? No way. Look at you. You have a copy of The Irish Times that just fell off your lap. I know you are a journalist there. You have a letter full of notes in your hand that, if you don't pay attention, will blow away. My Mum told me you are a very conscientious researcher and often lose yourself in facts. And, if you haven't noticed, you are the only person on this platform. Who else could you be but the person meant to meet me here – Jon McCormick Irvine?" She laughed. Jon swore the halo rose back up above her head.

He bashfully smiled. "I see ye're a true member of our family, then. Despite being different individually, we comprise a clan of devotees to wit and wisdom. Some of us Irvines observe others before making judgments; others jump to conclusions. Some of us McCormacks are quietly reserved; others are passionate engagers. And then we have our Smileys – of which you are one by extension, of course.

I'll be interested in learning more about you." Jon was surprised at expressing these reflections so quickly. He never initiated his personal thoughts to anyone he had just met and had not yet questioned in depth as the journalist he was.

"And I will be interested in learning more about you," Rose responded. "But first," she insisted, "we must get on our way to Lester and Louisa's. Come, take my arm and my satchel. While we walk there, tell me why it is called that."

Jon blinked for the third time. Was this how Americans acted – so assertively? This girl – or best that he call her a young woman – was causing him to refocus his mind and, strangely at the same time, his heart. He sensed both racing to compose a story he never could have imagined writing, or was he going to live it?

A muffled chuckle came from the beyond, followed by the comment: "That's me boy. Go for the truth."

34

Lovers on The Lough

March 24, 1940

Jon led Rose from the Helen's Bay train station down on a path that led to the Lester and Louisa tavern, before ending in the Belfast Lough. The twisting turns opened up to increasingly magnificent views. On the northern side of the water, the undulating emerald hills of North Carn Forest became more defined. At their foot, the ancient Carrickfergus Castle began to stand out on its rocky promontory. Built in the late 12th Century by Anglo-Normans, the strategically located castle had been the only British outpost in Ulster for over 400 years until it changed multiple hands during the next 400. Captured by the French then reclaimed by the Irish, it was currently in British hands. In this year of 1940, it was being secretly considered for a fourth set of hands – US naval and air operations. If the US joined the war effort, Carrickfergus would become the Lough's northern offensive outpost; Bangor Harbor, the southern. No German hand would grasp the ship and armament manufacturing center of Belfast.

Rose drew in her breath as she looked up from the path. Immediately below her, the verdant green landscape, dotted with yellow furze, rolled downward, disappeared into the languid, blue sea and, then, rose again on the opposing hills of velvet green.

She held that breath and, then, exclaimed, "Oh, what an absolutely splendid view. The entire scene is magical. It's as though the two sides of the Lough were ancient lovers who, for some reason, were separated. One is handsome and the other is beautiful, each looking longingly at the other across the water.

Jon stopped, turned and looked back at Rose. He pondered again about her presence of mind and imagination. How did this American know so much about Irish mythology? Surely her mother must have taught her well.

"Ah," he asked. "Ye know the tale of Master Moridan and Mistress Marion?"

Rose stepped closer to him. She paused her gait, saying, "No. I don't think I do. Tell me about it."

As the path was becoming quite steep and they had to quicken their pace to arrive at the tavern before dusk, Jon reached for her hand. He also needed a few minutes to recall the tale's details and relate them as eloquently as he could. A truly inspiring Irish tale had to be spoken in a truly enticing fashion.

"Well," he secured her hand. "Let me begin. I hope I can finish by the time we are at our destination."

"You will, for sure." Rose said, grateful for his security as she stumbled on the pebbled way. "And I promise I will not interrupt you for any clarifying details. You are supposedly very thorough in your writings; thus, you probably will be in your recitations." Together – hand in hand – they proceeded forward, Jon relating the tale.

"In the early years of the Irish, before kings took over land and laws, the druids led our people with intellect, spirituality and magic. Humans lived sympathetically with all creatures. Dragons lived next to mermaids; fairies next to leprechauns. All got along well until one season of incredibly frigid, winter storms. The fields were covered with snow; the lough covered with ice. All human and animal creatures were starving as the berries froze on their vines and the fish swam south into the great ocean. Two druid priests came together with their people to decide how they could survive the winter. They invited the little people and creatures to join a convocation that included leprechauns, fairies, furry animals and dragons. Much back and forth discussion occurred – as happens whenever any Irish community gathers. You know the term "craic", correct?" asked Jon.

"Indeed. I do," replied Rose. "My family in New York City participates in that every Sunday after church during our formal luncheons."

"Then ye know, there are always agreements, followed by disagreements, followed by agreements and more disagreements." He laughed as did she, eagerly nodding her head.

"Well, after a few hours, one of the leprechauns whistled a tune and his companion wolf started to howl in time. That quieted the cacophony of voices that had reached a deafening level. The leprechaun was Moridan, a formidable elder among the little people. His wife was Marion, a fairy of outstanding beauty despite being quite wizen with age.

The couple had lived over a number of centuries, sired a number of generations of little people and protected many an animal. The two believed it was time for them to enter the beyond, but not before they had left a legacy. That gift would benefit not only their own kind but all the "big and tall ones" plus the creatures with whom they had lived in peace and prosperity for so long.

Thus, Moridan and Marion proposed that, as they entered the beyond, they would weave their magic over the land beneath them and in the sea between them. Their favorite wolf agreed to join them. Before anyone had time to restrain them, Moridan placed his foot onto the snow. It began to melt as he stepped into and under the warming earth. Marion, on the Lough itself, kissed the frozen ice which began to melt as she descended into its ripples. Morrigan raced across to the opposite shoreline, his paws leaving sparks of fire on the hardened turf, burning the furze into the frigid terrain. Soon their bodies disappeared, embraced by the lands and lough. The Winter season immediately turned into Spring. Before the eyes of the remaining druids, fairies, leprechauns and animals, the sun began to shine and the land burst into colorful life. Ireland had been saved from an Ice Age extinction. The very same rolling hills and Lough ye see before ye have saved our nation throughout all kinds of seasons over the past centuries. They will do so today." He said wistfully.

He turned to Rose. "So, ye were right about the image of the lovers. They can, indeed, transform darkness into light, coldness into warmth, despair into hope."

Jon looked back across the Lough and focused on the castle. He knew what would be in store for Carrickfergus and the people of Northern Ireland. "Perhaps it's a tale not just about the seasons in the natural year, but those created by man." Turning back to her, he asked "What do ye think?"

"Hum," frowned Rose as she, too, had stopped on the path. She tightened Jon's hand and gazed at the opposite shore with him. "That is a question I will ponder. However, being the English teacher I was trained to be, I'm sure I'll have an answer for you soon."

"Perhaps ye will," said Jon, thinking to himself that she definitely possessed an American confidence by which answers would be quickly forthcoming. He wasn't so sure of his own.

"May I suggest, however, that ye wait and hear yere family members share their thoughts about the tale and today's seasons. Tonight, our Uncle Erin McCann is presenting his newest play based on this exact tale at Lester and Louisa's. Come, the tavern is just ahead of us."

"Oh, " said Rose ready to resume their journey. "I have yet to hear why the tavern is called that? "

Jon smiled. "Ah. Let's save that for another walk."

35

My Wild Irish Rose

March 24, 1940

As the couple approached the entrance of the Lester and Louisa Tavern, they could hear the laughter and song resonating from within.

The exterior structure had not changed from its early 1750's origin as a wayside inn for saints, spies and soldiers traveling south from Belfast to Portaferry along the coast of the Ards Peninsula. The inn's gabled roof of thatch and supporting mud walls had only been repaired or refreshed twice, never reconstructed. The stained glass window of the front door had been replaced only once, as well, after an incident of questionable sobriety caused great damage to its design and to the fist that went through it. No longer did the reflection display an engraving of a single lion harboring a sword next to a red shield, indicating to the illiterate the respite's original name of Beastie King. Instead, there was a perfectly soldered outline of a gold lion and ivory lamb dancing on green grass with the Morne Mountains behind and the Lough shimmering below. The Lester and Louisa was always open for refreshment– no matter type or intent.

The interior tonight was exactly as it had been in 1921 when the Smiley and Irvine family had joined the American McKenzies to hear about their island-wide inquiries and Erin McCann's reports on Collins' Anglo-Irish Treaty negotiations. That night, owner Mother Maud McCann had read her son Erin's discouraging note from London about partition. On this night, nineteen years later, Maud was in the beyond, probably walking with her dear Aunt Bridgette alongside

Grandmother Bella and Dr. Lizzie. What would the four women be thinking of this evening's gathering…and the decisions yet to be made?

As in 1750 and 1921, the performance stage next to the bar was large enough to host one performer at a time yet small enough to allow families to gather around numerous circular, wooden tables on the open floor before it. Tonight's fiddler, the inn's new owner and Maud's son Finbar, was tapping his feet and burning his bow across the strings. He was accompanied by the booming basses, altos and sopranos of merry elders and youngins in front of him. Any odd, off-key sibling was forgiven as his or her voice easily blended into the collective crooning.

Frosted glass partitions, perpendicular to the parameter of the open space, still sequestered private spaces for conversations where elbows leaned in from oaken benches onto worn and uneven table tops. Over two-hundred years, initials had been carved below those elbows – some from lovers in quiet repose, some from boisterous lovers of the drink, some from independence lovers in surreptitious exchanges. If only those tables could talk. What would they say to advise those alongside them in this year of 1940?

Around one such table top were several of the Irvine and Smiley clan members. They had been called together by Erin McCann to discuss the impact on Eire and Northern Ireland of Britain's declaration of war on Germany the previous September 3rd. Advice was not necessary from spirits in the beyond, nor from the inscribed initials or inanimate table itself around which the nine folks sat- five on one side, four on the other. Each person was ready to speak up without prodding.

Eamon and Kat Smiley sat next to their extended Smiley kin– Robert and Morna, wed now seven years and, finally, expecting their next generation any day. Billie and Agnes sat opposite them with Father Shawn O'Malley, the newly appointed Bishop in Rathmines. The priest was a family member by fiat after Ian McNulty had refused to kill Shawn in '19 along the Smiley's alleyway. He had been embraced by the McCormick household upon his mother's death in '21. Beside the priest was a second priest, twenty-three year old Wolfe. Lying on the floor below was his guardian and guide, the dog Larger. Erin sat with his back to the wall next to Rachel, watching the front door. Two empty stools placed at the head of the table awaited the young folks arriving from the train station: Jon and Rose. Erin was particularly interested in meeting Rose.

"We need to know if America is going to come into this war," said Erin, turning his head away from the empty seats and lowering his voice. "If it doesn't, we in the Eire will be forced to succumb to a stifling German alliance and ye in the North to a German dictator. I have no doubt our common sufferings under the British empire will be rewritten in history as an annoying discomfort compared, under the Nazis, to death in their gas chambers."

Billie's finger traced two sets of initials enclosed in a heart before him: an MC and KK. He imagined they stood for Michael Collins and his fiancé Kitty Keirnan who, in the 20's, had often stolen away for trysts at the Beastie King. What would Mike advise?

Billie shared his thoughts as quietly as Erin had posed his. "Our Dial is considering all sides being taken now in this war. As we know, Dev praised Chamberlain's peace alliance with Germany after the '38 Munich Surrender agreement. In return, Chamberlain was eager to support Dev's demand for Eire's neutrality, despite it being a member of the British Commonwealth. British Treaty ports along Ireland's western coast were returned to us then, and the tenant/landlord annuity payments required by London were dropped. It seemed like a very satisfactory collaborative arrangement.

Sadly, as we also know, just last September, you in the Six Counties of Ulster and we in the South were shocked by Hitler's betrayal of Chamberlain and the invasion of Poland. Churchill's warnings about the duplicity of Hitler were prescient. Chamberlain will never be able to govern as a former pacifist. Soon, the Bulldog will be Prime

Minister, and we in Eire will be faced with a colonial PM who dis-trusts our President. Since Winston never appreciated us Irishmen – except for Collins – I fear you in the Six Ulster counties will be sacrificial pawns in Britain's back door."

"Yes," said Eamon. "We must decide what role our people and we, individually, will play. A new government is being formed in London to guide Ulster through an active war. At the same time, Dev will maintain Eire's neutrality in what he's calling The Emergency."

Eamon was just about to say more when there was a bustle at the tavern's entrance and the fiddler stopped playing. Finbar announced: "Ach, here is our famous laddie, Jonathan Irvine. What news are ye preparing to write about our island today?" The elder McCann played the first notes of an Irish jig before abruptly stopping. He saw Rose in tow behind Jon. "Well, look at this. Is our good son finally seeing the value of a wild Irish rose?"

Rose looked around the open space and blushed. With her inim-itable American confidence, however, she curtseyed to the player, turned to the seated families and bowed. Then, to the fiddler, she requested "Do you know the song 'My Wild Irish Rose'?"

"Indeed, I do, miss. Do ye?" he queried.

"Of course, I do, " she stated, loudly enough for the sequestered Irvine/Smiley/McCann family to hear. "Let us all sing it together for, indeed, my name is Rose."

Erin chuckled in his seat. He knew immediately how Rose would fit into his country's Emergency.

36

Cigar Talk

May 24, 1940

Three months after Rose led the final refrain of "My Wild Irish Rose" with her newly found Irish family, so did another, confident woman before a gathering of Gaelic devotees. The setting of this May performance, however, was neither in Eire nor the Six Counties of Ulster. Rather, it was in Washington Heights, New York City. And the woman was not a young, twenty-three year old. Rather, she was that young one's mother, Margaret Smiley McKenzie, now aged fifty-four. It always seemed to Margaret that, whenever she sang the ballad, she could hear her darling Rose, over the pond, singing the same refrain:

> *My Wild Irish Rose*
> *the sweetest flower that grows.*
> *You may search everywhere,*
> *but none can compare*
> *with My Wild Irish Rose.*

The response to this New York City rendition was similar to that at The Lester and Louisa, three-thousand miles away. First generation, Irish American seamen, grocers, handymen and farmers joined their second and third generation offshoots of teachers, lawyers, doctors, bankers and prosperous businessmen in robustly applauding Margaret. They were all members of the Ancient Order of the Hibernians, New York's finest. At least, that was the assessment by Margaret's husband, Francis McKenzie, when he decided upon the invitation list for this Sunday's dinner and speech. He knew he had to impress the speaker: his childhood friend Robert Brennen, the Irish Head of Mission to the U.S.

"Ach, she sings like a nightingale," offered Brennen. "You chose well in making her a McKenzie. How many years ago was that marriage celebration? I fear I only remember that you offered the best whiskey that ever touched my lips."

Francis laughed. "Twenty-four to be exact. Yesterday was our anniversary, and I was keenly reminded of my darling's traits, both beneficial and, may I admit more often than not, ingeniously disturbing. She puts my thoughts into a spin, particularly now around this damn war across the seas or Emergency as Dev calls it. I swear Maggie has more understanding about our Irish American opinions and those of the families we left behind than any man here."

Francis continued, lowering his voice and leaning his head toward Brennen while keeping his eyes straight ahead on his bride. He never wanted Margaret to think he was not paying full attention to her when she engaged a crowd. Nor did he want anyone else but Dev's spokesperson to hear his concerns. Rumors could definitely influence the upcoming American Presidential election – Roosevelt's possible third term – and the fluctuating stock-exchange values.

Brennen reciprocated Francis by leaning his head toward his old friend, understanding the necessity for confidentiality. He also needed clear hearing of his friend's thoughts since he would relay back to Dev in a succinctly coded telegram that night Francis' trusted advice. After all, since childhood, this Irish Republican and Francis had been bonded by more than just common Irish birth and rights. They had been imprisoned together after the 1916 Uprising and, forever, honored its pledge of brotherhood. In addition, they were wise enough to greatly respect the role women played in listening to the common people and sharing 'lights out' information with their beloved partners. Today was a perfect opportunity for Francis to transfer to Dev's spokesperson what Margaret had heard from her

Daughters of Erin sisters, and, nightly, from their husbands.

"Maggie and I were going back and forth last night about Dev's stand on neutrality. He appears to be gambling with a hand of cards that ensures no current winner or loser. And yet, he is placing wild bets upon Ireland's future. Holding the British card, we hear that Dev is considering the return of Eire ports to Britain, but only if London reverses the Ulster partition. If Britain agrees and wins the war, surely, Eire will be blemished for that backdoor manipulation by its Protestant brothers and sisters in the North. At the same time, holding the German card, Dev must fear a German victory. Hitler's armies have already moved into France, Norway and Denmark and what's to hold them back from encompassing the entire island of Ireland in its victorious Empire? Hitler doesn't care about the Irish partition or Dev's pledge of neutrality. He only wants a pacified partner in order to obliterate Britain. There seems to be no win-win for Dev in being neutral."

Francis continued, becoming quite long-winded. "And just look at the folks in this room. Do they care if Eire is neutral? On the side lines of the game, they are literally making bets on winners and losers between Britain and Germany, not on Ireland. And soon, they will take bets on the US. Some businessmen can't wait for Roosevelt's Lend Lease efforts to increase their sale of supplies. Others, because of their anti-Semitism and desire for profits, plan to invest in German arms factories.

In the home, wives are protesting against their sons' conscription into the US army if war is declared despite those same boys emigrating in droves to serve in Canada. They even include my own boys, David and Edwin. And let me not forget our dear Rose who is in Belfast working for the International Red Cross.

It is a period of great indecisiveness, Robert, in games played across tables shrouded in the smoke of secrets, rumors and, regretfully, corporate profit-making. I fear Margaret was right in our discussion yesterday when she exclaimed in tears 'Where are our standard bearers – our Tone, Parnell, Pearse and Collins? Where are our morale compasses?' I couldn't answer her."

Margaret's song had ended. The crowd was now busily focused on eating rich dinner items: beef stews, potatoes au gratin and cabbage soup. Such Irish food did not harken back to famine, but to current American prosperity.

Brennan turned toward Francis and pulled out two Cuban cigars from the pocket of his Scots plaid vest. He gave one to Francis, lit it for him and, then, lit his own.

"Speaking of smoke, let's sit for a while," suggested Robert. He led Francis to a window, overlooking the lights of a bustling Broadway Avenue. The sill, covered by a plush green velvet cushion, was large enough for both to sit upon, broad shoulder to broad shoulder. For the next hour, Brennen shared as much as Dev had allowed him to relate regarding negotiations with Britain, Germany and the US. He emphasized that Dev's ultimate goal in any negotiation was the creation of a secure and independent island-wide Republic of Ireland. Discussions with the three global players had to ensure that. Brennan also shared some confidential details he trusted his friend would not betray.

"The current negotiations between Dev and Churchill's representative Malcolm MacDonald have not gone well," said Brennen. "MacDonald has conveyed to Dev the newly appointed PM's fury over Dev's neutrality and hostage taking of Irish ports for Britain's current defense and supply, released in '38 by Chamberlain. You're correct in saying that Churchill has offered to eliminate the Ulster partition clause of the 1922 Anglo-Irish Treaty in exchange for British use of these ports and Dev's neutrality reversal."

Francis let out a full-throated gasp at that last statement. "But there is no way Protestant Craig in Stormont would allow Churchill to do that!"

"Aye," responded Brennen. "Ye're right in that. Dev has already rejected Churchill's offer considering the past history of unkept

Parliamentary promises like those during WW1's Home Rule debates. You may remember a younger Churchill was against any Home Rule bill passing then. Nonetheless, the PM is prescient knowing that when Britain regains the upper hand in this war – which it will when the US comes in – Eire will look poorly in the eyes of the world, and, more so, to parents in the North. Their sons could have been helped by Eire lads fighting alongside them, sharing intelligence and guiding British supply vessels along the western coast. Such animosity by the North could set up another epoch of hatred across the island."

Brennen continued. "As for our own Eire citizens, Dev knows they too will suffer under a neutral stance. There will be a heavy tax on food and energy imports from Britain, and no arms would be offered by London for Irish self-defense if the Germans invade. Shipping will cease between British and Eire ports. Cross-border families will be torn apart by conflicting allegiances. These are conditions Dev will ask his followers to endure for what he deems will be peace."

"And what about the Germans? How is Dev negotiating with them?" asked Francis.

"It has been fascinating dealing with them. As you know, Hitler listens and, then, regardless of his advisors' opinions, makes his own decisions. Fortunately, Eduard Hempel, Germany's Minister to Ireland, seems somewhat sympathetic to us. With an incredible amount of diplomatic finesse and sensitivity, he conveyed to Hitler Dev's conflicting words of 'unimpeachable neutrality' followed, days later, by the declaration of a 'certain consideration for Britain'. I think Hempel likes Dev and so tries to balance the two leaders' egos by interpreting their statements as the card player's bluff and not, necessarily, imperial commands.

Francis chuckled at this, for he knew all too well Dev's attribution of saying one thing and actually meaning the opposite. The banker did believe, however, that the actions of an imperialistic Hitler needed no words to camouflage their intent.

Brennen picked up on the paradox. He continued. "Rest assured,

Hitler sees right through Dev's inconsistency. Already, we know that the Fuhrer doesn't care about nor trust Ireland's ability to create a united nation. After meeting with IRA agents in Berlin, some of them reported that Hitler would welcome the island into his victorious German Empire. Let us see what Dev does with that information in the next months."

Simultaneously exhaling their respective cigar smoke, both men agreed the report might influence Dev in rewording his 'certain consideration for Britain' statement.

"It is America that now must join the card game and share its moves with us. That requires the most sensitive of negotiations," said Brennan, "and is where Dev needs your help, Francis. Can you convince Roosevelt that all of Ireland needs his support?"

Francis nodded and looked over the crowd to see his wife exchanging pleasantries with the many attendees. She turned and waved at the pair indicating that it was time for Brennen to speak to the full group.

"Sometimes," Francis said, as he rose from the sill, and turned toward Brennen. "I feel Margaret has a spiritual connection with those who have passed before us. They seem to guide her in choosing the best words to convince me to be a just human being. Her sayings from Parnell, Pearse, Collins, and the Countess are quite inspiring. I can't get one of them out of my mind from our discussion yesterday. It was regarding the role Irish Americans should take in this Emergency. She quoted from a poem by Pearse: 'Of riches or of stone I shall not leave behind me...but my name in the heart of a child.'

Francis looked at his friend. His eyes began to glisten with tears. "Dear friend. I know the name Brennen will be remembered in the heart of many here tonight for what you are about to say. I only hope that the McKenzie name will be remembered similarly in years to come."

37

The Mule's Kick

May 24, 1940

While her mother and father were immersed in the global exigencies that a Second World War was thrusting on their American homeland, Rose was deep in the throes of a local war – that between Roman Catholic Church leaders and the women they deemed as "lost". Jon had found Rose a formidable sounding board on how to raise awareness in the Irish public to the plight of women. He and his cousin Maggie were specifically concerned about those working as indentured servants or slaves, as Maggie called them, in the Magdalene laundries. In addition, they were deeply moved by those shunned when returning home after the loss of illegitimate bairns. Maggie had found a sympathetic ear in Rose whose bravado confidence replaced that of Maggie's former mentor Rachel. Sadly for Maggie, Rachel's attention had focused away from women's issues and IRA commitments to those of her infant daughter, Maud. At least, that is what Rachel had told Maggie.

On this May evening, the three cousins were seated around a dining room table in their Aunt BB and Uncle Liam's row house in Rathmines. Windows and minds were open to new views of a changing season in Eire, particularly during the "Emergency".

"Which is worse: to return to formerly loving families that judge you horribly and to have lost a child forever or to be employed by an institution that enslaves you, all in the name of a loving and forgiving God?" Rose forcefully thrust onto her lap the first draft of Jon's editorial ready to go into the Dublin Irish News. "What is the real emergency Dev is addressing?

"That depends on your perspective, doesn't it?" asked Jon, turning to Maggie. "Tell us what you have heard from your interviews with women. How might they answer Rose's question?"

"Ach," replied Maggie "They provide a complex set of thoughts, nestled primarily in guilt and, generally, in fear. As our resident philosophers Uncle Eamon and Robert tell us, there are multiple sides to a just man and woman, I'm sure they would add. The women I have met are certainly just, despite the wrongs done to them, because they want desperately to improve their lives and those of others like them. Some have overcome the guilt of abandoning their newborns; others have not. Some have prevailed over the cruel shunning by their church members and neighbors; others have not. So many have had to leave their towns and start their lives over. Rarely does that happen with the help of their religious leaders. Those betrayers have abandoned, rather than saved, the 'lesser of these."

Jon frowned and positioned his pencil to take notes. "Tell me what happened when you met with the Dail's Teachta Dala (TD) Maureen McCarthy, sister of Bishop Carney in the North. Was she supportive of the women?"

"Nay," replied Maggie with unbridled distain in her voice. "She just kept nodding her head saying 'I know. I know.' Even though her own, younger sister Grace cried when describing to me how she had to give up her baby son, TD McCarthy would not take a stand. She kept saying the constraints on her were too many as her constituency is primarily Catholic and indebted to the church for employment, education and charity. As Britain tightens the trade channels to Dublin during this war, many a husband is out of work. There is little cash to support his own family let alone those who come back home besmirched. His wife doesn't want to be seen in public as sympathetic despite saying so in private. TD McCarthy won't even open the door for us to her brother in Belfast, let alone her own priest here in Dublin. All seem consumed by German or Catholic ideologies to care about abandoned women."

Maggie and Jon were silent. Rose picked up Jon's draft and quickly reread the first sentence.

She suddenly looked up at the two. Her eyes widened. Her cheeks began to redden and expand.

"I have an idea," she exclaimed. "My mother Margaret said that when an Irish person is perplexed and feeling awash with contrary thoughts, he – or she – calls on the spirits, not the church, to offer guidance. We have so many departed in our family, there must be at least one spirit who can help us."

"Rose," replied Jon. "Ye must be blaggin' us. This is the 1940's, not the 1540's or 1740's when the mythical spirits of CulCochain governed the minds and actions of our people. What are ye thinkin'?"

"Wait, Jon. She might be right," cautioned Maggie. "You say that Uncle Aiden speaks to you and Mother BB always recites words of wisdom from the past. We all know Uncle Erin is constantly including judicious words from the past in his plays. Rose, what are ye referring to exactly?"

Rose considered what she should tell her companions. Over the past three months, she had been recruited by Erin to act in his Dublin theater on the weekend while working during the week at the Belfast Red Cross center on Falls Road. He had also asked her to secretly relay messages between the outlawed IRA in Dublin and its Belfast brigade. The naïve thrill of being a spy was contributing to her decision to stay in Ireland. Jon as a possible paramour also contributed. For now, though, she refrained from sharing her subterfuge role and offered only a few lines from Erin's play in which she was currently acting.

"Here is the final line from Erin's new play Resurrection II, a revision of his 1919 original given in tribute to Padraig Pearse after the Easter Uprising. I understand that Aunt BB and Uncle Liam attended that first showing with Uncle Billie and Aunt Agnes. Grand Aunt Lizzie was there, too. Tomorrow, I will play the ancient Phantom Queen

Morrigan who, in the final scene, asks what the audience must do to continue Padraig's mission. We three need to answer her ourselves tonight. Rose began her recitation.

> *"The departed ones are with us tonight. They have always been with us.*
>
> *I ask you: What will ye do to honor their names, known and unknown.*
>
> *Will ye transform our struggle into the resurrection and eternal life of freedom for all?*
>
> *Let yere hands reach out; let yere voices be heard; let yere words reawaken the dreamers; and never, ever let those who are more powerful than ye suppress ye."*

Rose continued in her inimitably passionate manner. Her words sounded like the bullets shooting across the historic trenches in Loos.

"Maggie, you and Morna can reach out to the women who are brave enough to speak up in public about their pasts. Jon, you can write your articles and help Aunt Kat and Aunt BB include excerpts in their IndePen publications.

I'll tell Mother and Father about your findings, Maggie. I bet Mother knows several Daughters of Erin who immigrated to America because of their own persecution by the church. Perhaps Mother could organize them to contact New York City's Bishop Angus Wellman at St. Patrick's Cathedral. He could communicate their concerns to Bishop Carney in Belfast.

Jon, can you also convince Uncle Billie to read Maggie's report and consider a bill in the Dail to investigate the industries first, then, the church hierarchy's role in other crimes against women? We must act now! This tragedy has gone on for decades under the guise of a holy church and loving God. Our women deserve better!"

Rose was standing before her cousins acting like a Brian Boru warrior for Parnell, Pearse and Collins. She paused, mid-sentence, though, when a rush of cool air blew through one of the dining room windows and shuffled her hair over her eyes. A small Belleek vase engraved with shamrocks fell over on the table. Rose blinked.

Jon and Maggie winked at each other.

"Ach, dear Rose," said Jon. "That's the spirit of Grand Uncle Aiden. He always visits us when he thinks we're getting too passive and need a good, mule kick in order to take action. Welcome to your activist family."

"Nay, Jon. Ye're wrong, " corrected Maggie. "It's the McCracken sisters, Sarah and Mary, along with Christine O'Leary and the Countess urging us to think carefully about what we propose during a war and how we act. Rose, welcome to your careful family."

38

A Pause In The Beyond

June 30, 1940

So much has been happening in these first six months of 1940 that we, in the beyond, must pause our interventions and reflect on their value. Many of us are at our wits end with, not only ourselves, but those below for whom we feel responsible. Let me explain.

As Uncle Aiden always does, he is moving much faster than he should. Before we can contain him, his words have blown in through too many open windows. His advice to several of our young ones seems totally void of sober and careful contemplation. We must bless him but, truly, I think only God and Bridgette know how.

Collins and Griffith are absolutely apoplectic – although that is a misnomer here as we are free of such earthly maladies. Nonetheless, Dev's decision on neutrality has greatly agitated them, and try as they can to advise him, he is not listening.

Lizzie and the Countess are shocked at Rachel's transformation from rebel to mother. They want to focus on Jon, Rose and Maggie, not on her. However, they know they must adjust their priorities and address Rachel quickly. Caring for four young adults at the same time is quite challenging.

Our most esteemed elder Bella is deeply concerned about Devlin and Neil taking such different roles in this second World War. She fears that both positions could bring the lads to us much sooner than any of us wants. And of course, Robbie is praying – for the first time, I must admit – that his sons David and Edwin survive the Canadian assault in France.

When we look down upon Robert and Morna, they look exhausted at the end of each day, as does Ian. Caring for the minds and physical welfare of neighbors and strangers during these complex months is definitely wearing on them. When do they have the time and energy for their own wee ones?

Maud and Thomas McCann are very concerned about their sons Erin and Finbar playing covert roles at the Louisa and Lester Tavern and Abbey Theater. Maud, particularly, believes they are flirting with destiny while allowing Finbar's daughter, young Fiona, to court a similarly precarious fate. Thomas argues with Maud since he applauds their actions. Ah, we must conduct as much marital reconciliation here as communally down below.

In addition to these challenges, we have forgotten our other, more, quiet family members. Thon, while working with his Thomas family and Foyle classmates in London, has become more British every day. Wolfe is studying with Sean O'Malley to be a priest. Little Kieran's curiosity is growing faster than an alder tree whose branches are spreading north and south, east and west. Liza is watching everyone around her, but no one is watching her. As an Inde Pen youth author, Kate is writing articles that raise her parents' concerns about her safety. And our youngest Irish-American relative, Arthur McKenzie, is picketing outside the White House in America against the war despite his step-brothers fighting in it. Who among us is guiding these young folk?

As for myself, I fear I am failing as the spirit assigned to bring unity among our earthly family members. All I see are individual ships sailing out from various ports in different directions across tumultuous seas. Their sails are untethered and flapping uncontrollably. I am in great need of advice from my spiritual partners. To whom should I turn?

Ah, as with every question posed in the beyond, an answer now comes to me. Along the garden pathway I see Sister Bridgette, followed by her blessed canine entourage of Bigger, Sceo and Boru. Indeed, she will comfort me today.

My darling, Una, ye look so distressed, come her words. Over a century here in the beyond, I swear her cheery countenance has not faded a bit. Perhaps it's because of her eternal faith in a loving God. I never question her about that resolve, despite wanting to. I so admire her.

Tell me what is troubling ye, she asks.

I am befuddled, I tell her. How can we comfort our continuously growing family below when such confusing choices lie ahead of them? We can certainly intervene and guide our beloveds, but there are so many of them now and so few of us. And who knows if they will even consider our advice?

She laughs and looks at the three companions now seated at her side, tails wagging. They cock their heads. Their ears flap open.

Me love, she says. Look at our fellows here. What they are telling ye?

I must admit I look at the three canis familiares and don't see anything of import.

She smiles, that beautiful half-circle that radiates such patience. What are their ears and silence telling ye, dear Una?

I am suddenly struck by the countenance of the trio. All they are doing is sitting patiently and listening.

Ah, I realize. Must we do the same as these knowledgeable souls: open our ears to listen to those below?

Slowly, I admit that I am using the terms guidance and comfort incorrectly. Our role in the beyond is not to tell our living family members below what to do. Rather, it is merely to listen to them first and, if they desire, guide them in making their own decisions. They alone must experience the impact of their choices. Then, and only then, can we welcome them home. If it is at a time we may consider premature, so be it.

Bridgette and the three dogs bow their heads toward me.

My dearest Una, she concludes, reconciliation between the two worlds of beloveds – those here in the beyond and those below – means destiny aligns with free will, action with thought, and warp weaving with woof in a fine tapestry. Whatever choices are made by those of our descendants will inevitably lead them to their destinies and, eventually, to us.

I sigh, knowing that what she says is true: they will find comfort here no matter whatever occurs on earth and whenever. After all, in the end, they will join us in our wonderful world of unconditional love. And, for sure, the conversation, weather and flowers here will be absolutely spectacular!

39

The Kiss

September, 1940

Park Lane, Bangor,
September 20th, 1940

My dearest, loving Momma,

My heart broke when Uncle Eamon shared your telegram last week about Edwin's death in France. Among all those whose lives were certain to be lost in this war, I had not wanted to consider his – my own dear step-brother. Perhaps it was my power of denial that permitted such avoidance? Perhaps it was some subliminal spirit that did not want me to worry? Perhaps it was your admonitions that hope was more comforting than fear? But now, reality denies any denial; its pain is absolutely undeniable.

Your transatlantic call yesterday from Father's office broke my heart even more upon hearing your voice tremble. What is it about the role of mother that requires strength when a son or daughter goes to the beyond before that parent? You truly should be released from a requirement of stoicism, but I know you will never relinquish it. Instead, you will insist on being the strongest of the strong, helping each of us cope with Edwin's loss while you mourn in silence. I beg you to hear me when I say you must share the weight of your sorrow with us. Our family here has more experience with the tragedies of life and death than I had ever imagined nor you had ever shared with me. Please let them and me comfort you.

Momma, you were – and still are – the best of mothers. How many times did you settle the petty arguments Edwin and I had during our childhood and recent years? I remember the Christmas of '26 when he and I argued about who got to read the Wadsworth poetry books first. In '28, do you remember we argued about the Wilkie Collins' mysteries? Then, in '30, we bared our verbal fisticuffs on where our family would spend that summer's vacation – the Pennsylvania Poconos or the New Jersey shore. Those seem so ridiculous now. On more serious topics, he was like Father, an advocate for requiring that the unemployed work during The Crash. I can hear him arguing: "They should just pull themselves up by the boot straps". I, on the other hand like you, would be pleading him to join us on the soup line at St. Agnes' in the Bowery. You always calmed the roiling waters between Edwin and me. You made us see that each of our ideas was worthy of consideration and just a different petal on the same shamrock.

I wish we could have been there with you today during Edwin's memorial service at St. Patrick's in New York City. Likewise, I wish you could be here with us tomorrow at St. Mary's Refuge in Belfast. Cousin Wolfe will assist Father O'Malley in the service. Wolfe has just been ordained and serves as St. Mary's priest for Community and Youth Outreach. Father Wolfe – which I find so difficult to call him – and I spend each Monday at the Belfast Red Cross Center. Despite his blindness, he has such insight into people and how to draw their feelings out, especially in times of loss. I have learned much by just watching him and hearing his comforting words. I know he will provide solace to our entire family, including you whenever you need him.

Aunt Kat and I will be here in Bangor with Jon and Kate for the entire week and are determined to support you, Momma. Uncle Liam, Aunt BB and Maggie are arriving this afternoon. Uncle Billie and Aunt Agnes come tomorrow morning. Morna and Ian will attend the service with Rachel and Robert. The four are working so hard, but insist on being with us. Only Thon, Devin and Neil will be missing from our Irish family. Thon and Devin, now in Algeria, are among those Great Britain soldiers for whom we pray on a daily basis. Neil is still recuperating from his injuries in Scotland with Lily McCarthy, but he sent a beautiful poem for Wolfe to read during the homily. We will dearly miss you, Father, David and Arthur – our Irish-American family. We know, however, that you will be with us in spirit as we will be with you.

Momma, the gathering of our family today and tomorrow – whether in New York, North Africa, France, Scotland or here on our Emerald Isle – brings tears to my eyes. Those tears are not just because of Edwin's passing, but because of the love surrounding us during this time. I know that blessing will support each of us in the days and months ahead but, also, whenever any loss occurs as the years proceed. Who knows what our fates will be. Who knows what may happen to David, Devin and Thon or to us here in Northern Ireland as Germany increases its attacks on our ports. Who knows what the next decade will present us- what sorrows and joys, challenges and opportunities.

Whatever our present and future, we need each other every day. You have taught me that. And, isn't that what families are for? Whatever I can say or do to comfort you now, I know everyone in our family can offer as well. Together, we will always be here for you.

In ending, Momma, let me share something quite strange. Last night, I felt an unusual waft of autumn breeze come through my window. It carried a warmth that, first, embraced me like a shawl and, then, placed a gentle kiss on my forehead. I remember you telling me that our grans and grandads and their grans and grandads visit us during times like this. Do you think they were with me last night? Do you think they are always with me?

I believe they were and are.

So, with that belief, I say good night and hope you can feel their kiss and mine on your forehead.

Your loving daughter,
Rose

40

Monday Memorial

September 9, 1940

St. Margaret's Refuge in Belfast was never overcrowded during its regular weekday services. With men fighting overseas, mothers working overtime in factories, and children reciting math tables over and over again in schools, Bishop Seamus O'Malley and his new assistant Father Wolfe Irvine did not expect many attendees at this special Monday Memorial service. Most probably, they thought, only round-shouldered elders would grasp the brass heads of their canes or arms of caretaker relatives to successfully navigate the cobbled bricks from secular stoops to spiritual front steps.

How wrong the two priests were.

Every one of the forty rows abutting both sides of St. Margaret's nave was filled with folks of every age. At the regular weekend masses, men in uniform, business suits, or working trousers sat near the narthex for their quick exit to pubs after the service. Women in hospital whites, factory garb or formal dress sat in the middle section to entertain children on laps or the hard wooden pews. The elders positioned themselves closest to the chancel for hearing the priest's guidance and homily. Today at this special service, however, members of varied ages, positions and roles filled any available seat. Overflow chairs were already unfolded and occupied in the side galleries and chapels.

The two priests were stunned. The bishop saw what his blind assistant could only hear – the shuffling of feet and the bustle of affable greetings or hushed condolences. As they waited behind the newly installed organ during its opening prelude, the two officiates considered this new environment.

"Why are there so many attendees today?" whispered Father Irvine, pulling his guide dog Larger closer to his side.

"I'm not sure, Wolfe," replied his mentor.

"Perhaps God has announced a Papal dispensation for those who join us today," joked Wolfe, trying to bring levity to the growing anxiety he felt as a newly ordained priest. After all, even religious celebrants suffer trepidation when performing their public roles. God – nor men – weren't always kind critics.

"Ach," offered Seamus. "I think it's the presence of our Thespian in residence Erin McCann. I heard he announced at the Lester and Louisa on Friday night that he would be doing a reading here today – not only in honor of his nephew Edwin Smiley, but of all of the boys, Catholic and Protestant, lost or serving in the war. Ye know how news travels up and down the Lough during a weekend of pints. Last night in the manse, my housekeeper Millie McGregor reported that even our colleague Reverend Ian Crossley from Fisherwick Presbyterian encouraged his congregants to attend our memorial."

"Is he here?" asked Wolfe.

"Aye," said Seamus. "He's seated right between your father Billie and uncle Eamon. For sure, the Right Reverend knows that his attendance will be related to Edwin's father in New York City before the evening sun sets. Irish Americans who are friends of Roosevelt will know as well." Seamus sighed. "How quickly a sacred ritual honoring the souls of the dead becomes a political event honoring the policies of the living. We'll have to watch our words today so no one claims sides have been taken, be they pacifist or warrior."

Wolfe was now more than anxious. He could feel his heart beat increase and his hands sweat. His original homily offered the Smiley/ Irvine/McCormack members an intimate, familial comfort. Wolfe had asked Erin McCann to read the very personal and partisan poem Devin Smiley had written on behalf of his cousin Edwin and all the sons of Ireland. With an inter-faith congregation now present, a revision might be required by Wolfe to provide more inclusive solace and grace. A voice, however, whispered through his angst. "Do what is right, me boy. God and I will forgive ye." Larger nudged his nose into Wolfe's shaking hand.

The prelude finished. The two priests plus canine faced the expectant congregation.

Bishop O'Malley began the service.

"Dear brothers and sisters, we welcome ye to this solemn memorial honoring our sons who, in this past month, have given their greatest sacrifice for our nation and families."

For the next ten minutes, he led the congregation through the liturgy of the word prescribed by the Catholic church. A gospel and two lessons were read by only the bishop. Psalm 23 was read antiphonically by the congregation: "The Lord Is my Shephard. I shall not want…"

Then, to the surprise of all of the congregants, Catholic and Protestant, Seamus introduced Father Irvine.

"While I welcomed you earlier to what I called a solemn honoring of our cherished sons, Father Irvine and I also want us to celebrate the lives that they lived. Who were these young men and how did they contribute to our lives before their too early departure from this physical world? How can they remind us of how we must live before death?

"I turn now to my colleague, Father Irvine."

Larger led Wolfe to the front steps of the chancel. A gasp of amazement was inhaled into the lungs of over one-hundred souls.

"My good friends," started Wolfe. "Today we gather to say farewell to those whom we have cherished over the past two or three decades. Some of us birthed them. Some washed their faces, fed them potatoes and cabbage, and held them when they were sick." Silent weeping was exhaled.

"Others of us played soccer alongside them; flirted with them;

bent an unsteady elbow in the pub with them." Chuckles followed.

"We sang with them, argued with them, learned from them or rejected their ideas. There is probably nothing we did – positively or negatively – without them being part of our lives. That means there is nothing they did without us being part of theirs."

Wolfe paused, then continued. "But ye may ask, 'I didn't even know them. How can I have been part of their lives?' "

"I submit to ye that ye did know them and still do. We have been together with them despite our different faiths, different neighborhoods, different schools. For, ye see, we and they are always together in the eyes of God. My cousin Edwin is among those whom we honor today. He with the other sons of St. Mary's Refuge – Patrick, William, Anthony, Charles – have just joined the saints above. And I know there are sons of Holy Trinity Anglican and Fisherwick Presbyterian like Arnold, George and Frank who are with them as well. Those lads know each other well, for they fought together in the same war, died together, and, now, live together in Heaven. They are eternal brothers in the family of our Lord Jesus Christ and God. And we must, in honoring them, be brothers – and sisters – as well in this earthly family."

"Let me ask someone ye know well as a champion of Irish culture to read a poem that reflects that universal family of which we are members. The poem is written by Edwin's cousin Devin Smiley."

Wolfe raised his voice and called to the back of the church. "Master McCann, can you join us?"

Erin rose from his seat, strode to the middle of the center aisle. He bowed first to the two priests before him. Facing Seamus and Wolfe, he raised his head to look up at the cross hanging over the frontal altar. He remembered the homily at Michael Collins' funeral in '22 wherein Father Sullivan described the spiritual directions of the cross: the vertical connecting God to earth and the horizontal connecting man to his neighbors. Today, that image needed to be made real again.

Turning around, he gazed out at the congregants before him, to his left and, then, to those on his right. In the most eloquent of Gaelic tones, Erin McCann recited Devin's poem by heart.

May the shields of Cu Chulain protect ye,
The Uilleann pipes praise ye,
The Celtic Sea carry ye,
And the Mourne falcons guide ye
On yer Heavenly journey.
May ye hear the greetings of our ancestors
As the farewells of yer kin begin to fade.
May the warmth of yer great granma's shawls
And the handshakes of yer great grandpas
Pull ye inward to yer eternal home.

May ye visit us once ye are settled
To guide us on our earthly journey.
May yer smiles greet our eyes
And yer wisdom reach our ears.

And may we forever look upward to ye
And reach outward, in yer name, to each other.

41

A Winter Proposal

November 1940

"My mum told me of this spot before I left New York", said Rose, holding tight to Jon's hand.

"Tell me what ye know," he asked.

Jon wrapped his woolen scarf tighter around his neck and put Rose's gloved, left hand deeper into his coat pocket. An unpredicted light snow was falling during their late afternoon walk on the path to Ravine House in the Belfast Botanic Gardens. He didn't want his newly found love to fall, especially today. Nor did he ever want to be separated from her. How magical was the happenstance of time and place that had brought her to him. Now, he hoped another magical occurrence would forever link them with each other and those who had walked here before.

Jon led Rose to a bench underneath an expansive, tropical fern next to the glistening reflection pool. With the cold weather, each element of nature was adapting to the seasonal change. No longer as relief from summer heat, the fern branches, instead, served as a blanket protecting Rose and John from the soft powder of this first winter storm. Rather than absorbing the sun's rays, the pond captured icey flakes to rejuvenate itself and reflect the grey clouds above. In addition, neighboring swans tucked their beaks underneath wings and sparrows burrowed their heads within plump, tufted chests. As the human pair reclined into the wooden bench and its worn back, they also adapted by settling into each other's warmth, regardless of the cold.

"No, my love," replied Rose. "You are so much more knowledge-able than I about this place. You tell me its history."

Jon began. "This is the place where my ancestors from the McK-night, Irvine, Smiley and McCormack families have honored each other in both life and death. Here, in 1834, my Great-great Uncle William Irvine proposed to my Great-great Aunt Bella; here, a decade and a half later in the midst of the Great Famine, she spread his ashes into the pool before us. On this very bench in 1912, your Uncle Eamon proposed to Aunt Kat. Seven years later, they buried the ashes of your Great Aunt Lizzie in the bushes behind us. So many more passings have been honored here. So many celebrations of love."

"That's what my Mum told me. She also mentioned a tradition you all follow when scattering a family member's ashes." Rose tight-ened her pocketed grip on his hand. "Tell me about that."

"Aye," he continued. "In the Spring after one of our loved ones passes, we gather here for an Irish goodbye that, I must admit, is quite unique to us. Great Aunt Bella began it out of respect for her brother Anthony's burial wishes in 1919. They were: 'Ashes, no coffin; ale, no whiskey; and laughter, no tears.' She collected his ashes in an old urn that her mother McKnight had sent from Scotland in 1834 as a wed-ding gift. During each beloved's passing since then, we have lined up in family groups and passed that same urn from family member to family member – young and old. Each dips a teaspoon into the urn, scoops up some ashes, and says a prayer or relates a remembrance. He or she, then, throws the ashes into the bushes behind us or into the reflection pool.

"After that, each person receives a kiss on the forehead from the mother or father in that family. If the person who has passed were a man, it used to be the father who gave the kiss; if the person who passed were a woman, it used to be the mother. Now, the kiss comes from both parents and is returned by the recipient. It was Rachel who changed that tradition two decades ago when she was such a preco-cious child demanding suffragette equality. All our women agreed at the time, as did the men, knowing better to do so.

But back to the actual customs. When all have had their opportunity to say their blessings and receive their kisses, we sing the departed's favorite song. Thereupon, of course, we imbibe in a sumptuous meal spread out on picnic blankets around the pool. Rachel has now dubbed this tradition the "Outdoor Wake". We have never missed one yet.

Rose laughed. "We would never be able to do all this in New York City's popular Central Park. The police would say we were disturbing the peace or holding an illegal meeting. It's a lovely tradition for your Irish family, Jon, like so many others I am learning about."

Jon hesitated, held his breath and proceeded in adding his own story to the spot's family history. He pulled a tiny, velvet covered box from his jacket's left pocket and turned to Rose. He took her hand out of his other.

"Ye heard me say there are not just blessings given here by our collective family when those we love have passed. Family members have also come here alone to make decisions or with a loved one to share their sentiments.

He opened the box.

"Rose McKenzie. Ye are the most beautiful and ingenious lass I have ever known. These last months getting to know ye and working together on so many important issues facing my island have been the happiest I have even known. I can only hope ye feel a little like myself and, perhaps love me as I love ye." He started to stutter. "I...I..."

In true, American style, Rose finished his sentence: "You wonder if I would consider spending the rest of my life with you, Jon? Are you asking me to marry you?"

He blushed. She took her hand out of his right pocket, faced him, and placed her two mittened ones upon his cheeks and around his ears. She pulled him toward her and kissed him on the forehead.

"Oh, you wonderful and silly man. I am honored to accept your proposal. Indeed, I love you as much as I have always known you've loved me."

As they kissed again – this time on the lips, they knew it would be first of many kisses they would share during their engagement and long marriage.

They did not realize that another couple was watching them from above the ferns.

"Ach," said Uncle Aiden. "Our Jon didn't even get to ask her to marry him. Instead, she asked him."

"Now stop, ye old fool," warned Bridgette. "It's a new day in Ireland and we need to accept that women and men are becoming equals in many ways unfamiliar to us. They shared in the proposal, and both had the final say."

"Ney, that's not right," blustered Aiden. "I'll show Jon." And with that, the snow that had been held up by the fern's branches fell upon Jon with a swoosh. Rose and Jon stood up from the bench and laughed, brushing off the white layer from their coats. Jon gently placed the emerald engagement ring on Rose's left hand finger. He sang the love song that would become their anniversary ritual: My Wild Irish Rose. She joined him in the last verse.

"See, ye old goat," laughed Bridgette. "Not even the happenstance of nature – nor yer interference from afar – can inhibit the happiness of our young ones. Ye better get used to that!"

42

Engaging Traditions

February 8, 1941

Holding engagement parties had not been a tradition in the Irvine/Smiley/ McCormack family. Weddings were followed, at least a year later, by baptisms. Baptisms were followed, about sixty years later, by an "Outdoor Wake". These had established three customary traditions.

Over the decades, however, additional rituals began to take prominence at annual family gatherings. Christmas Day dinners were hosted at the Irvine's Dublin house followed by exceptionally creative charades, thanks to Erin McCann. Easter luncheons preceded afternoon egg hunts intricately designed by Neil Smiley around the backyard bushes of his family's Bangor home. On the beach at Killiney Bay, July picnics accompanied constant craic under the noon sun until the first light of the moon.

Some traditions evolved into mere expectations, albeit absence was duly noted: attendance at first communions of Catholic family members, initiations of Protestant sons into the Boys Missionary Brigades, and graduations from university studies. Liam and BB hosted these celebrations at their Rathmines home, no matter how many weeks afterwards.

More honored by the family were the "rites of passage" created over the years. The 13th birthday of all the young boys was memorialized by a first "approved" pint at Lester and Louisa's. The 13th birthday of the lasses was commemorated by reading Pearse's 1916 Declaration of Irish Independence before the statue of the Countess

Markievicz in St. Stephen's Park. And, of course, there were the Sunday luncheons held at 3 PM by each individual household. Extended family members who might be away from their respective homes because of studies, jobs or covert assignments were always welcomed into the extra chairs.

These traditions – formal or informal, expected or spontaneous, joyful or mournful – kept the family's emotional ties strong. Each ritual was also a means by which important political news was shared, keeping them well-informed and, thus, protected from or, at a minimal, aware of potential physical harm. Of course, the most honored tradition was the forehead kiss, an assurance of love and safety offered by those living and those from the beyond.

The engagement party tradition would add a new design on the ancestral tapestry of this family's history. Its warp and woof would be strengthened and colored by how the beloveds, earthly and heavenly, practiced these rituals. And, recognizing the potential width and length of their tapestry, that new tradition would now be added by none other than an Irish-American.

In a conversation with Maggie and Liza earlier in January, Rose had first mentioned her desire for an engagement party.

"Why in heaven's name do we need an engagement party?" Liza had asked. "If a marriage proposal has been made, the boy only needs to seek her father's permission. If permission is granted, a church is chosen and the banns posted. Then, the wedding date is set. Why add another step? Aren't these four quite enough?"

Rose had laughed.

"Yes," she had replied. "One would think so; but, the time between proposal and the father's permission can be quite lengthy. And, the time between the permission and the banns even longer. If, God forbid, someone objects, more time is wasted on resolving the accusation. One has to keep the fires of attraction and commitment burning, don't you think?"

Liza and Maggie had looked at Rose as though she were a

foreigner which, despite her being already loved dearly by the family, she was indeed – at least to Irish customs.

"Given our current anxieties about war, rationing, loyalties and IRA subterfuge, don't you think it behooves us to plan a joyful gathering before the wedding? Our families need to come together, laugh, sing and have a grand time. I think my engagement to Jon is a perfect occasion for great craic! And, since Father McKenzie and Mother are coming here next week from New York, I'm sure they would be ready and raring to host such a celebration."

Not understanding the Western equine metaphor "ready and rearing", Maggie and Liza had laughed, accepted Rose's enthusiasm and noted its rationale. So, as she had predicted or had mandated her parents to do, today was going to be their hosting of the first engagement party tradition for the family.

At the Lester and Louisa, Fiona and Finbar McCann had prepared a magnificent feast and festival to initiate the new tradition. With Father McKenzie's open wallet and long-distance connections with Belfast merchants, he had been able to provide many of the rationed items for a buffet display of glazed ham, milk, cheese and various coveted condiments. Butter (not lard), salt and sugar were prolific. The feast began at 3 PM, the same time every Sunday luncheon had been held by ancestors Bella and Lizzie and now by their descendants. Individual tables in the Inn's common room had been aligned in a row to accommodate the twenty-plus family members... babies et al. Abutting the common area, side enclosures of benches and worn tables remained sequestered for the individual conversations sure to happen after the meal and before the evening singing, music and blessings. Such craic would enable the exchange of news of partisan import to the men and, of course, to the women.

By 5 PM, Francis McKenzie was already holding court in his enclosure with Billie, Eamon, Robert and Jon. The Irish-American banker had to share FDR's potential Lend Lease bill that would support Britain militarily and agriculturally against the Germans. Liam,

Ian, Wolfe, Kieran and Erin had settled into benches around a partitioned table far from McKenzie. The latter group had no intention of learning whatever the Irish American alliances had for either the UK or Northern Ireland. Erin had news from the Belfast IRA Brigade.

The women remained in the central room. They had moved their chairs closer to each other at the end of the extended dinner table to better hear each other and to facilitate the constant exchange of Rachel's and Morna's infants from one comforting woman's arms to another. They were also deciding activities they did not want their respective men to question, let alone know.

All three groups were making plans, not for the wedding, nor confirmations, nor baptisms. Rather, they were anticipating the covert actions to be taken in this year of '41 – a year they knew would be full of unpredictable events, probable losses but, if prayers went well, potential successes and blessings. Each group was ignorant of the other groups' ideas.

The only souls who would hear the plans shared by all were not of the fore-mentioned humankind. Rather, three earthly canines would take in the words and sense the various emotions of hope, angst and fear. Before the music and dancing livened the air, the three guardians would have accompanied their respective humans. Grua would be with Billie, Larger with Wolfe, and Fai with Morna.

Only after the evening's merriment would end, would these three share among themselves what each had heard in the private discussions. After the guise of sleeping soundly by the fireplace, they would arise and call upon their heavenly counterparts – Bigger, Sceo and Boru – to consider the earthly interventions.

All six would then practice their own tradition: protecting their loved ones as best they could.

43

Triage

Wednesday, April 16, 1941

1 AM :

Robert grabbed blankets and a basket of tinned food. Morna held tight to her medical kit and a sack of extra bandages. The air raid sirens had sounded in the middle of the night outside their Falls Road home. Soon they had begun hearing the foreboding hum of German Luftwaffe and successive explosions. Along with their tiny daughter Meg and dog Fai, they had quickly entered into the underground tunnel that served as their neighborhood shelter. About fifty others had gathered with them underneath the Belfast Clonard Monastery. Morna began administering emergency aid to late arrivals suffering from burns, crushed bones and fear. With Meg in his arms, Robert led both Shankill area Protestants and Falls Road Catholics in hymns. He also offered whatever comforting words a philosopher could to anyone. Fai nestled along the sides of trembling children and, not a few, adults.

5 AM:

No one was certain at what time the bombing ceased. They felt relief from the terrifying barrage overhead, but it was tempered by the terrifying fear of what might greet them above ground.

"Hurry, hurry," cried Morna. "We must get to the hospital as quickly as we can."

Neither Robert nor Morna cared about certainty; they just knew it was time to leave the shelter, assess the damage before them, and find their family members. If the couple could offer assistance to others during their search, all the better. A kind novitiate at the Monastery agreed to keep Meg as long as was needed for her parents' to complete their mission. "She's in God's hands here," said Sister Eunice, smiling at the wee bairn. Robert looked at Fai and rolled his eyes. Fortunately, neither Morna nor the nun saw his doubt. Ach. "Who is the God that takes Meg in his arms but doesn't protect others who surely have died tonight?" Robert said to himself. "Perhaps this is not the proper time to ask that question." He hesitated while petting Fai. "May we put you, not God, in charge of Meg's protection, dear friend?" The faithful dog wagged her tail.

It was only at the end of the day that Robert would ask about God again.

The couple left the Monastery just as dawn peeked over the smoldering city-scape. They turned from Falls Road onto Grosvenor Street and followed it east to Templemore Avenue and Belfast City center. The Ulster Hospital for Women and Sick Children was located at the end of that avenue. Morna's brother Dr. Ian McNulty was assigned to the hospital as its lead Administrator. Just yesterday, Morna had been beside him on an outreach immunization program held in the hospital's clinic. She knew he would have gone to the hospital the minute the sirens rang out. Since then, he had probably transformed their program into a rescue and emergency aid mission. Little did she imagine it would also include so much triage and so many sacraments, the final signs of crosses over foreheads going cold.

The devastation before them as they traversed cross street after cross street was horrific. Former three story buildings of bricks had collapsed into rubbles of shattered edges and dust; flickering flames were consuming the remains of household furniture, grocery products and church pews. More disturbing were smoldering bundles of charred objects, indistinguishable between manufactured or human. The smell of thermite and magnesium from incendiary bombs that had created this horror was mixed with gas leaking from pipes connected to houses and stores. Robert and Morna covered their faces with handkerchiefs embroidered by Aunt Kat with their initials for decorative usage, now for survival. Each wished they could have had transparent versions for their eyes.

It had taken the couple four hours to go twelve city blocks to the hospital. At each street, there were soldiers and citizens emerging from the debris and moving quickly into action – some used their hands to dig through the rumble for crying victims. Some used their arms to lift injured onto improvised carriers. Some used their knees to bend over those whispering their last wishes. All were listening for cries. All were praying under their breaths. Morna used her medical acumen to provide immediate treatment or advice. Robert used his muscles on borrowed shovels to uncover the buried and lift them onto blankets. By the time, they reached the hospital, they were exhausted. What greeted them took not only their last bit of energy but their remaining hope to find Ian alive.

9 AM:

The Ulster Hospital for Women and Children was demolished. In its place were jagged stakes of bent steel and charred wood. Dust rose from one end of Templemore at its right turn onto Albertbridge. Bodies covered with torn sheets or ashened coats and shawls were lined up across from what had been the hospital's entrance. Ambulances and private cars on Albertbridge Road awaited the barely living. Hospital staff who, like Robert and Morna, had sheltered in their neighborhoods during the night, were arriving to join their soul-weary colleagues. Soon they, too, were performing triage through unconscious recall and pure stubbornness. Soldiers and constables were trying, to no avail, to control the crowds of family members seeking their loved ones, to no avail. Chaos reigned.

"I must find Ian," cried Morna, racing ahead of Robert to the ambulances.

"Morna! Morna!" Robert yelled. "Let me go first." He could not keep up with her as she darted over and around the fallen debris.

When he did catch up, she had stopped abruptly behind an ambulance. At its rear was Ian, staring silently at a still body on the pavement below him.

"My darling, darling, brother. You are alive." She murmured as she wrapped her arms around him.

"Morna. I tried to save him. I tried. I tried. He was next door giving a lecture last night and ran over here when the sirens first arose. Despite his leg, he helped us carry so many patients to the shelter. We were almost finished when the bombs fell and he was…he was." Ian pulled back from her embrace.

"Who is it, Ian?" she asked, not wanting to look at the covered figure below her.

"It's Uncle Eamon. We just lost him." Ian began to sob.

Morna straightened her stance. Then, like a tree branch split from its bark by a lightning strike, she folded down to the remains of her dear uncle. Robert knelt by the body, too. He had just arrived and heard Ian's words. For the first time in Morna's relationship with her husband, she heard Robert cry out a long moan, followed by what she recognized as his continuous, existential query. "My God," he exclaimed. "Why?"

A wisp of wind blew across Robert's forehead. He thought he heard the faint bark of a dog.

From the monastery, Fai had beckoned Sceo.

44

The Second Coming

Sunday, June 15, 1941

Rachel sat before the statue of Mother Mary in a side chapel of St. Margaret's Refuge in Belfast. The Blessed Mother was standing on a small, sandstone altar before a delicately embroidered tapestry of Ireland's natural gifts – verdant green hills, gurgling streams, yellow fruze and wildlife – elk, wolves, fox and rooks. The Blessed Mother's arms were out-stretched and head bowed. She was illuminated by two beeswax candles set upon brass stands placed at opposite sides of the altar. Each stand was engraved with intricately designed thistles and butterflies. Before them, tiny flames flickered in amber votive cups placed along tidy rows on a table to Rachel's right. To her left was a wooden donation box for the troubled – present or distant, alive or dead. Rachel was not sure which group consumed her thoughts the most at this moment.

Despite being an avowed agnostic, Rachel often came to St. Margaret's to think. She had never accepted the teachings of priests whom she considered as hypocrites. To her, they espoused religious dogma without practicing the tenets themselves. Having overcome so many challenges by herself to reach her own goals, she could not accept an ethereal being guiding, let alone determining, her life.

That assurance was being tested tonight. She had asked Ian to care for their infant daughter Maud while she conducted a house visit with an ailing woman whom she had befriended first in Cork at the Sisters of St. Mary's and, again, after meeting her twenty years later in the Belfast Gallagher Women's Center. Tonight's house-visit, however, wasn't just for a friendly chat. Rachel's decision-making, usually set after her emotions were quieted, was racing uncontrollably between her moral conscience and her partisan duty to the IRA.

It was almost nine and no one other than Rachel was in the church. At least, that's what she thought until she heard a quiet voice behind her.

"Is someone here?" The shuffle of feet, more than the question, brought Rachel out of her agitated state. Actually, it was an additional four feet tapping upon the marble floor that focused her attention and brought relief.

She turned to see Father Wolfe and his canine companion Larger approaching her.

"Don't be afraid of me," the voice continued. "If ye are in need, I can help."

Rachel stood as the pair reached her. Wolfe could feel Larger's tail wag and torso move excitedly.

"We know ye, don't we?" Wolfe asked.

Rachel sighed. "Aye, Wolfe. It is I."

He immediately recognized her voice.

"Rachel. I would normally say 'What are ye doing here at this time of night?', but I know ye too well. Come sit next to me and tell me what's bothering ye." Wolfe reached for her hand which she readily offered, leading them both to sit upon one of the chapel's wooden pews. Larger lay down at their feet.

"Ach, Wolfe. I fear I have taken on a task I truly don't want to complete, but know I must. If I tell ye about it, can ye promise to forget it?" she asked.

"Rachel. I am a man of God and a priest of His faith. What ye tell me is a confession of what ye are thinking, not of what ye have already done. As such, I won't forget what ye say, but I will not share it with anyone." Wolfe turned towards her. "Speak and I will listen."

They had not released each other's hands and did not until Rachel finished describing her task and the dilemma it raised. She had been assigned by the Belfast Battalion of the IRA to determine who had betrayed one of its members. Six had escaped two days before from Belfast's Crumlin Road jail. They had been charged for murdering several informants during the confusion of the recent blitz. Five were successfully on their way to Dublin. One had gone to a safe house on Falls Road to meet his family before returning to Eire. The reunion offered no comfort for he had been captured by the RUC this very morning in that house.

The house was that of Rachel's friend whom she was to visit this night. Grace McCarthy Magee, a former Magdalene laundry worker who had fled the laundry in Cork, moved to Belfast and married an IRA member. It was Grace's husband, Frank Magee, whom the battalion thought turned in the sixth escapee. If, during Rachel's visit, Grace mentioned that Frank had not been home when the RUC arrested the escapee inside, then it would be certain that Frank was the informant.

"If I do hear that from Grace, I must go back to the battalion tonight, and Frank will surely be dead by the morning. Wolfe, they have two teenage boys. They will be fatherless, and Grace will be a widow in the poorhouse if Frank is killed." Rachel began to raise her voice. Wolfe could feel her angst and held her hand tighter.

"Rachel. Ye have always thought through challenges before with yer heart first, then yer mind. Can ye close yer eyes for just a minute or two. Can ye put yer mind and heart at rest just for those minutes?"

Wolfe could feel Rachel shift away from him to face the altar. Her tight grasp on his hand relaxed. Her breathing quieted its pace. He sensed that she had closed her eyes.

He started to pray, first, silently to himself. When he next spoke aloud, he did not mention God, Jesus nor Mother Mary. Instead, he recited, in part, a William Butler Yeats poem, The Second Coming.

> *"Turning and turning in the widening gyre*
> *The falcon cannot hear the falconer;*

Things fall apart; the centre cannot hold;
Mere anarchy is loosed, upon the world,
The blood-dimmed tide is loosed, and everywhere
The ceremony of innocence is drowned;
The best lack all conviction, while the worst
Are full of passionate intensity.

Surely some revelation is at hand;
Surely the Second Coming is at hand..."

Rachel opened her eyes; she did not look at the statue before her, but at the tapestry behind it. Letting go of Wolfe's hand, she stood up.

"My dear, dear Wolfe. Ye are certainly a man of strong faith and scholar of our culture. Thank ye for listening. And I thank ye for yer promise not to share what I have told ye." She turned away from him and, after petting Larger's head, walked out of St. Margaret's. She could not wait for the second coming.

Wolfe sighed. He reached toward Larger who was now standing up. The dog's tail was not wagging. "Aye, my pet. As a man of God, I didn't reach her at all, did I?" Wolfe asked.

"I did, however, tell her I would guard what she said. Now, I must consider how to forget, and may God help me to forgive whatever she has decided to do."

By noon the next day, Frank Magee was dead.

45

Unpredictable Predictability

October 3, 1941

"I think of him every day." Kat quietly shared with her sister BB.

"Whenever, I hear the latch click on the front door, I think he'll be opening it. Whenever I hear the back door open, I think he'll be walking in. Whenever I reach for the second pillow on our bed, I think he'll be pulling me close. I think of my beloved Eamon every day – almost every hour of the day."

Kat stared out the kitchen window of the Bangor home where she and Eamon had raised their three children, two dogs and many a voice on the issues facing Ireland. Here, they had entertained young and elder family members, Catholic and Protestant friends and adversaries, political leaders and followers. Here, there had been laughter and tears, arguments and apologies, debates and resolutions, songs and recitations by famous and not-so-famous poets. Many such activities had been accompanied by the occasional slurring of words and toppling over of unsettled glasses. Now, the kitchen and entire house seemed silent.

"I know you miss him terribly," said BB to her, beloved sister. "We all miss him. He was a distinguished philosopher who offered such balance among our differing family members. He helped us remember the larger questions in life." BB smiled. "Do ye remember that night when Devin and Neil were arguing about whether Devin should go to England? The two boys were yelling like banshees when Eamon raised his hand as a referee on the rugby field and quietly said to each: "What is your purpose in a just and ethical life?"

"Aye," Kat smiled. "I remember that well."

BB continued "And do ye remember when Collins and Griffith sat across from each other right at this table debating how the Executive Council should address the pro and anti advocates of the Anglo-Irish Treaty? Eamon listened quite a while, didn't he? And, then, he just leaned forward between the two leaders and simply asked: "How should we treat our fellow Irishmen? Does the end really justify our means?""

Kat didn't respond. Instead, she brought out a handkerchief, the one that had been embroidered by her mother Lizzie as a gift for Kat's marriage to Eamon. For over thirty years, it had comforted her. Now, despite its frayed edges, it retained its magic. Twirling it around her slender hand, she knew what Eamon would be saying to her today. He would recite lines from his favorite Mary Katherine Tynan poem, urging Kat to be the resilient shamrock he loved:

> "Shamrock stayeth every day
> Be the winds or gold or grey...
> And it laughs o'er many a vale.
> Sheltered safe from storm and gale...
> Soft it clothes the ruined floor
> Of many an abbey, grey and hoar
>
> And the still home of the dead
> With its green is carpeted...
> But my shamrock, brave and gay,
> Glads the tired eyes every day...
> But my shamrock, one in three
> Takes the inmost heart of me.

Being the spiritual member of the family, BB recognized that her sister was in a place far from the table and let her be.

But it wasn't for long. The front door opened and a bustle of voices and laughter soon filled the hallway leading to the kitchen. Kat came back to the present time and place.

"Mum, how are ye?" Liza asked as she entered the kitchen and placed her arms around Kat's shoulders. The twenty-two year old kissed her mother on the top of her head and turned to see her cousin Maggie doing the same to her mother BB.

"Ach, what is it about our family?" asked Liza. "We are so predictable!"

Maggie laughed at Liza. "My dearest Liza. Weren't we just laughing about how we wanted Mother and Aunt Kat to help us be predictably unpredictable?"

"Indeed, we were. So let's get at it." Liza pulled out a chair from one side of the wooden table at the same moment Maggie did on the opposite. BB stood up to retrieve two more tea cups, placed one before each lass. She took the copper kettle whistling on the stove and poured the steaming contents into each cup. At the very same time, each lass reached for the one slice of soda bread remaining from Kat's and BB's earlier breakfast. The piece was split in half.

Kat and BB looked at each other and beamed. These two young women, born in the same month twenty-two years before, had been raised almost as twins. In their secondary school years, they had gone together to St. Enda's in Dublin before it closed in 1935; in the summers, they had volunteered with their mothers in the Gallagher Clinics of the north. Both were now finishing up their studies at Trinity College in Dublin; Liza in philosophy, Maggie in religion.

Kat straightened her back and focused on Maggie's last remark about predictable unpredictability.

"Ach. Explain thyselves," Kat encouraged, using the phrase Eamon always did when asking family members to justify their statements.

Maggie began. "Aunt Kat. Ye and Mum have been writing your IndePen articles for over thirty years. Grand Aunt Lizzie did for decades before, and Great Grand Aunt Bella even longer before then. Just last year, didn't ye celebrate the 90th anniversary of the column?"

BB and Kay both remarked in unison. "Aye, we did."

"Well, " said Liza. "That's predictability. But, let's chat a bit about your articles' predictable content. Great Aunt Bella wrote about major issues: the Great Famine, tenant rights on plantations, labor strikes on the docks, and the terrible Penal Laws. Aunt Lizzie continued that brilliance by covering issues facing Ireland at the turn of the century: the Easter Rising 1916, World War 1, the War of Independence in '20, The Civil War in '21. In this decade alone, you have raised equally important issues such as cross-border relations, negotiations with Great Britain, health and welfare deficits, and now another world war. Always you have described how those issues impact citizens in both The Free State – now Eire – and Northern Ireland."

Liza was about to go on when Maggie jumped in which was a frequent mode of communication between and by the two. Each seemed to finish the other's sentence.

Maggie looked first at her mother, then, at her Aunt Kat. "Let me ask you both a question. How often did you, Grand Aunt Lizzie or Great Grand Bella describe these issues and, summarily, call women to take action?"

The two elders glanced at each other. BB folded her hands, positioning them as if to pray. Kat knew exactly what her sister was thinking: Where in God's name are these lassies going with this question? Kat placed her handkerchief on her lap, folding it into a square, another square and a final square. BB knew exactly what Kat was thinking: Where in the nation's name are these lassies going? Both women sensed their next, similar question: What has Rachel been saying to these girls?

For the next two hours, the four went round and round on the possibility of moving the column from 100 years of predictability to a new present. Could the column's content change? Should it? They finally focused on two key questions: What was the purpose of the column today and who was its key audience?

Another hour and a full dinner helped them answer those; but not without a few predictable stances conflicting with unpredictable ones. The audience was easy to determine – women. All four welcomed writing about issues facing that population. After all, the other newspapers were primarily focused on what men were saying. Rarely did they publish women's voices.

The purpose was not so easily resolved. Kat and BB were fearful of proposing controversial actions to address issues. They did not want to put the column, its authors and audience members in jeopardy of public criticism or, worse yet, physical harm. Liza and Maggie countered that their family had always stood up for solutions that were ethical and just. Hadn't Uncle Anthony and father Eamon taught that in their philosophy classes? And wasn't Cousin Robert teaching the same? Hadn't Great Grandfather William died for that in Macroom during the Great Famine, Grand Uncle Aiden in the Belfast labor strikes and now Cousin Edwin in France?

"Where are the women among those activists in our family?" exclaimed Liza.

Kat wanted to share the many secret accomplishments of Grand Aunt Bella and Holloway Prison Superintendent Fanny McCarthy; BB about Grandmother Lizzie, Sister Bridgette and Grand Aunt Maud McCann.

Those tales would have to wait, however, as Maggie quickly interjected. "We're not saying that women must die when standing up against injustice. They already are dying because of it. Shouldn't our sisters know they can mitigate, rather than succumb to it? Shouldn't they be included in what that effort looks like? We need to offer them more than just words on a page. Better yet, we need to let them tell us what changes they desire, are willing to advocate for, and act upon. That's what a good journalist does, correct? We seek out the injured and report on what they believe will help them."

Kat and BB knew that Rachel had, indeed, been talking to the two daughters. They also knew their daughters were right.

Thus, previously unpredictable compromises were reached. The four resolved that the purpose of the column was two-fold: To voice the concerns of Irish women and to call them to action. Specific content would come directly from women who were rarely heard. Along with national and international women leaders in both Eire and N.I., marginalized women would identify solutions and determine how to enact them. IndePen would publish all three: problems, solutions and actions. Perhaps there could be a series on a particular issue with quotes from those effected, if they wished to go public. Each column would encourage women to participate as they felt comfortable doing so. By the end of the evening, the first column announcing this new purpose and inviting women's ideas had been composed.

Calling All Women and Girls

The IndePen women are inviting you to a meeting on November 15 at 6 PM in Linen Hall, Belfast and on November 22 at 6PM in the Trinity College Library. For over ninety years, we have been predictable in our mission: to share national information and viewpoints for all citizens on challenges facing our grand island ranging from the Famine of 1845, to the Easter Rising in 1916, to World War 1, the Great Depression, and now this new World War. We have decided to alter that predictability by changing the purpose of our column. As such, we would like to focus directly on the challenges facing women today and offer actions we can take together.

If you are interested in helping us make this change, please attend either of these meetings. You can RSVP your attendance by writing a letter to IndePen, Our Ireland Newspaper, 84 Crumlin Road, Belfast. Or you may directly contact any one of us.

In an historic change to our predictable fashion, we are sharing, for the first time in the publication of this column, exactly who we are.

Most sincerely yours,

Katherine Irvine Smiley, Belle Bridgette Irvine McCormick, Elizabeth McKnight Smiley, and Maggie McGregor McCormick

In the beyond, Eamon paused his walk with Bigger and dear friend Michael Collins. "Ach," he exclaimed, referring to the women below with great pride. "Those are my ethical and just Shamrocks." Michael nodded in agreement.

46

Voices Raised and Recognized

December 6, 1941

The four IndePen writers had been thrilled by the attendance at their two gatherings, one in Belfast, one in Dublin. More than forty women had come to the former on a blistering cold evening November 15th; about sixty to the latter a week later when another storm raged. Weather had not deterred will nor wisdom.

The Belfast Linen Hall library had buzzed with the voices of women, fearless despite the previous April's blitz. Bombs had struck the roof of the Belfast City Hall directly across the street. Local citizens quipped that the Luftwaffe never took aim at the historic library because their pilots were so ignorant and illiterate. No explosions destroyed centuries of Irish history contained within the cherished repository. At the Trinity College Library meeting in Dublin on November 22nd, about sixty women came. Like their peers in Belfast, their voices buzzed excitedly and fearlessly, but not because they were experiencing military blitzes. In contrast, they were suffering from household bruises and broken bones. Despite deValera's State of Emergency nationwide, there were domestic bullets and bombs unchecked within families. Furthermore, so many unmarried, young girls were still suffering from the indentured status dictated by the will of the church.

Notwithstanding their common Irish heritage, the attendees at the two separate events were also not of the same mindset nor emotion. They portrayed different demeanors and even wore different clothes.

At the Linen Hall Library, most of women had on military uniforms for serving in auxiliary services, bulky trousers for working in the munition factories or ship yards, nursing bibs for hospital work or out-of-fashion suits for teaching in schools or sales-clerking in department stores. With most Northern Irishmen serving in the battlefields or administrative war offices in Great Britain, women at the Linen Hall gathering had taken on many a role previously designated as male. Thus, they dressed accordingly. Kat and Liza had not been surprised at the variety of dress nor initial expressions on faces before them – some glum, some tired, but not too glum nor tired to speak up. All were soon animated and expectant. The volume of chatter evidenced there was much to be shared publicly.

At the Trinity College Library a week later, BB had been amazed at the type of women there who had faced Maggie and her. She had reflected back on her time in 1912 attending her first Daughters of Ireland meeting in Dublin. Then, she had encountered so many notable women leaders: the Countess Markievicz, Patrick Pearce's mother Margaret and his sister Mary. They had been such impressive individuals both in social stature and in fashion. Now, thirty years later, dress indicated equality, not class. No fancy hats with peacock feathers appeared nor fur trims on any coat. Instead, the common tweed skirt just below the knee, woolen sweater and linen blouse bowed at the neck characterized at least ninety-percent of the attendees. The other ten percent wore pants and solid shoes coming directly from factories or warehouses packing rationed foods or exported goods to be shipped to London, at least, those the emergency laws allowed. Only, in part, had the faces of these women been similar in expression to those in Belfast: glum and tired. The Trinity College Library women, however, were not animated. The volume of their chatter was much lower than that of the Belfast contingency. The Dublin women had much to share, but not publicly. Their husbands and the church had sobered them too much.

On this December night, about a month after the two gatherings, the four family members had returned to a kitchen to discuss their findings and the next IndePen editorial. BB was hosting them at the Rathmines home she and Liam now called their empty nest. Ian, Morna and Rachel had moved out and on with their respective spouses. Maggie was rooming with Liza and two other girls in a small walk-up at Trinity. Kieran was living with Liam's sister Shelly at the Lester and Louisa while studying at Queen's. BB could empathize with her sister Kat at the silence that reigned in Bangor. There was one difference, though. Liam was still alive. Eamon was not.

"Come, let us look at what we have heard in our two meetings," encouraged Kat. "What fascinating stories were shared, full of angst and sorrow."

"Aye", said BB. "It reminded me of my early days back in the '10's as a novitiate when the Mother Superior would tell us to rid ourselves of all earthly feelings and replace them with prayers for redemption and forgiveness, as though we were to blame for those feelings and had to forgive the source."

"But wait," exclaimed Maggie. "I heard many words of bravery and strength, of pride and motivation. For sure, women spoke passionately about their troubles, but many said they wanted to address them straight on. Some already had. I didn't hear any claiming to be victims of their circumstances."

"'Tis true, dear Maggie," added Kat. "Like your Mum, I recall planning meetings during the Easter Rising during which women...."

Liza jumped in. "Mum, that was over twenty-five years ago. Can we please consider what the women are saying today? It seemed to me that the voices I heard weren't interested in gaining independence from Great Britain. Rather they wanted their children to be safe and, sadly enough, many wanted that for themselves as well, specifically from the bombs or belts they felt daily at home. Can we focus on the current ideas shared for our editorial?"

Kat looked at Liza with an expression of both guilt and pride. Hearing her mother Lizzie for a fleeting second, she thought to herself. "How had this child become so perceptive and so resolute?" Kat smiled. "Ach, Liza, forgive me for reminiscing so. Yes, let's focus on what we heard, not what I remember."

BB and Maggie glanced at each other, knowing that Kat was often referring to the past in these last months, a way by which she could keep Eamon in her presence. A short silence followed.

Liza brought them back to the task at hand. "Do you remember the comments from those two women in the back of the room at Linen Hall? They soon started to yell at us. Maggie and I were astonished and taken aback by their fervor."

"Girls," chided BB." We must remember that – as in a medical clinic – whatever or however someone speaks in our meetings, we must listen carefully to the words and respect the feelings behind those words. The women must trust us first, which only happens after we let them air their true pain and anger. What do we remember that they said, starting in Belfast?"

Maggie took out her notebook in which she kept meticulous annotation of what the attendees had shared. "Remember the first of the two young women, the one in the brown jacket and grey pants. She had radiant red hair in a long braid over her shoulder?" BB and Maggie nodded. Kat frowned.

"Here's what she said:

'I am tired, tired, tired every day. First, I cannot stomach what is going on in the shelters. We are called out of our homes by the sound of the siren and the drum of the planes overhead almost every night. No one, especially the children, can sleep soundly before being abruptly awakened. In anticipation, they have terrible nightmares. Then, we race into the shelter and never know what's happening outside until we hear the all-clear. Fear of the unknown is horrific. Finally, we leave the shelters to see such horrible sights, crumbled buildings and, dare I say in public, crumbled bodies. No child should have to see that devastation. They are so scared during

the day that they won't play outside. Their schools are closed. The
church kitchens are overwhelmed. Our men are gone. What can we
do for our children who are suffering from this emotional debacle
called a war?'

Maggie stopped reading her notes. They were blurred by the tears emerging from her eyes.

Kat's face flushed. Suddenly, she widened her eyes and exclaimed. "Wait. Wait. Didn't the other woman say she was sending her young son to a sister in Scotland where there haven't been any bombings? Didn't she complain how there was nothing anyone was doing here to provide safe havens for the children?"

"Aye, she did." Liza replied, turning toward her mother who had a curious glint in her eye and a smile beginning to form. Liza noticed both. "Mum, what are ye thinking?"

"Well... why don't we organize a children's evacuation service, just like they are doing in London. We can find safe, temporary homes for our Belfast children in the countryside of Tyrone or in the hills of Fermanagh?"

BB stared at her sister and began to speak, but couldn't before her own daughter jumped up from her seat.

"Better yet, why don't we ask some of the families just over the border in Donegal or Cavan to open their homes temporarily?" Maggie was becoming more and more spirited.

"I'm sure some Eire families would welcome Northern Ireland children, especially those who want to make a subtle complaint to deValera about his neutral stance. Many of the women in our Dublin gathering were furious about that, stating how their cousins in Ulster – Derry and Belfast, particularly – were suffering worse than they in Dublin. What a generous and loving action to provide safe havens for the children of Belfast. And what a peacemaking effort it would be for mothers to collaborate across the partition. The Belfast children could become friends with those in Eire despite the prejudice of their grandparents and their parents today. And the children of Eire could carry their friendships with those from the North into their adulthood. Think of the understanding gained by everyone, children and mothers and, then, perhaps fathers as well? We can call it the Families Together program."

Kat, BB and Liza sat stunned.

Maggie summarized her idea with great gusto. "Why are ye so surprised looking? Doesn't IndePen represent the voices of women from both countries?"

Slowly yet deliberatively over the next hours, the four discussed the benefits and challenges of such a plan. How could families be convinced to give up their children temporarily and partner with host families they might not initially trust? Would there have to be financial incentives or would compassion be enough? How could government leaders in both countries be moved to approve of such a program? Would London's input be excluded? Who would manage the program, etc., etc., etc.?

More questions than answers were raised among the women. Liza finally brought the discussion to an abrupt halt by proposing what her three writers eventually considered a clever next step.

"In this week's IndePen, let's report on the need women raised related to children's welfare. We can also share the Families Together plan as a solution we heard them offer. We'll raise the questions we just posed and solicit readers' answers by the following week. We know that the women in Belfast are deeply concerned about their children's safety. We know that the women in Dublin were equally concerned for their sisters in the North. If we put their common concern and this solution in print publicly, I can only imagine how it will spread, like wildflowers on both the Mourne and Tara hills. Politicians on both sides of the partition will read constituent suggestions. They'll also hear demands for the plan after their wives, sisters and mothers convince them it's a grand idea. Voila! Women's voices will have been heard, not just in angst and sorrow, but in strength and motivation."

BB brought out Grandmother Bella's four, tiny, crystal wine glasses and a bottle of wine Liam had brought from the reconstructed Cistercian Monastery in Kilkenny the previous week. She poured a thumb full into each glass.

Raising their glasses, BB toasted to their resolution: "Let us thank God for the blessing of our first enterprise."

"Oh, Mum," said Maggie. "Can't we just give thanks for the blessing alone? What does God do, anyway, for women who speak up? He, his priests and nuns haven't been listening to women for ages. So, let's keep God at a distance and women close."

"Don't forget, "Maggie continued, frowning. "Our next IndePen issue will address the main concern raised at our Dublin gathering: women worrying about their own welfare."

47

Inside and Out Parallel Lives

December 20, 1941

Agnes and Rachel had taken parallel paths in their journeys to support the independence movement. Over Agnes' fifty-seven years and Rachel's thirty-five, they had never participated in a common IRA activity nor were they actually certain of the other's membership. Their particular "circles" had moved in different areas of the island and taken very different actions. Rachel never knew about Agnes' exposure of the informant Nathan Dickson at Four Courts in June of 1922. Agnes did not know of the Countess' betrayal of Rachel and, thus, Rachel's implication in the April '22 murder of Father O'Hare in Macroom. Numerous other actions had taken place over the past twenty years, too many to assume by either about the other.

Over their lifetimes, however, they had been together during many a family gathering, picnics in Killiney, lunches in Rathmines, burial ceremonies at The Botanic Garden, and performances of plays by Erin McCann. Each had guessed the other's participation in the IRA but had respected its rule of secrecy. At Rose and Jon's recent engagement party in the Lester and Louisa, an obvious truth had begun to emerge. Separate from the men, the women had spoken about the death of Frank Magee. Agnes had noticed Rachel's frown followed by her somber withdrawal from the conversation. After twenty years of avoidance, their IRA paths were finally crossing. At the end of the party, exposing her own role and fairly certain of Rachel's, Agnes whispered only three coded IRA words to Rachel: "Tiocfaidh ar la" (Our day will come.) Rachel did not look surprised and retorted in kind: "Aye. Uncle Mick lives."

Today, the two women had returned to the Lester and Louisa where, for almost ten months after the engagement party, they had begun clandestine meetings on behalf of their respective circles within the IRA Belfast battalion. They came to the traditional Sunday family luncheon well before the rest of the family arrived. Fiona McCann escorted the two IRA members to their assigned table at the back of the dining area, knowing full-well the purpose of their monthly meetings. After all, Fiona, like her father Finbar and Uncle Erin, was also a respected member of the movement.

Agnes and Rachel sat facing each other for a few moments of silence. Agnes began the conversation.

"My darling, Rachel. It's so good to see you. You look well, but tired, as a new mother. How are you faring?"

Rachel's hesitant smile drew a thin line across her face. She nodded in agreement with Agnes' assessment. "Yes, I am tired; but aren't we all? Now that the US has come into the War and so many more vessels are arriving in Bangor's harbor and Carrickfergus' shipyards, we have more opportunities to keep the movement alive. Regardless of being tired, we have to keep going. We have to keep moving forward."

Agnes grasped Rachel's hand. "Yes; indeed we do and, if I can be so bold to ask, Rachel. How do you keep going forward?"

Rachel looked at Agnes. "Aunt Agnes, let me be honest. It's not my responsibilities that exhaust me; it's my doubt that wears me down. I can't stop thinking of Frank Magee's wife Grace and her two teenage boys. Whenever I see his boys outside their father's store in Belfast, they seem so angry and lost. I feel incredible remorse about my part in his death. I am torn between wanting a better life for them and a better life for my little Maud. Can those two ever be the same? I don't know." Rachel turned her head away to conceal her distress. She fell silent but quickly continued, as though she were speaking to someone behind the three glass partitions enclosing the wooden table and chairs.

"I keep thinking of Auntie Lizzie. You may not know this, but, when I was just twelve in 1918, she and I were once at the Linen Hall Library designing posters for a suffragette march. A woman approached us whom Auntie said caused the death of Patrick McCann, Erin's brother, during the Easter Rising. Auntie Lizzie said that this woman's truth about patriotism needed to be washed 'inside out'. I will never forget Auntie's explanation of those words.

Agnes remembered Lizzie's story about Christine O'Leary. In 1919 as part of an IRA vendetta, Christine had murdered the Orangeman Samuel Acheson behind the Smiley's house in Bangor. Samuel was attempting to kill Eamon. As revenge for Samuel's death, Christine was murdered by Samuel's nephew Chester Acheson in 1921 outside the home of Countess Markievicz in Rathmines. Subsequently captured in Macroom by Anti-Treaty members, Chester was killed. It was the historic 'tit for tat' within Irish conflict.

Agnes asked Rachel. "Tell me what the words 'inside out' meant to Aunt Lizzie then and to you now."

Rachel turned toward Agnes. "Aunt Lizzie told me to always take the facts, opinions and arguments I hear from outside and cleanse them, inside my heart, with a bath of justice and compassion. Only after doing that should I follow my heart's insight in deciding any outside actions. Aunt Lizzie said that our family had always practiced the art of 'inside out' no matter what faced us. And that has served us well, as Uncle Eamon always said, to live an ethical life."

Her voice trailed off. She paused. "You ask a second question, Aunt Agnes," regaining her focus. "What do these words mean for me now? I don't know."

Agnes shifted in her chair. She leaned across the table toward Rachel and placed a hand on Rachel's left arm, holding it there as she next spoke.

"Dearest, Rachel. Whenever there is doubt or troubles surrounding you, like Aunt Lizzie wisely said, you have to collect your facts,

opinions and arguments. You decide how they inform your understanding of the circumstances. Then, you ask what truth can you
glean from them. Once you form your belief, the hardest part may
not be to cleanse that belief through a bath of compassion and justice, but to cleanse the actions you are considering to take. You have
to choose whether or not they will exacerbate, mitigate or eliminate
whatever causes the trouble."

Rachel bowed her head and placed her own hand on Agnes'.
Agnes continued.

"Our whole family has had to deal with uncertainty, almost
always regarding some evil going on around us. Your brother Ryan
McCormick chose to fight against Home Rule by planting a bomb.
He died by the hands of an accomplice he thought was a good friend,
your own brother-in-law's father Robbie Smiley. Your brother Liam
and my own husband Uncle Billie have taken another route. They
work as TDs in the Dublin Dial promoting laws supporting justice.
Look at what Ian, your own husband, is doing by bringing health to so
many destitute families; our IndePen lassies by identifying women's
needs and promoting the Families Together program; Erin McCann
by writing plays; Wolfe by preaching kindness and forgiveness to the
masses; and, lest we forget, our dear Neil in Scotland, Devin now in
France and God only knows where Thon is. Each one of them has
had to consider their own 'inside out'.

Agnes finished, almost breathless. "I know you can choose what's
best for you, your loved ones and your country, Rachel. Look to your
heart and see what 'inside out' means to you."

Rachel closed her eyes. The pattern of her inhaling and exhaling
began to slow down, like the ebb and flow of the Killiney tide until,
not surprisingly to Agnes, Rachel was asleep. Agnes did not with-
draw her hand resting on Rachel's arm. Instead, she began to stroke it
like a mother calming an anxious child.

For a good five minutes, Rachel dreamed. And as she did, she felt the same warmth she had felt surrounding her like a shawl on the Bennetsbridge road in 1922 after she had fled the shooting of Father O'Hare. Just as it had that night so many years ago, a figure swirling in light approached her. The Scots-Irish lilt she had heard then spoke to her now. As Rachel had before, she questioned: "Who are ye?"

Ye need not know exactly who I am, replied the figure. Just imagine I am those who understand the tangles in yer mind. There have been many a soul before ye who also had to choose a right path for their beliefs and actions. Like ye, they had to determine loyalties based on what they deemed as true and just. "I don't know how to determine that truth." Rachel asked, no longer in a whisper but rather in an impassioned plea. Rachel. Dear Rachel. Again came the melodious refrain. Look for times you felt loved. Listen to and see where love lies and it will reconcile yer doubts. Then, ye shall know the way to truth.

Rachel suddenly awoke. She opened her eyes to see her aunt before her.

"Oh, Aunt Agnes, how long have I been asleep?"

Agnes withdrew her hand from Rachel's arm. "Long enough, me love."

"Did I speak at all?" Rachel asked.

Agnes looked fondly at her young companion. "Do I really need to tell ye what ye said and with whom ye were speaking?"

"Nay, ye need not," replied Rachel softly. "Thank ye, Auntie, for being with me today. I think I know what I have to do."

A bustle at the Inn's front door interrupted the two women. Many of the family had begun to gather for their Sunday ritual. Ian approached Rachel with little Maud in his arms. The child reached for her mother, and Rachel embraced her.

48

Tempus Non Fugit

December 31, 1941

Una's Epilogue

It has been eight earth years since we last held our New Year's fete to celebrate the ways we guide our loved ones. Over that period, we have had many a discussion about the meaning of time. What is it? What does time require of us? How does time influence the impact we have on our loved ones below? Is time so illusory that we can never capture it?

Uncle Aiden called for today's gathering to come to some resolution about our understanding of time and its influence on our powers. Aiden entitled our agenda as 'Tempus fugax'. He never liked following the dictates of renown Latin phrases. Rather, he would adapt them to his own Gaelic propensities. After all, his ancestors had won wars, survived famines and created one of the finest oral and artisanal cultures known to man and women, as Bridgette and the rest of us remind him, well before the Roman alphabet existed. Aiden would forever claim that Gaelic creativity came centuries prior to Roman and British usurpations. Thus, for him, time never flies. Rather, it's fleeting and best described as 'Tempus fugax', like a coy mistress' wink to a passionate lover.

As timeless spirits in a timeless place, I agree with our resident bard and know that time often does appear misleading. Sometimes it flits from place to place, person to person, animal to animal, nature's bounty to nature's bounty. It can't be measured until it has flown quickly away. We ask ourselves 'Where has the time gone?' Sometimes it rests longer in one place, person or animal than another before moving on. We ask ourselves 'When will whatever pain we are experiencing finally pass on?' Sometimes time repeats itself, as with the seasons. Flowers blossom, fade away and blossom again; a daughter is born, grows up and dies, but her smiles carry on in a grandchild. It is then that we embrace time's passage into eternity and are grateful for its gift of creation, of re-creation actually.

I question myself. Is time flying away or is it just flitting from moment to moment, purpose to purpose? Might its mission be to offer us second and third chances at recreating something or someone, just as perfect as that which was created the first time around? Or is it continuously changing in both purpose and form?

Earlier today, others had questioned Aiden's announcement. Our newest philosopher had been discussing the phrase with a number of our family members. I laughed as I heard Eamon Smiley debate, in his gentle manner, of course, with Uncle Aiden, Margaret Pearse, and Christine O'Leary. Thank goodness, he had his mentor Anthony McGregor as well as William Smiley and Bridgette McCann on his side.

In the late morning, Bella, Lizzie and I kept our distance. Collins and Griffth kept score as the debate continued into the afternoon. Padraig Pearse sat back the entire day to take notes for his next poem. The McCann men – Patrick and his father Thomas – had been tending the garden so had not heard the animated discussion until their arrival just minutes ago. Neither had the Achesons nor Ryan McCormick who were off playing rugby. Robbie Smiley had been orienting his son Edwin, newly arrived to our surroundings. As we finally gathered in the garden, the sun had just lowered itself over the hills. Fireflies were twinkling above the lilies, and the moon was shimmering off the *top nettles of the firs.*

The fete's intent was to shed our own light on the events of the last eight years. Had our prophesies from '32 actually been met? Had the national and global events of the last two years brought predictions to fruition or to failure? Had time flitted from place to place, person to person, animal to animal? Or had it flown away for naught? Was our dear island better off or did we still need more chances to return it to its perfect state? Could we really measure our influences on time or were they as Uncle Aiden quipped 'fugax', fleeting?

The debate continued into our fete.

As always, Uncle Aiden spoke up first.

"This new war has divided us as badly as the 1798 rebellion and the 1921 Civil War. We can't seem to get the bloody English out of our lives. They have turned us against each other in every century since we fought Strongbow and Henry II in 1167. That's almost eight-hundred years. Time is not flying away; it is leaving us unresolved – betrayed and lost behind. It never allows us to finish our battles."

Smiling at his elder, Eamon approached Aiden with a book in hand.

Since we are in the 'beyond', we naturally have access to all literature, regardless of when spoken or written. Our libraries are miles wide and deep, collections that span the world and universe multiple times. How blessed we are by their content. But do they always contain the answers we need?

"Dear, Aiden," began Eamon. "You are correct in saying that it appears time may be flying away and, thus, betraying us. For sure, we Irish seem to be repeating losses to the British time and time again. Those tragedies have haunted us for centuries. Here is my counter argument to your negative portrayal of time. The actual translation of the phrase 'Tempus fugit" is not that time is flying, but rather it is fleeing. If we were to say time is flying, we

would need to say "Tempus volant", not "tempus fugit".

Aiden frowned. "Laddie, what difference is there between flying and fleeing? Ach, ye professors and high-brow thinkers always believe ye know more than us activists. Look over there at Padraig Pearse. Didn't he just sit back after giving his declaration speech on Easter Monday in '16 and let the others like Clark and Connelly die? Words mean nothing unless followed by action. See him, now again, sitting on his duff just writing away. He had flown away from us then and is fleeing his responsibilities now. deVelara is doing the same below. Likewise is that pig-headed Churchill and the supposed president of our Irish Americans, FDS or R or Y, whatever that last letter is."

"'Tis true, good sir," replied Eamon. "Often writers and politicians present proposals that are never carried out in daily lives. However, humor me, just for a minute while I tell ye more about the words 'Tempus fugit' and your words 'Tempus fugax'.

"Back in 69 BC, the Roman philosopher and poet Virgil wrote this book, The Georgics." Eamon offered the book to Aiden who scowled and raised his hand in defiance of taking it.

Eamon continued nonetheless. "In his writing, Virgil used the term 'Tempus irreparable fugit', meaning that time flies away and we can't retrieve it back. However, Virgil didn't say that we have lost the lessons time has taught us, nor did he say there isn't more time that follows. Time is like the repeated seasons of the year, the annual harvesting of the soil, the daily ebb and flow of the Killiney tides. Time allows the birth of descendants and keeps offering them new opportunities to correct mistakes, to proffer new ideas, to take new actions. Time provides the chance to redeem ourselves by proving our grandchildren have learned much from us and our own ancestors." Eamon paused. I, of course, nodded in agreement.

Aiden leaned on his cane and bowed his head. The entire membership was silent. Even the birds stopped singing. The *blossoms of the lilies leaned toward the elder. The ears of Sceo, Bigger and Boru perked upright.*

Aiden raised his head. "Laddie," now facing Eamon "whether ye say flies or flees, fugit or fudgit or fridgid, time is passing us by with nothing concrete to show. We keep fighting the same battles for the same goals, but they elude us. Time has not brought us closer to independence from Great Britain, determination of our own future, nor the respect of our free will to be Catholic or Protestant or Jewish or whatever that Asian religion is."

Bridgette interrupted his tirade. "It's Buddhism, my dear."

Aiden scowled his acknowledgement, but continued.

"All I can say is that we are contaminated with British flies and fleas just like a mangey mutt on a cold, rainy night." Bigger released a plaintive whimper. Aiden looked at the aggrieved companion. Bending down as well as he could to stroke the animals head, he added. "Ach, Bigger. Rest assured. I'm not referring to you, dear friend."

"Nay, not true." said Collins who had been anticipating a moment when he could jump into the debate. "Indeed, while victories have been elusive at times, their lessons have not. To wit, look at the Constitution recently passed to form Eire. It uses the very same words Pearse wrote in the 1916 Declaration of the Republic. In addition, consider how deValera has remembered British duplicity during the negotiations of the Anglo-Irish Treaty in '21. That's why he sticks to Eire's neutral stance in this war. He has no trust of Churchill to alter the Ulster partition if Eire takes up arms against Germany."

At that point, the Countess jumped in. "Aiden, ye old fool, didn't ye hear that women now have the vote as of 1928 and that they can hold office just as I did? We have learned much over time not to repeat mistakes. Just ye wait, more women will rise in the ranks of decision-makers and more victories will be won for all the people in Eire and, dare I suggest, in the entire island."

Bella took her brother's hand. "Dearest brother Aiden! Look at where else women's voices are being heard. Consider what BB, Kat, Maggie and Liza have done in the last months with IndePen. The needs of women and their own solutions are not only being heard throughout the island but, more importantly, acted upon. And what about Jon and Rose with their journalism, particularly regarding the Magdalen laundries? Never doubt, good sir: 'Tempus docet.'"

Bridgette leaned toward Aiden and whispered "Time teaches." Aiden grunted, but added reluctantly, "Perhaps ye are right. I'll give this round of the debate to ye, Eamon. But don't think I won't be back to argue with ye again in our next fete."

His companions clapped and whooped for his admission and for his endearing stubbornness.

I called our formal gathering to order since much more needed to be discussed, debated and decided.

Time – whether flying, fleeing or indefinable- had much for us to still teach and for us all to still learn.

Part 3

1945

49

First Day

January 1, 1945

Jon McCormick Irvine had established himself in the professional field of journalism both at the Irish Times newspaper and, as a lecturer, at Queen's College in the literature department. Over the past two years, he had traveled widely around the island of Ireland noting the domestic impact of the war and across the British Channel in Europe documenting the global impact. His eyes and words had transcribed the destruction on minds and hearts as well as bodies, most recently in the D-Day invasion of Normandy. When he returned to Belfast last month, Rose held him during many a nightmare.

The war was wearing not just on Jon, but on many Northern Ireland citizens as damage and death had devastated their communities over six long years. Rationing had diminished pounds; fear had diminished courage. Jon was now constantly trying to convince his students to speak up about their concerns and fears, to give them hope for the future through writing about their lives and their plans when peace eventually would arrive. He recognized the struggle many felt personally when their own families were impacted. Despite enlistment being voluntary in Northern Ireland, many Unionists served and died. Many Nationalists did neither. Tensions were growing between the two groups as Catholics were a majority of Nationalists and Protestants a majority of Unionists.

To confront the differences in a civil manner, Jon had assigned his journalism students to write an editorial. The headline was to read "Living Together in Peace After War: What Germany and Japan

Have Taught Us In Northern Ireland?"

On this first day of the New Year, Jon read one submission to Rose.

"On this first day of what we pray will be the last year of a horrific world war, it is time that we consider the challenges of living in peace that lie ahead – today, tomorrow and thereafter. I find myself thinking of historic leaders who successfully guided their nations during similar times of reconstruction and renewal. Certainly, we have our Irish leaders – Brian Boru, Grace O'Malley, Wolfe Tone, Charles Parnell, Countess Markievicz, and Michael Collins to name just a few. Some lost their lives before knowing success; others lived long enough to celebrate it.

One leader who speaks to me today does not come from our Ireland; nor does he come from the United Kingdom or Europe. Rather, I'm referring to the United States President in the late 1800's who led his country through a civil war similar to that which we experienced in 1921 and may now suffer from again. That President was Abraham Lincoln.

From 1861-1865, the North and South of the United States had split apart due to economic and cultural differences: cotton and slavery. The North had taken on manufacturing as its focus for wealth, leaving bereft the Southern cotton plantations dependent on slave labor. Over 620,000 lives were lost during the subsequent conflict: 360,000 Northern soldiers (Union) and 258,000 Southern (Confederate).

Lincoln wanted unity despite these differences. As a matter of fact, he was consistently remorseful at having to declare war between the two sides in the first place. His second inaugural speech, given in 1863, attests to that and his commitment to a peaceful, unified nation afterwards. Here is an abridged version of his pledge.

'Fellow countrymen... four years ago all thoughts were anxiously directed to an impending civil war. All dreaded it – all sought

to avert it.... And the war came.... Both [sides] read the same Bible and pray to the same God and each invokes His aid against the other. It may seem strange that any men should dare to ask a just God's assistance in wringing their bread from the sweat of other men's faces but let us judge not that we be not judged...

...Fondly do we hope – fervently do we pray – that this mighty scourge of war may speedily pass away...

With malice toward none with charity for all with firmness in the right as God gives us to see the right let us strive on to finish the work we are in to bind up the nation's wounds...'

The world war we are now experiencing in this year of the Lord 1945 is based on similar economic and cultural rationales to those during President Lincoln's time. The Allies support democracy and equality while the Axis powers act out fascism and discrimination. The slaves of America in 1861 to 1865 are the Jews, Romani, artists and intellectuals of 1932 and now. How similar these conflicts sound to our own between Catholics and Protestants, Republicans and Unionists? Are the American slave owners equivalent to our former plantation owners, now replaced by manufacturing tyrants exploiting underpaid workers? Are the Nazi, anti-Semites equivalent to our governmental leaders setting Catholics against Protestants – Irish speakers against English speakers?

We have much to do in the next year to conduct the same reconstruction tasks stated over 150 years ago by Lincoln. Let me close with his final words from that second inaugural. May they guide our mission after this war: to live together in peace.

'...to bind up the nation's wounds, to care for him who shall have borne the battle and for his widow and his orphan – to do all which may achieve and cherish a just and lasting peace among ourselves and with all nations.

Jon raised a linen handkerchief to his tear-filled eyes. Aunt BB had given Rose this last remnant of the Irvine handiwork created in the early 1820's by Great Aunt Lizzie. Rose, in turn, had given it to Jon before he had left for Normandy. Its worn edges belied its enduring comfort.

"Who wrote this?" asked Rose.

Jon turned the paper over to its second page.

"It's signed Kieran Irvine McCormick." Jon looked at Rose. His eyes cleared.

She sighed. "Ach, another virtuous soul in our family. I must talk with him."

50

The Kharma Tea House

February 1945

Mrs. Quinlon's Tea House had changed considerably in the last forty years. Still on the corner of Stranmillis and University roads near the Botanic Gardens and Queens College in Belfast, it had been transformed from a traditional establishment for English aristocracy into a multicultural salon for members of the Commonwealth and college. Mrs. Quinlon had passed into the beyond – or perhaps elsewhere, given her irascible temperament – just after the Great War ended in 1918.

She had died on November 11, Armistice Day, when, without diminishing the political import of that very day, her husband raised his hands to the Almighty and praised His wisdom in answering the beleaguered spouse's prayers. Strangely, Mr. Quinlon died the following week. Rumors attested that Mrs. Quinlon had raised her own ethereal hands, but not to God. She had found her revenge from the beyond. Their children, Sam and Florence, attempted to keep the establishment going for the next two decades, but to no avail or profit. The linen table cloths were never so clean as when Mrs. Quinlon had washed them herself nor were the centerpiece flowers so beautiful as when Mr. Quinlon had tended the establishment's garden. The place was sold in '37 just before the war began. The next generation Quinlons immigrated to Canada to manage a Labatt Brewing Company in Ontario.

The new owners were the Srinavasans, with roots in the Commonwealth country of India. The father, Sanjay, had come to Belfast in 1900 to study law, never to return to his homeland. He had married Irene, his Irish-born, Catholic wife in 1905 and the rest was family history – two sons, a daughter, and now the new tea house, aptly and simply called The Kharma House. It was noted as the first Indian restaurant in Northern Ireland. Mother and daughter managed the enterprise. Like Irish Brotherhood members who had frequented Quinlon's before them, the sons (also lawyers like their father) resided over client meetings. Plans for the independence of India from Great Britain were covertly at the top of their agendas. It was not a paradox that, on this early evening, Kieran McCormick was going to meet his cousin Rose McKenzie McCormick at The Kharma about a similar plan for Northern Ireland. It was also not surprising that he had been smitten by the Srinavasan daughter Manjula.

As he waited for Rose at one of the dining tables, he was amazed by the cultural effects surrounding him. The former teahouse's traditionally somber, dark amber interior had been transformed by the Srinavasans. The main dining area was alight with stained glass, Kharbuja lamps hanging from the ceilings. Their brilliant rays of red, green and yellow landed on the interior walls like fireflies, shimmering warmth and light. Statues of various gods – Vishnu, Lakshmi and Krishna – watched from the mantelpiece above the recessed fireplace that took up most of the back wall. To accommodate the meaning of Commonwealth, wealth among common entities within the British Empire, and to satisfy Irene's business acumen, the Gods' neighbors were miniatures of Christ and Mother Mary, St. Bridgette and St. Stephen. Around the walls, alongside photos of British and Irish soccer teams, were those of Commonwealth cricket players – some from India, some from the Caribbean, some from British East Africa (British Kenya). Large silver ornamented trophies from local, national and international victories were placed in a glass display that reflected the multi-colored lights of the lamps and universal unanimity.

All players in the empire were welcome, especially during this war time period. Irene Srinavasan claimed that the only reason the

Kharma House had survived the Belfast Blitz was because all the gods from different religions had protected the building. Kieran believed the same. As a child, he had always been curious about different cultures, particularly those within the Commonwealth. His mother Bridgette had introduced him to the Folk-Tales of Bengal by Lal Behari Dey. Uncle and playwright Erin McCann had shared the poems of Rabindranath Tagore, a friend of Yates. His father Liam had brought Kieran every Commonwealth newspaper delivered weekly to the Dail. For certain, these sources had led Kieran to his interest in literature and, specifically, journalism. He was fascinated by India's customs, its history, and how it was approaching its own independence. Couldn't Northern Ireland do the same as India by following Gandhi's non-violent approach?

Of course, these were the intellectual reasons Kieran was intrigued by India. There was a personal one as well. That was Manjula, his fellow student at Queen's College and the daughter of Kharma's reigning proprietor. Manjula was one of the most exotic girls Kieran had ever met. He knew she considered him a bit of a bumbler, for that's how he had introduced himself to her just months ago. He was entering a row of seats in the Lanyon Hall amphitheater of Queens and tripped on the step leading from the aisle. Two Modern World Literature tomes he had been carrying would have fallen onto her lap as she sat in the first seat if she had not quickly moved. Despite politely acknowledging his apology, she had ignored him for weeks thereafter. It took an entire semester of lectures, questions and debates for him to garner the courage to initiate a longer conversation.

When he did, she had listened to him since he had spoken up quite a bit in their class about Indian literature. That had both surprised and intrigued her. Manjula was particularly impressed when, in that first lengthy conversation, Kieran said he was reading the Bhagavad Gita, a sacred Hindu scripture of universal truths. Little did Kieran know that Manjula's best friend was also influential in her agreement to speak with Jon. That friend was none other than Rose

McKenzie McCormick, the wife of his cousin and Queen's professor Jon McCormick. Rose had read Kieran's journalism assignment for Jon's class. She had immediately sent it on to Manjula. After a class during which Kieran referred to the writings of Gandhi related to the post-war territorial negotiations among Churchill, Stalin and Franklin Delano Roosevelt, Manjula had decided this friend of Rose was someone of interest. If Rose trusted him, perhaps Manjula could, too.

Rose had also sent Kieran's essay to her Aunt Agnes which was why Kiernan was at the Kharma House tonight. Since the beginning of the war, Rose and Agnes had bonded as IRA sympathizers, if not outright activists. They had determined to play obscure roles that would be both surreptitious yet effective, subtle yet purposeful. Rose's actions had to be carefully chosen. Married to her dear beloved Jon, she could never jeopardize his position both at the university or at the newspaper. Like Agnes' protection of her husband TD Billie and her sister-in-law Bridgette's of husband TD Liam, the clan's women constantly had to weigh their love of family against love of country. Involving Kieran in their respective circles had been well determined. Being closer to his age and idealism, Agnes knew Kieran would listen to Rose more than to a six-decades old, cynical aunt.

For that reason, Rose, not Agnes, had invited Kieran to meet. The Kharma House was chosen as the least likely place any Ulster Unionist member would think an IRA member would frequent, let alone themselves. Most UPC would never be caught alive, nor in a tipsy state, at an Indian restaurant. However, the two women could not think of a better place to meet than where the owners had empathy, if not sympathy, for anti-colonialism. Rose also knew that Kieran would never turn down an invitation to explore Manjula's lifestyle and customs. To ensure he came, Rose had indicated that Manjula would be stopping by later in the evening.

Turning his attention now to the woman approaching him, he rose from his seat.

"Auntie Agnes. What are you doing here?"

"There has been a change in your evening plans, Kieran. Sit thee down and I'll explain."

Hidden behind the kitchen door, Rose and Manjula watched them through to its circular, beveled window.

"He'll join us for sure," said Rose.

"I'll pray to Tara, our goddess of compassion, empathy and action, that he does," offered Manjula.

51

The Star

February 1945

Kieran pulled the chair out from the circular table for his aunt to join him. She settled in and looked across at her nephew. His upper body and face were silhouetted by the late afternoon light streaming from a window directly behind him. There, thirty-four years before, Agnes, Billy and Lizzie had been enlightened by Eamon's tale about a twin brother. That brother, not Eamon, had just attempted to assassinate the Irish Republican Brotherhood leader Thomas Clark. All these years later, Agnes could visualize the philosopher Eamon in the outline of his nephew Kieran. How strange, she thought, that, today, we would be sitting at the same table where Eamon had proven his innocence and took on his alliance within the Irvine/Smiley/McCormick family.

Will Kieran be his uncle's nephew or will he be stronger? Agnes wondered. She had never considered university philosophers or intellectuals like Eamon as the activists Ireland required before, during or after a critical historic event. Presently, as the European front would soon be in Allies' hands, Northern Ireland Republicans needed tested soldiers and activists for its own front against the British. The island must be re-formed into one independent nation.

She brooded to herself. Where are the Theobald Wolfe Tones, the Thomas Clarkes, the Countesses, the Michael Collinses? Where are Uncle Aiden, mother-in-law Lizzie Gallagher Irvine and Patrick McCann? How can I convince this young intellectual to join our Belfast Brigade?

Agnes knew her conversation with Kieran today had to be substantive in words and yet sensitive in feelings. Having read his classroom essay, she wondered if Kieran might be contemplating two opposing paths in his life's journey. His own conflicting words, quoting US President Lincoln, suggested that: "How may we propose to 'achieve and cherish a just and lasting peace among ourselves'?" Would Kieran choose a path to achieve or just cherish peace? Would he consider taking physical actions in Northern Ireland or only writing esoterically about peace? How did the young lad differentiate the word achieve from the word cherish? Would he be a Pearse or a Clarke? Agnes wanted him to act first. Later, he could write about cherishing peace.

Agnes started. "Oh, my Kieran. You remind me so much of your Uncle Eamon. How we loved him. I'm so sorry he has passed."

Kieran nodded his head, cleared his throat and thanked her for her sympathy.

"He was a truly good man, wasn't he, Aunt Agnes? How often I remember his sharing life's imponderables on Sunday afternoons with Uncle Billie and you around your Dublin, dining room table. You probably never knew that I would sit on the stairs up to the playroom and listen to you all. Of course, as a buachaill-og (Irish for young boy) of seven, I would have to ask cousin Kate or sister Maggie what many a word meant. But I remember the back and forth of fascinating banter and the laughter as well. I would say there still is good craic at your home whenever any of us young folk join you and Uncle Billie. but most topics discussed now are so very serious."

"Aye," said Agnes. "We will always welcome you and the other young ones to our home, " Agnes said. She paused.

Kieran noticed her eyes misting over as she gazed over his head at the window behind him. Evening shadows were beginning to dance onto the individual panes from the light of street lamps outside. She imagined the figures of her own father, sisters and cherished Grandfather McCracken, all now in the beyond.

"Are you alright, Aunt Agnes?" he asked, reaching over the table top to her hand poised on the tweed handbag she had placed there. He touched the tips of her fingers, but she quickly pulled them away and tucked them into a closed fist.

"For sure, lad." He saw her back straighten and her eyes look directly at him, as though a restored soul had taken hold of her. She cleared her throat. "My sixty plus years have given me so many fond memories at our house. I'm so grateful you remember them.

Nonetheless, let's get to our business here, Kiernan. I know you expected Rose, not me. That must be explained first. Once done, we'll get to the purpose of my visit." Agnes took a deep breath and was about to begin, when she was stopped by Kieran.

"Wait, Auntie." He placed a menu before her. "Let's order something for our tea first. What would you like? And do not refuse me paying for you. One of my essays was just accepted in the Galway Chronicle. I have some loose coins. Choose whatever you'd like from the items here." He offered her the one-page menu with various selections in both Hindi and English.

Agnes was taken aback by his interruption and suggestion. If she had not known him from birth, she would have attributed his digression to being an informant for the British or RUC. Was he biding time to catch his own breath or set her off-balance? Was this diversion an innocent move on his part or calculated?

She wondered what she was going to learn about him tonight or he about her. Perhaps, she thought, he needs time to contemplate the import of her replacing Rose. Perhaps he's not as undecided in his journey as I thought. Despite knowing him for years, her IRA years of suspicion colored her thinking, even of family members. She would assume nothing about him.

"What a joy, Kieran. Thank you for this treat, but you'll have to ask the wait staff to help me understand the items or perhaps you know them well already?"

Just at that moment, The Kharma House's matriarch, Irene

Srinavasan, approached their table.

"Ach, if it isn't our dear Agnes," came a Macroom lilt Agnes recognized immediately. Agnes turned toward it and rose to embrace the woman approaching her. "Blessed Mother Mary! Irene Corcoran, is it ye?"

"And despite that Blessed Mother, it certainly is!" came the words along with two strong arms embracing Agnes. "It's been almost twenty-five years since we threw kisses at each other across the station platforms of trains going in opposite directions between Macroom and Dublin. What a surprise to see ye tonight and, especially, with this young man."

Agnes wanted to continue the conversation with Irene who had been more than just a friend in their respective youths. She had been Agnes' IRA circle contact for the Macroom brigade up to 1925. Agnes wondered if Irene was still playing that role in Belfast. When Irene grabbed Agnes' hand, pressed it within her own two, and said "Let us meet again when the fairies dance," Agnes heard an answer in the coded message.

"Right now," continued Irene, "you and this fine fellow must eat. I'll get you some beef and cabbage, not a foreign item from the menu. Except, how does a pot of excellent Indian Darjeeling tea sound to start?"

Not waiting for a response, Irene turned toward the kitchen and disappeared.

Agnes and Kieran were stunned and started to laugh. "You must agree," offered Kiernan, "that, despite how small our island is, on any single day we will encounter a family member or an old friend."

"Indeed," replied Agnes, retaking her seat. "And speaking of the first, that is why I am here tonight, instead of Rose." Kieran sensed her tone change. Serious conversation was ahead.

"You may not know this," she restarted, "but your parents, aunts and uncles decided a while ago that it was time for a new family tradition. We agreed that, when one of our younger members turns twenty-two, he or she would meet with an elder to discuss the roles our ancestors have bound us to play in the future. You have heard much over your years about the various ways each of those grands and great grands chose his or her place in Ireland's history.

"Tonight, I have been assigned to talk with you about the role you may choose in our family's gallery of patriots."

Kieran was not surprised by his aunt's description of the new tradition. His sister Maggie, just a year older than he, and exactly like her loquacious Aunt Kat, had impetuously described her own 'twenty-second' conversation with Uncle Eamon before he died. Maggie related that her cousins Thon, Jon, Liza and Kate now secretly called it the 'birthday upside down'. It mimicked the Irish myth that when a baby was lifted by his feet and its head was bumped (gently) on the floor, he was gifted good luck. Kieran laughed to himself. It would be quite a feat to currently lift him upside down and bump his head on the floor. However, he returned to a sober demeanor, reflecting respect for his family's more deliberate ritual.

Irene Srinavasan brought out a large tray with their dinner plates and tea. She sensed a crucial conversation forthcoming so quickly left the two alone. They ate in silence, a rarity when two or more Irvines and McCormicks were gathered together.

Kieran finally spoke.

"I know a bit about the various roles our ancestors have played, Aunt Agnes. Their work during the famine, the Easter Rising, the War of Independence and Civil War has been told during many a bedtime storytelling, Sunday lunch, and picnic at Killiney Bay. No one ever bragged or praised our relatives. Their deeds were described merely as matter-of-fact activities that, during horrific times, had become routine.

"I know, despite their modesty, that our family members have been courageous in all the independence movements against Great Britain, labor strikes between the privileged and poor, protests against religious discrimination, policy negotiations among IPP, OR,

UPP, IRB, IRA, RUC, UVF and all the other abbreviations representing groups in conflict. I could go on and on as I just have."

He paused to summarize: "The impact of our family's participation in these activities has been incredible and, I know, renown over the centuries."

Agnes bowed her head in agreement.

"Uncle Patrick McCann, Great Aunt Lizzie, Great Great-Aunt Bella and my own father Liam are my heroes. And now that includes you, yourself, who have done so much over the last half century. Exactly what I will never know. I truly want to be part of your legacy. I want to be part of Ireland becoming whole again." His speech raced as did his mind.

Then, suddenly, he stopped, clutched his napkin, and rolled it into a ball. It went round and round, slowing his thoughts.

Agnes waited, recognizing Kieran's need to carefully parse his next words.

He spoke honestly. "While I want to be worthy of our family, I am not an activist. One could say I'm too cerebral and think too long before making decisions. I'm ill-equipped to stand up and protest in a timely or effective fashion.

Agnes did not say anything. She knew him well enough to continue waiting for his next words.

"But there is another reason I don't consider myself an activist. When we Northern Irelanders were asked to fight this war, I refused. I had to admit to myself that I couldn't kill anyone, even an enemy. I must apply that commitment to whatever role I play in my future, Aunt Agnes. You know more than anyone in our family whether that's possible. What do you think?"

Agnes gazed at her nephew. Did he know more about her past than she had assumed? She paused and, then, quickly decided she would not pursue that question tonight. Her task was to help him decide his future, not to share her past. Despite being disappointed at his pacifist reflections, she also loved him dearly. Whatever he chose to do would be blessed by her and the rest of the elders.

"I had an idea you might say these things, Kieran." She reached for his hand. "Please know I respect them and your desire that they inform the role you play. Let me share some thoughts that might put you at ease."

She offered him two options. One was to serve as a writer for which he was already being trained at Queens. He could be a conveyor of information about what the general population was thinking post-war. Particularly, he could focus on Unionist opinions regarding the steps Northern Ireland might take to become part of the Republic. Kieran, as an objective writer, could be paired with his cousin Jon. Agnes would not share that Jon might not be so dispassionate as he was already taking on a covert IRA role sharing information he heard about specific RUC actions against the Belfast Brigades.

Agnes knew that many Brigade members believed Northern Ireland citizens were ignorant about the plight of Catholic and Protestant minorities who were Nationalists. The British newspapers and BBC never shared accurate news about the poor housing, health and labor conditions of both groups in Ulster. Protestant evangelicals misled their congregants in sermons about their suffering. Catholic soldiers returning from the war front were being treated differently than Protestant veterans. All this needed to be publicly exposed. As a writer, Kiernan could play a huge role in informing the public about these prejudices. Readers would benefit on the island as a whole, in Great Britain and throughout the world.

Thus, the second option was to share information that portrayed the Irish Republican Army as a political, not paramilitary organization. Kieran could meet with current Belfast Brigade members to collect their ideas for a peaceful, post-war Ireland. Many had felt abandoned by the Dublin IRA. Many had felt dismay at the lack of leadership in the NI IRA itself. Many had died during incarceration in either the Crumlin or Derry goals. Prison conditions had been horrific. These elders, however, wanted an end to violence. Instead, they supported reconciliation among partisan groups through votes, not guns.

Kieran had listened carefully to her two options. He placed the balled up napkin on the table, unfolded it and spread it out flat before him.

"Aunt Agnes. May I offer a third?" He asked quietly.

She took the edges of the napkin and folded two corners into the center of the piece. She grinned, saying, "We knew you might come up with a third, dear Kieran. Like all of our ancestors before us and we who are still on earth, there has never been a family member who was not a free thinker when determining a role in our country's future. Please, tell me what you are thinking?"

Kieran explained a role that amazed Agnes.

"May I document the ways we can promote peace in Ireland that is based on the philosophy of non-violence? As you know I have been reading about that in my class with cousin Jon. My own feelings about being a pacifist have led me to ideas from other countries and faiths, particularly the non-violent Satyagraha movement in India led by Mahatma Gandhi. Believe it or not, there have been similar movements here in Ireland. For example, there was our own Irish Catholic Association strike led by Daniel O'Connell in the mid 1820s. That was followed in the 1870s by the passive shunning of tenants who were exploiting the British land laws and undermining their poorer neighbors. Parnell supported that in his initiation of boycotts against those traitors. Did you know that the man after whom the term boycott was first used in the 1880s was the Irish Captain Charles Boycott. He was among the first to be shunned. I could go on and on with examples such as food strikes by women suffragettes and trade embargoes by commercial giants."

As he spoke, Kieran followed his aunt's lead, folding the napkin corners nearest him toward the center. When he finished his proposal, the napkin had formed a star.

"My boy," she said, placing his hand on the folded cloth. "Look at what you have just created. Take that star and make its points guide your role. You will definitely honor our family."

She rose and reached over to kiss the top of his forehead. He bowed to receive it.

Kieran would always remember her parting phrase. "May the light of your star shine brightly now and in the future, Kieran. It will guide you and others to peace."

As she left by the front door, she thought to herself. "I have learned much from this young man. Perhaps there is hope, after all, for a peaceful Ireland."

His cousin Rose and Manjula had been watching the interaction behind the window of the kitchen door. After Agnes was out of sight, the two young women turned toward each other. Rose spoke first. "I wonder what she told him to do?"

Manjula hesitated. "Nay, Rose. She didn't tell him what to do. He merely listened to something or someone else, perhaps a spirit who graced him. Look at his face. It's catching all of the light from that far window. He's at such peace."

And, indeed, Kieran was at peace and so was Uncle Eamon.

52

Train of Thoughts

July 13, 1945

By the Spring of '45, British troops had won the offensive in Northern Italy and Belgium. The Canadians had secured the Netherlands. The Red Army had moved into Poland and was on the outskirts of Berlin. US war planes were bombing the German capital. The Battle of Berlin which had begun on the 16th of April had resulted on April 30th with Hitler committing suicide along with his newly, legitimized wife Eva Braun. On May 8th, the Western powers had declared VE Day (Victory in Europe Day) over Germany. That war was over for most Irish and British military men and women, volunteers and families.

Able to travel freely without war limitations, Kieran and Manjula took the Saturday evening, Great Northern Railway Ireland (GNRI) train from Portadown, south west of Belfast, to Derry. Formerly restricted to the transportation of military personnel and supplies, tonight's passengers and baggage gave credence to the formal end of the war in Europe. No longer were the windows in the train's carriage blackened by shades pulled down nor drapes pulled across. Kieran and Manjula saw before them the beginnings of post-war Ulster.

Only a few of the passengers were dressed in military uniform. Many didn't need to wear battle apparel for the couple to know who had served. Several had crutches; some displayed bandages under their tams; most reflected a somber look on unshaven faces. Kieran knew these were the lucky ones to return home after recuperating in hospitals or requisitioned estates in Scotland or Wales. The Irish

Times had just reported that over 4,500 Irish and British soldiers had been liberated in May from prisoner of war camps in Germany by RAF Lancasters. Kieran surmised, by the vacant expression on his face, that one of them was seated near him across the train's narrow aisle.

Scattered among the returnees were a few civilians. Two middle-aged businessmen carrying weathered briefcases seemed to recognize the angst among several young soldiers. Kieran heard the elders speaking reassuring words such as "patriots" and "heroes". Three passengers were young women with heavy suitcases. Manjula focused on them assuming their jobs in the Belfast armament or ship-building factories had just been taken over by returning male veterans. Or were they some of the Magdalene girls coming home? Regardless of the reason for their journey tonight, Manjula wondered what roles they would take on – or be allowed to take on – within their families.

Kieran and Manjula knew each face told a story that had to be captured in words and shared in print. They were ready to do both.

The young couple was going to meet Catholic elders of the Derry IRA battalion who had just been released from jail. Their experiences in captivity would definitely publicize the hypocrisy of a government (Stormont and London) that had just triumphed over Germany's fascism and prejudice without acknowledging its own. In addition, Kiernan and Manjula would interview Protestant members of the Nationalist movement in Derry, who had supported the incarcerated. One assigned Protestant had been part of the hunger strikes protesting prisoners considered as criminal, not political. Finally, for a view of what could create peace among the Unionists, they would speak with former soldiers, loyalists to the British crown who had just returned home.

Until the interviews began, however, Kieran and Manjula were happy to spend time with each other. They had definitely come to a full-stop agreement about their impressions of each other. Manjula thought Kieran was a genius – naïve, but still a genius. She enjoyed his interest in her family, her religion, her secular beliefs, and specifically, his curiosity about why her Indian father had married her Irish mother. Kieran was fascinated by Manjula's ability to live comfortably in two worlds, a traditional Buddhist society and a traditional Catholic one. She had shared much about discussions around the Srinivasan table and now around the kitchen in The Karma House. He wanted to know what caused her to be so open to new and different ideas. She, in turn, wondered the same about him.

Tonight in the overnight train, there would be no such thing as a physical romance between the two. Rather there would be in a romance of words, verbal passions openly expressed and embraced. They would not argue, raise fisticuffs nor demean the other. Rather, they would model the reconciliation process which so intrigued Kieran – that of nonviolence.

Manjula began the process by asking Kieran questions. "I am intrigued by what you had said about Gandhi in our last class at Queens College. I don't understand how you are so unlike other Irish Catholics who never even look at me, let alone ask about me or my culture. What made you so interested in people different than you?"

Kieran thought before responding to her. "Manjula, I have no idea. I think it was just by osmosis. You know, it happens when someone is within an environment where ideas just seep into your body like the warmth of a woolen sweater knitted by your grandma. Some thoughts come as insights that sneak under your eyelid and fall asleep in your brain. My family and its extended members are always talking and listening, listening and talking about differences. They discuss how first to understand and, then, to resolve them. Sometimes I feel we are a clan of different animals that gather, somewhere in the Mourne Mountains, to sing in harmony with each other. The birds chirp, the wolves howl, the sheep baa. But they eventually blend in together – and we do, too.

"I remember a story once told by Michael Collins to my older cousins. He talked about the animals of the forest not getting along until they all could hear each other's voices and sing in harmony with each other. Then, and only then, could they make the music of a symphony. Our Sunday lunches are like that. Each of us is a different animal with a different voice. But, by the end of the afternoon, we all are part of the most eloquent concert. Everyone has shared an idea, even the young ones like my sister Maggie, my cousins Katie and Liza. Now, tell me about you? How did you become so open to people different than you?"

Manjula frowned at Kieran. "I fear I am not that open, especially to people with whom I disagree or find judgmental. My mother is like that, too. We're like two buds on one potato or two cross stitches on an embroidered hankie. I think it was my father who influenced me more than anyone about exploring and, then, accepting differences. His courage to come to Ireland, to study hard and become the honorable person he is has inspired me. You know, he's been a lawyer in the courts of justice for over thirty-years listening over and over to so many stifled voices while making their cases for justice and equality. He has witnessed the devastating impact of poverty and prejudice. Yet, he never tires from fighting that impact through the law. By the way, he doesn't practice for the money as he has way too many pro-bono clients. That's why my mother insisted we open The Karma House. She claims people pay more to fill their bellies than their brains!"

Manjula laughed as did Kieran.

"My father has taught me so much about the necessity to understand by listening before speaking, by asking questions before making assumptions, to be open to contrary information. I must admit I find that hard."

Kieran looked out the window, which now at the midnight hour was not allowing him to see outside. Instead, the window reflected his own face and Manjula's.

"Yes," he quietly answered. "I find it hard, too. Recently, I had a disquieting discussion with my cousin Rachel. She has had a very checkered, or should I say plaid, past. She has not been as innocent or nonviolent over her thirty years as she now wants me to believe. I know she has had some very disturbing experiences, starting with one during the 1916 Uprising. That was when our Uncle Erin McCann's brother Patrick was shot dead protecting her from an Orangeman's bullet. Now, she has vowed to be a peacemaker across partisan groups, but I wonder if she's telling the truth."

Manjula saw Kieran's doubt and softly queried. "Perhaps as a mother responsible for raising two children, she wants to live in a peaceful nation."

Kieran looked back at Manjula. "Maybe that is what causes one to reconcile differences. When one thinks of others, particularly those to whom you have given birth, you rethink being stubborn or winning arguments or having your own way. Since I have yet to experience giving birth, I guess I don't really know."

Manjula chuckled. "Well, good sir. Since you will never experience childbirth, you better find some other ways to understand reconciliation."

Kieran laughed aloud. He knew he would learn from her.

Manjula looked out the window. She saw her reflection next to his and wondered to herself. I see the two of us reflected in this window. I wonder what that means for our future?

As the train wheels raced across the tracks toward Derry, her mind also raced, around and around and around. To where would her mind lead? And more importantly, to where would her heart?

53

Interview 1
Charlie Magee

July 20, 1945

Charlie Magee had been a brute of a man. That is brute in the physical sense of muscular and brute in the emotional sense of certitude. Three years ago, at age 42, he had weighed a solid 190 pounds (just under 14 stones) and was at the height of his boxing career. From his childhood, during his teens and young adult years, he had rarely lost a fight – on the street or in the ring. He was Charlie The Grand to his male schoolmates, fellow ironwork chums, and members of his boxing club, The Belfast Irish Athletics. To his female admirers, no matter which epoch, he was Charlie The Gorgeous; for, like many an Irishman with curly red locks, rosy cheeks and tidal-pool blue eyes, he was very handsome.

However, when Manjula and Kieran met him on this rainy Sunday afternoon at the Magee's flat in Derry's Bogside, he was neither grand nor gorgeous. His five-foot nine carriage supported only 110 pounds (8 stones). His muscles were so deflated that, when he shook the couple's hands, the skin on his arm wobbled like apple jelly. His face no longer bore a reddish glow. Instead, gray freckles were tucked between wrinkles in horizontal streams like rain on the outside of a foggy, window pane. Charlie was no longer a brute after spending the last three years in the Derry Jail – his fourth incarceration since joining the Belfast Battalion in 1925 at age twenty.

Today, Kieran and Manjula were not surprised when they saw

him shuffling toward them with assistance from his wife Rebecca. Informed by Agnes Irvine about their purpose, Rebecca had not shared it with Charlie. Instead, referring to the young couple as sympathizers on a special assignment from Belfast, she had only encouraged him to "hear them out" and respond as he wished. There was no other way with her partner. He did whatever he wanted no matter what others advised.

As he settled into a rocking chair near the kitchen window, she placed a woolen shawl around his shoulders and a sheepskin blanket upon his lap and lower legs. A handkerchief was rolled up at the wrist of his shirt's left sleeve. Despite the July heat, he was always cold and often coughed, not from any external weather but from the weathering of internal lungs. The kettle was placed on the stove. The gas lit. A tea pot and three porcelain cups were set on the counter below the window. A small plate of potato crackers, flour still being rationed, accompanied the fare. Charlie gazed away from the visitors to look out onto the back garden. A silence followed.

Rebecca would not join them. She would listen instead while sitting on the hallway bench. This was her husband's time to talk openly, if he wanted to. She had heard so many questionable truths from him during their courtship and marriage of twenty years that she could recite them all: word for word, boxing match by boxing match, arrest by arrest. Their courtship had started when he was a wee lad, she a wee lass. He had pulled at her red braids from his desk behind her in Kilkenny's primary school. She had tried to ignore him, but couldn't because he was so handsome and entertaining – laughing, joking, and playing the violin given to him by his father. He was ready to enter secondary school and become either a musician or actor, but his plans were foiled when his father was killed in '18 during The Great War. As the only son with two younger sisters and an ailing Mum, Charlie went north at age thirteen, straight to the Belfast factories. Rebecca went on to secondary school. They promised to marry once she finished her teacher training.

For five years, Charlie tolerated work at a metal shop where bolts and screws were made for Harland and Wolff ships. The job offered a stable income, built his muscles and provided male models in his father-less life. He was introduced by his shop foreman to boxing and quickly excelled. His frustration at leaving school early and anger being his family's sole bread winner finally had an outlet; and his good looks had an audience.

On June 6 of '25, he had won the national, bare-knuckle boxing championship. At the end of the next Monday's shift, his foreman Jack Sullivan came to congratulate Charlie and invited him to the pub for a celebratory round. By the end of the third round, Charlie had been recruited to join the Belfast IRA. At first, he just delivered messages, using his leg muscles to run if any RUC suspected his assignment. Then, he used his arm muscles to dig ditches for storing arms in various dump sites around the Curry Street and Short Strand area. Upon securing the trust of battalion leaders, he moved to a Derry shipyard and learned to place his bare knuckles around a Webley Revolver or Lee-Enfield rifle.

All the while, Rebecca knew nothing of his role in the IRA. She had been happy to meet his factory chums at their wedding in '25, then the men who, over five years, became the godparents of their four boys. His boxing matches introduced her to other men, but she never guessed their covert roles. With Rebecca and Charlie, these men, their wives and offspring attended services and festivals at Derry's St. Mary's Catholic Church. Alongside the Sisters of St. Mary's, Rebecca taught fourth grade and served with neighborhood wives at the church's soup kitchen during the depression years. Charlie never shared his Battalion assignments. He wanted her to be protected by ignorance if any Orangemen interrogated her.

It wasn't until his first arrest in 1930 and six month imprisonment at Belfast's Crumlin Jail that Charlie told her why he spent so many nights at the local pub and traveled with Sullivan so often away from Derry. The news struck her like her father's leather strap across her bare buttocks. Charlie insisted that she not ask nor discuss with anyone what he whispered in the jail's visitors' room nor from the pillows of their settle-bed. At no time did she feel he told her the full truth. She obeyed him, though, and never shared his words until this last imprisonment in Derry's Bishop Street jail which she felt had destroyed his body and spirit. For the sake of their boys, she needed to know her husband's past before he crossed the bar. That was why she had agreed with Agnes to bring Kieran and Manjula into their home and why she was secretly listening.

Kieran pulled a wooden-backed chair up to Charlie's side. Manjula placed a foot stool behind him and bent down into it. She balanced her tea cup on the floor, a notebook on her lap and pen poised in air to capture his words. Kieran and she knew Charlie would not be forthcoming talking to a young girl, particularly a foreign looking one. Thus, she was behind Charlie as the scribe of his tales.

Kieran began the conversation telling about the Irvine family, starting with his great-grand William who had been killed in Macroom during the famine of 1847. By the time he had spoken the names of Aiden McKnight and Patrick McCann, Charlie had raised his head and faced Kieran.

"Ye're Liam McCormick's lad, aren't ye?" Charlie asked.

Kieran nodded his head, covering his surprise that Liam would be known to Charlie.

"Ye come from good stock, then," Charlie offered.

Kieran agreed, responding "And so do you, Master Magee."

For over two hours, Charlie opened up to Kieran. He told of numerous assignments he had completed – and many at which he had failed – never mentioning any names of fellow activists. He detailed the treatment he and they had received once imprisoned: beatings, hunger, verbal derision, and humiliation. He described the prisoners' reactions: hunger strikes, metal cup poundings, synchronized recitations of Irish poems and songs. The efforts to consider IRA members as political not criminal prisoners were to no avail, instigating instead ever more severe punishments by the RUC and British military than given to common murderers and thieves.

Just as Charlie was sharing his most recent incarceration, he started to cough. Rebecca quickly entered the kitchen and placed her arm around Charlie's shoulder, looking at Kieran.

"I think ye are done, don't ye?" she asked the young man.

Charlie raised his hand and pushed her arm away.

"Ah, Becca, I will never be finished and nor should our boys," he growled, placing the handkerchief up to his mouth. He coughed again and red sputtered onto it.

"Now that the British war is over, our Irish one restarts. Ye must talk to my boys," Charlie said to Kieran. "When I'm gone, they will be the next boxers in our rings."

Kieran and Agnes exchanged looks. Manjula watched from behind. All three knew Charlie was fighting his last match.

54

Interview 2
Thon McCormick Irvine

July 25, 1945

Kieran knew very little about his cousin Thon McCormick Irvine, the son of his own father's brother Ryan. In 1912, Ryan had been killed after attempting the assassination of Irish Republican Brotherhood (IRB) leader, Thomas Clark. The circumstances of Ryan's death were merely stated by family members, not explained. And why Thon and his brother Jon had been raised by the Irvines in the South instead of the McCormicks in the North was equally obscure.

Family folklore was full of rumors. Some said Ryan was killed in retaliation by an IRB collaborator for the attempted Clark assassination; others by a rival Orangeman to frame the IRB; several alluded to an unknown family member, perhaps even Robbie, the twin brother of Uncle Eamon Smiley. Regardless of the hearsay, the family protected the boys from any retribution by partisans, IRB or Orange. That was why Thon and Jon took on the Irvine's last name and why no one talked about Ryan McCormick. He was dead, and dead he would stay.

Since no elder would confirm the truth about Thor's father, Kieran's generation could not differentiate fact from lore. But, it didn't matter. The family honored forgiveness of or, at least, silence on questionable past alliances and actions.

Today, as Manjula and Kieran approached the Londonderry Guildhall, Kieran wondered about his cousin's background and current alliances. Thon was a decorated officer of the British Intelligence Corps assigned to Northern Ireland's post war deliberations. His staff were specifically responsible for the disposition of forty-two German U-boats just surrendered in Lisahally on Lough Foyle, north of Londonderry. Kieran wanted to know exactly how Thon felt about the future of post-war Ireland, free from German occupation but not from British. Where did Thon's allegiance now lie?

Kieran and Manjula entered the lobby of the neo-gothic hall just as the late afternoon sun was streaming the colors of its stained-glass windows onto the parquet floor. Manjula admired the red and yellow patterns taking shape on the white and black tiles. A soldier's red vest from one window and a yellow skullcap from another seemed to design a Dharma circle below her. Manjula wondered if this symbol of the Buddhist path to enlightenment was foreshadowing their conversation with Thon.

After all, he would be the first British intelligence officer she had ever met but about whose role she had heard much in her youth. India had suffered under the rule of men like Thon imposing the Empire's interests. Today, Manjula wasn't going to prejudge. Rather, as Kieran and she had discussed, they would be open minded to Thon's ideas. Kieran would ask the questions. She would take notes. Both would listen intently and learn from him.

Thon was standing in fully decorated, brown military uniform under an arched hallway off the Guildhall's reception area. His six foot, one inch stature made the circular curvature above him seem like a heavenly crown. In contrast, his leather-belted waist and visible cross-chest pistol holder conveyed an earthly authority. As he walked over her imaginary Dharma circle, Manjula was shaken by the power he seemed to emit.

His first words, however, caught her off-guard.

"Kieran, my lad. What a surprise to hear from you and, now, see you face-to-face after so many years. You were just twelve when I last played rugby with you outside your Rathmines home." Thon grabbed his cousin by the torso, pulling Kieran into a full court embrace, as though they were fellow teammates celebrating a victory match. "How grand it is to have you here in Londonderry."

Releasing Kieran, Thon turned to Manjula. "And who is this fair lass accompanying you?"

Manjula was taken aback by the gregariousness of this man. She had expected him to be a reserved British gentleman, formal and staid. Instead, he was like her Irish mother's three brothers, vast in verbiage and glee. What was a person of such personality doing as an intelligence officer for the colonizer? Manjula blushed at his question and her own assumptions. That's what she felt, at least, for the moment. Let's see what this man is really about, her emotions cautioned.

Before either she or Kieran could express their own greetings, Thon turned and led them to the main staircase off the entrance lobby saying "Let's go to my office upstairs. We have much news to share." Taking two steps at a time up the massive wooden staircase, Kieran and Manjula could hardly keep pace with his energy. By the time they reached the top, he had already opened the door to a lovely sitting room off the chapel.

"Here we go," he said as he waited for them. "We can talk privately here."

They followed him to a sofa of plush, red velvet bordered by two satin covered, highbacked chairs. Its pillows, embroidered with the crest of Londonderry – a skeleton on a rock, a three towered castle, and the arms of London – caught Manjula's eyes. The motto inscribed below the figures – Vita, Veritas, Victoria – caught Kieran's. A coffee table was in front of the sofa; a set of three wooden backed chairs on its opposite side. The circle formed around the table by the furniture looked staged for unity, except for the papers randomly scattered upon seats, sofa, table and floor.

Thon quickly gathered them up and stacked them upon a desk under the side windows facing the Guildhall's western courtyard. As he did so, Kieran noticed they were newspapers from countries all around the world: Britain, for sure, and also the US, but primarily from the Commonwealth: India, Kenya, Jamaica. Other papers were from Europe: France, Italy, Portugal, and farther East: The Soviet Union, China and Japan. There were also local papers from The Republic and Northern Ireland: Dublin, Cork, Galway, Londonderry, Belfast. Why so many papers wondered Kieran.

He didn't have to wait long for the answer.

"Please forgive my disorganized, reference library," offered Thon. "I have always loved newspapers, particularly how they reveal truths, or, more interestingly, what national leaders want their citizens to consider truths. Many provide opinions on the front pages, but, as you read more carefully, you can also glean a number of hidden concerns. As we move into a new era here in Ireland, the world around us is readjusting to a future where those concerns will occupy the frontline of governance and prosperity. That future rests on what people never want to experience again: war. I hear you want my prediction of that future. Not sure you have come to the most knowledgeable soothsayer, but you should be happy I have read most of these and can give you a global perspective." Thon sat down on the edge of one high chair and beckoned his two guests to the sofa.

"So, ask away whatever you want to know. I'll have an opinion on anything and everything."

During the next few hours, Kieran asked his formal questions. He constantly wondered if he was hearing his cousin speak opinion or truth. The topics ranged from his experience during the last months of the war – advising on the unconditional surrender documents signed by Germany's General Alfred Jodi in Reims France on May 7, assisting on the Allied Control Council's role in Germany's governance on June 5, and finally being reassigned back home to Northern Ireland five days later.

Kieran and Manjula both noticed Thon's enthusiastic renditions lessen as he mentioned the last assignment. Had his Irish roots raised questions about his loyalty to the British Empire now that the war was over? What had been the rationale by his superiors to send him to the backwater of Londonderry? Kieran posed the question and Thon skirted the answer.

"What can you tell us about your current assignment here in Derry?" asked Kieran, subtly trying to focus his cousin on national issues by using the Catholic and Nationalist revised title for Londonderry.

"Ach, that's a very direct and interesting question, good cousin, which, as you can surmise, I fear I'll need to be careful in answering. Don't want any national secrets to get out into the Irish News or Stormont speeches, let alone Dail minutes." He laughed.

"I will only say that the disposal of those German U-boats will be a priority. Then, we'll see what I can do next. My time in the Queen's service is up in just a few months. I welcome coming home after fifteen years away to again join our family's Sunday gatherings and discussions. Perhaps my Uncle Liam will have ideas for me. I'm sure my brother Jon and I will again toss those between our opposing goal posts, just like we did before I left in '32 to work in London with my Foyle classmates in their father's London firm and then, like they, in the war effort."

Thon's eyes wandered toward the window as he paused. "That was over thirteen years ago when I was only twenty-four. Both of my pals died, one on D-Day, the other in Italy." His silence hushed all sound and thought hovering in the room. Manjula noticed his eyes began to shimmer. "Was this man more sensitive than she expected? What had he experienced during the war that affected him so upon its end? Had he somehow begun a journey that was leading him beyond the political requirements of choosing sides?"

She knew she had to ask the final question of today's interview.

"Do you believe in beloved reconciliation?" she asked.

Thon quickly redirected his gaze at her, as though seeing her for the first time. Kieran was surprised at her directness and specificity.

Thon regrouped his thoughts and composure. "What an interesting question, young lady."

He abruptly stood up, placed his hand upon his belt and turned toward the door leading to the hallway.

"I look forward to your insights in conversations we'll have with our family about my next role. Perhaps then I'll be able to answer your question. For now, let's continue our tour of this magnificent hall. The chapel is just next door."

55

Preparing for Interview 3
Anna Crossley Lawson

July 27, 1945

Anna Crossley Lawson was a lost soul. The wife of Tom Lawson, Thon's classmate at Foyle and co-worker in London, had suffered too many tragedies to find a way back to joy. Growing up in Belfast as the daughter of Bishop Crossley of Fisherwick Presbyterian Church, she had been unconditionally loved and happy. She was devoted to her parents' evangelical ministry working with the poor, the sick and the "fallen". She had dedicated her hands and heart to the church's mission: converting infidels, convincing agnostics, and committing to the one and only faith – Protestantism.

At the age of ten in 1920, she was a leader of the Fisherwick Children's Brigade, the first in a series of youth training programs for future evangelical ministers. At age twenty, she represented the Brigade at its annual revival held in Londonderry for the blessed, Christian believers, i.e. Presbyterians. It was there that she met young Thomas Lawson whom she married five years later in 1935. The two had settled into life in London where Thomas and his brother had taken over their father's insurance business. When war broke out in '38, Tom considered his family's safety before his own as an enlisted officer. He convinced Anna to return with their two children to her parents' home in Belfast. He left for North Africa.

Tragedy took its time to strike her, but strike it did. First, the youngest Lawson child was killed in the August '41 Belfast Blitz.

Little Sadie had been running across the street with her grandmother to reach a shelter on Malone Road when a bomb fell too soon and too close. The second tragedy occurred in June of 1942 when Tom's 4th Armoured Brigade was captured after the Allies' disastrous defeat in western Libya's Tobruk. Through Thon's intelligence connections, he confirmed Tom's death six months later in a German POW camp. The final blow to Anna's grasp on hope came when her remaining child contracted diphtheria and passed in '43.

Anna had relied on her father to confirm and reconfirm her belief in a loving and compassionate God about whom she herself had preached in many a setting. She had convinced so many others to rely on Him in times of trouble. Now, it was for her father to counsel her through her own despair. He had failed. Instead of reassuring her, Bishop Crossley had himself turned away from God, bitter about the loss of his own wife and granddaughter in the Blitz. His personal grief and doubt were compounded by the loss of his son, son-in-law and so many others among his young parishioners. Half of the Fisherwick Boys Brigade was lost in the first three years of the war. He had also come to grieve with his Catholic neighbors who had lost their children during the blitz. Both he and his daughter now doubted the power of the God of the Covenant who had led Israel out of the desert. Why couldn't He lead them out of the pain of their daily remembrances? Their despair fed off each other's.

Ironically, it was the Catholic Father Wolfe Irvine who had sat with Anna, listened to her and guided her day by day through the challenges of loss and doubt, with or without a belief in God. In seminary, Wolfe had attended many of the Fisherwick revivals when visiting his Aunt Kat in Belfast. Aunt Kat, Aunt BB and his own mother Agnes were intrigued by the power of prayer espoused by evangelists, so the three accompanied Wolfe in his own exploration of faith and belief. As Catholics, of course, they were considered a quartet of "infiltrators" in the predominantly Protestant meetings whose participants tolerated them more than questioned their attendance.

Knowing Thon's family through her courtier Tom, Anna, in contrast, warmly greeted the four. She could be heard, at a distance from them, convince her followers: "How can we convert the lost if our message isn't shared with them?"

Using his refined sense of hearing, Wolfe's blindness had enabled him to actually catch her words. "I'm going to remember those," he had told himself. "I know they'll come in handy someday." And indeed, they did…. at least, somewhat.

After the death of her second child, Father Wolfe would remind Anna of that message. They would stroll once a month for an hour with Larger through the Botanic Gardens, just next to Queens University. Anna appeared pensive whenever he repeated what she herself had preached back in her revival days. "You may remember what you declared emphatically to your followers: 'The message of hope must be spoken and heard before being believed, particularly by those in denial'. Might you be open now to hearing your own message?"

Their last walk was right after Christmas of '44. Anna seemed particularly anxious. Whenever Wolfe asked her how she was doing, she would lower her head, turn away from him and gaze somewhere into the beyond. He knew it wasn't at a God above, behind, or in front of her. I'm losing her, he warned himself. Physically, he had. One month after that walk, Anna had fled Belfast to seek refuge at the Lawson family's homestead north of Londonderry near Greencastle on Eire's Inishowen Peninsula. The most northern point of the island, the area was renowned for long winter nights, fierce storms and ancient spirits.

Wolfe feared that Anna's declining faith and despair were taking her farther and farther away from reality, leading to a final tragedy. But Wolfe, the consummate shepherd, was not going to give up on a lost lamb so he turned to his elder brother Thon recently assigned to Londonderry. Wolfe encouraged, if not begged, Thon to visit Anna. "Be a good shepherd, " said Wolfe. "You've had lots of practice with your soldiers."

Thon had chuckled at his younger brother. "Ach, I think you're putting too much trust in my capabilities and beliefs, dear Wolfe. It's you, not I, who have the secret intelligence about your God. I willingly agree to meet with Anna, but only as a mortal being, not as a faithful shepherd. I leave that magic up to you."

When Thon finally met Anna in Greencastle in mid-June upon his return home, he was shocked by the physical and emotional toll imposed by seven years of loss. The vibrant zealot he had last seen with Tom and the children in London had regressed into a dark space, emotionally and spiritually. Like Wolfe, but as a seasoned warrior, he was not going to give up on restoring his friend's wife to her former self or, at least, to a renewed self. He visited her weekly.

At first, Anna was silent during Thon's revels of Tom's pranks and escapades in and outside Foyle's confines. After a while, Thon saw her grin and once actually laugh at his tales. Soon, she was asking a few questions about Tom's mischievous behavior and if he ever displayed that at work. She also began to ask Thon about himself and his family – Wolfe, Agnes, BB and Kat. The two never broached the circumstances of Tom's death, nor did Anna refer to her children. By the end of July, he noticed that her eyes seemed clearer, her cheeks rosier, and their conversations more focused on the future.

That was when he asked if she wouldn't mind being interviewed by Kieran and a lovely, young Indian woman. Thon explained that the two were gathering ideas from community members to help government leaders make post-war plans.

He and Anna were walking arm in arm along the Greencastle Hill overlooking Kinnagoe Bay on a surprisingly sunny day. "They want to hear your ideas, Anna. As someone who has lost so much during the war but has survived, you have many gifts to offer," he suggested.

"Ach, Thon. I have nothing but sorrow to share. Why would they want to hear that?" she pulled her hand away from around his elbow.

He was determined to bring her back into the secular fold of

Ireland's flock of sheep. He knew her previous talents and dedication to others. Both were desperately needed in rebuilding Northern Ireland after the war and linking it with Eire. He noticed that his wartime intelligence skills of assessing situations and convincing others of essential actions were now required.

Quickly, he placed her hand back under his crooked arm. "Anna. What do you think Tom would want you to do? Wrap yourself up in a dried sheepskin and let the banshees carry you off? I don't believe he or your little ones would want to unwrap such an unattractive package in the next world, let alone such a rigid one. Come on, Anna, where is that old revivalist spunk?"

Anna stopped walking. She again withdrew her hand from Thon's arm and turned toward the vast expanse of the Ballyhillion Beach below and the North Atlantic beyond. She appeared to be in a trance.

"Tell me," he carefully continued. "Did you always think people listened to your revivalist words, let alone believed and acted on them? Nay, I doubt it. Because of your faith and hope as a determined missionary, you knew you had to keep going on, didn't you? Surely, in the past, you had many ways, other than just preaching about a God they doubted, to change the minds and hearts of those you considered lost in this world? You acted out your faith and compassion by helping the poor. You comforted the elderly. You listened to those who needed an ear to hear their grievances. You modeled hope. You can do that again, Anna, without believing in God."

She did not move. He recognized her angst and indecision. He had seen it on the faces of his military comrades as they considered the fates awaiting them before a battle. He had seen it in his own mirror when preparing for any undercover assignment from which he doubted he would return.

Thon heard a quiet voice carried toward him on the sea breeze. It soon swirled around him. He recognized the same calming lilt that had encouraged him in Algiers, in Sicily, in Rome and in Berlin just months ago. It offered him these words as his final plea.

"What about the children of widows who need your help? What about returning veterans who lost their families in the blitzes? Are you going to give up on them just because you don't believe in a compassionate God? Maybe He or She or It – or just your heart – is waiting for you to hear what's right for you to do? That you can certainly share with our people."

Anna paused and looked at Thon. Her face seemed to catch the sunlight just right. Her cheeks began to radiate. Thon sensed that, like the Goddess Morrigan that shape-shifted between the afterworld and earth, Anna was transforming right before him. He felt that he was, too.

Anna faced him directly. "Since when did you become such an evangelist on whatever you think I need to dispel my despair? Have you become a healer like our Irish Goddess Brigid? I bet your Aunt BB has been talking to you. Or maybe it was that brother of yours, Father Wolfe." She began to laugh. "Ach, you Irvines and McCormicks are all the same – great storytellers and leaders. You've persuaded me. I'll talk with your next generation."

Thon smiled. He heard a diminishing voice whisper in his ear on the wind. "Good job, Thon McCormick Irvine, and welcome home. Now, you know your purpose, too."

56

Interview 3
Anna Crossley Lawson

July 30, 1945

"Help her know God is present, even when He can't be seen," said former nun BB.

"Help her pray again so God can show her the way forward," said Father Wolfe.

"Help her imagine the future with or without God," said agnostic Irene, Manjula's mother.

"Help her reflect on her family, community and country so she renews her purpose," said veteran Thon.

"Help her believe again in her strengths to move ahead," said activist Agnes.

"Help her talk about anything," said loquacious Kat.

"Help her feel her heart beat, so she knows she is still alive," said Una.

They were all right.

Anna had reluctantly accepted the visit of Kieran and Manjula. On this surprisingly brilliant summer afternoon, the three sat around an iron cast table under the shade of a walnut tree in the backyard of the Lawson family home in Greencastle. Anna had prepared tea, scones, and some letters that her husband had written during the first years of the war. Whatever she was going to share with Kieran and Manjula had to be through his eyes and voice. She did not consider

her words purposeful. They were too sad, too bitter, too angry to contribute any worthy insights.

The couple knew they would have to apply all the advice offered
by family members to convince her to the contrary. She had much to
offer them.

"We thank you for agreeing to meet with us, Mrs. Lawson," began
Kieran. "You have provided such delights here. I hope you don't think
we came just to devour them?"

Anna smiled and poured three cups of tea in silence. When
finished, she sat back and tucked a strand of grey hair behind its
waiting ear. Leaves, stretching along extended branches of the oak
tree, danced above. They spun in rhythm with the afternoon coastal
breeze.

The letters she had chosen rested in her lap. A green velvet ribbon
circled them. The table's small diameter determined that the knees
of the three individuals around it almost touched each other. Anna
moved her seat out of range to avoid such contact. Kieran and Manjula did not. Together, they would temper each other's concerns for
this widow by nudging one knee against the other's whenever a question had reached beyond acceptable protocol or required kindness.

When Anna had settled herself, Kieran began again. "I understand that my cousin Thon has told you the purpose of our visit.
However, perhaps you have some questions about it?"

"Yes, Thon has told me your purpose. No, I have no questions.
Please, just go ahead and ask what you must."

Kieran sensed her reservations and knew he would have to be
strategic, yet gentle, in his questioning.

"We have already spoken to several people about their experiences during the war and their hopes for the future. None have yet
been women so I'm hoping you can share your experiences from a
daughter's, wife's or mother's perspective. Would you mind that?"

Anna held Thomas' letters tight. She began to review them in her
mind despite having read each so often that she had them memorized.

His continuous message had been of love for her. He wished that, if he didn't return, she would raise their children to be as kind and compassionate as she. He vowed that he would always be with her, if not in the flesh, in spirit. And he would be with her as she continued life serving her Christian community. Anna shook her head, hoping to dispel the sorrow about to overwhelm her. She cleared her throat.

"Ach. That's a fine question to ask as there are many wives and mothers who have suffered in this war, not just from the loss of a life partner but when their own children succumbed to the vestiges of war. I'm sure your family members have shared my own losses with you so I will not belabor them. Let me tell you, instead, of the bravery and strength the women around me have displayed. That is the experience of the war I want you to report."

Over the next half hour, Anna described so many incidents of women helping each other and the war efforts that her normally sallow coloring awakened to a pale pink followed by a vivid red. She talked about nurses, teachers, military drivers, factory workers, foster mothers, farmers, coast patrollers, civilian guards. The list of roles and examples went on and on. It seemed that a flood of her memories had been released like the rush of water when a high tide flashes through a sink hole.

Kieran and Manjula realized that Thon was right: help her focus on family, community and nation. Aunt Kat was right, too: help her talk about anything.

Manjula wanted to pursue another line of questioning that would elaborate on Anna's descriptions and perhaps lead her to speak about herself. Manjula interrupted Anna's flow.

"Excuse me for interrupting you, Mrs. Lawson. I am comforted by your words about the strength of so many women. But I am also curious about them. How did these women stay strong despite their challenges and sorrows?

"Perhaps you can help me understand my own mother who lost her brother in Algiers two years ago. She just kept working daily in our tavern and at night with the Bangor coastal watch patrol. She never talked about him. She never wept before us. To this day, I don't know how she managed. Do you think holding all that sorrow inside was good for her? How did you stay strong?"

Anna paused mid-breath. She could feel her heartbeat quicken. Clutching Thomas' letters, she questioned herself: "Did I stay strong? Nay, I didn't. I withdrew from my family, my faith, my service to others, my friends. Now, I am a recluse walking the cliffs along the sea and wishing I no longer existed. How could I have missed Thomas' most important message: to live on for his sake and our children. How selfish I have become. Dear God, please forgive me. I must act as four people, not just one alone, to rebuild our nation"

Manjula saw Anna's demeanor change. Her back straightened. She drew her seat closer to the table. "My dear, Manjula. May I call you that?" Anna asked.

"Of course, Mrs. Lawson."

"Let me tell you how the women I know to this day, like your mother, draw upon a strength we can hardly understand, let alone measure. They want to make sure the present and future are not shaped by sorrow, but by hope. Many rely on their faith; many on the spirit of their ancestors; many on their family and friends; many on pure stubbornness. No matter how they have survived, I believe they feel the future will be better because of the strength they have shown in the last six years. Regardless of religion or class or nationality, as you know so well Manjula, we are alive today and must create that future on behalf of those who are not with us. They cannot have died in vain."

Anna abruptly stopped. "Oh, heavens. I seem to have resurrected my overpowering style of evangelical preaching. Forgive me."

"To the contrary," interjected Kieran. "You have shared eloquently exactly that which we hoped we would learn from you today. If more women in our nation feel as you do, our future will certainly be bright."

"My lad, I know many women do. We just have to call them to action."

Anna rose from her chair. "Join me in a walk along the beach, won't you? I want to hear the ideas you are hearing about peoples' hopes."

"It will be our pleasure," Kieran rose as did Manjula. They had been advised well by their family members on how to help Anna. Now, Anna would help them.

57

Interview 4
Netty McNeill Campbell

August 4, 1945

"She may still be like I was," professed Anna. "You'll need to be cautious and not compromise her trust by any presumptions you may have. I can't divulge why I say that as it may influence your questions. So, let me just wish you blessings when you're in her presence."

Anna had arranged for Kieran and Manjula to interview a former classmate of Anna's from her days at the Senior School for Girls of The Belfast Royal Academy. Anna had studied religion; Netty, history. Both had learned their primary role in the social structure of society. Caring for the family came first as daughter, sister, mother or grandmother. In sewing classes, however, they had learned surreptitiously about other roles such as business women and politicians. These they could not openly share with male family members or fellow students. The two girls pledged a bond as each other's "forever counselor". They had honored that pledge for over twenty years and served as god-mothers of each of their children before Anna's little ones had passed.

Their bond was solidified not only by their early pledge but by one common experience from the war. Each of their husbands had died in a German prisoner of war camp. Netty, her two boys and baby girl had moved to Londonderry in '36 so did not suffer, as Anna had, from the Blitz of '41 and diphtheria in '42. Both, however, had lingered in the pangs of spousal loss until Netty had remarried in '40 to a stout man of stout Loyalist beliefs.

Netty McNeill had become Netty Campbell, married to John, a widower in his fifties who brought three adult sons with him to her household. John had also brought his membership in the Apprentice Boys of Derry, an activist organization defending Northern Ireland's union within Great Britain. Over the last four years, Netty had been coping with what this meant for her own teenage children who had been influenced otherwise by the former evangelism of their god-mother Anna and a growing belief in non-violence.

As Netty waited for Kieran and Manjula at the parish hall of First Derry Presbyterian within the walled city, she considered what she might share with them. Anna had prepared Netty with the intent of the two, but intentions for Netty always seemed to transform them-selves over time. As a Campbell, she never knew what was specifically under the coverlet of words. For years, she had four men around the dinner table talking a form of code. She was suspicious of the unaired, and what she feared were unclean, linens they covered.

I trust dear Anna, Netty thought, so will assume these young people will say what they mean and do what they say.

She watched the sun stream through the stained-glass windows of the hall. She was entranced by the designs of nature glazed into each frame – flowers blooming, rivers streaming, animals peace-fully grazing. How bucolic these scenes, she deliberated. If only life reflected the same.

Her reverie was broken by footsteps approaching her from behind, accompanied by a lively greeting.

"Mrs. Campbell," Kieran spoke in his most jovial voice. "Thank you so much for meeting with us."

Netty rose and extended her hand to Kieran. He shook it warmly as he turned to Manjula. "May I introduce you to my companion, Manjula Srinavasin?"

Netty's eyes could not refrain from staring at Manjula. "Oh my," said Netty. "Forgive me being forward, but you are related to Irene

Corcoran, aren't you?"

Manjula smiled. "I am. And, you'll be pleased to know my Mum sends you her best. When I told her yesterday that we were meeting, she could not stop praising you. What have you done to earn the accolades I have failed to earn over 20 years?"

Netty laughed, reaching out her hand to grasp Manjula's. "Oh, my dear child. Your mother talks about how blessed she is with you and all you are achieving at Queens. She's just not the type to mother through compliments. Rather, look at her face when contentment is there. That's where you'll get your praise."

"Hum. You may be right, Mrs. Campbell. I just focus on her frowns and silence. I should remember the smiles more. Thank you for that advice."

The three drew chairs from a stack at the back of the hall and placed them at the end of a long dining table. Netty sat at the head; the two younger folks, one on each side of her. Within less than five minutes, Netty felt an ease in sharing her thoughts about Ireland's future. She desperately wanted peace among the various factions she knew all too well living with John and his boys. While she never shared details, it was obvious to Kieran and Manjula that she knew quite a bit about the activities of the loyalist Apprentice Boys of Derry and their two affiliates, the Ulster Defense Association (UDA) and Ulster Volunteer Force (UVF). Netty had become well-versed in reading the code of the Campbell men.

"I fear there are undertones of pre-war attitudes about the north's partition from Eire that have been exacerbated by the war rather than alleviated. On one side, so many young men, both Loyalists and Unionists, have died. That sacrifice rationalizes their support of partition from Eire. On the other side, many Nationalists, both Catholic and Protestant, also died. Their sacrifice on behalf of a colonizing and exploitative nation begs the opposite. Unifying with Eire is their answer for a future of peace. It will become a very bitter time ahead between the two sides if we can't reconcile based on mutual respect and trust."

Netty looked at Manjula. "You need to convey that message to whomever you are reporting your findings. But don't quote me."

Kieran nodded his head. "We won't, Mrs. Campbell. Please trust us."

"Aye, for Irene's sake and Anna's, I do. But I warn you both. Be careful with whom you talk about your task here. I have already heard from Charlie's wife what you're about. You don't want her to share that with others, although I think it's too late. Watch where you walk at night and always keep your eyes open. Look ahead, around and behind you."

Manjula took Netty's hand. Any reservation about interviewing an honest Netty was no longer warranted. "You're just like my Mum. That's exactly what she said last night. But, she also had a message for you."

"Ach, she was always telling me what to do at school. Is she doing the same again?"

"Aye. She thinks you need to run for the Northern Irish Parliament out of the Londonderry constituency."

Netty laughed out loud. "You tell your Mum that I will only run here if she does the same in Belfast West!"

58

Interview 5
St. Stephen's Wolf and Fox

Sunday, August 5, 1945

St. Stephen's Church of Ireland was eerily somber after the morning service. A congregation of Derry 's walled city residents had knelt in the church next to the Apprentice Boy's meeting house to commemorate the end of six years of fighting on European soil. Many had prayed for their sons, husbands, brothers and fathers – soldiers sacrificed for the United Kingdom and its allies. Many prayed for those civilians lost at home, the elderly and babes, mothers, wives, sisters, daughters, and aunties. Others had prayed for forgiveness of nefarious deeds recently committed or those yet to come.

A curious whispering was still swirling across the nave's pews and up the granite, arched pillars. At the top of each pillar was a sculpted head of one saint or another, all martyred – John The Baptist, St. Sebastian, St. Alban and, the church's nomenklatura St. Stephen. Most were not easily recognized by Kiernan nor Manjula who had remained after the formal service. They sat in a middle row waiting for their last interview. Kieran believed that the statuary figures should have been accompanied by Ulster men now resting in French and German fields or by Jewish children in unmarked graves. Manjula noted the absence of women.

"There is something about this place of worship that is quite foreign to me, " said Manjula. She shivered and tucked her arm around Kieran's elbow. "I am so used to Wolfe's mass on Sundays in Belfast.

His church has such brightly colored windows and tiers of candles that shed light on cloudy days and illumine the lovely flower arrangements. Despite his blindness, Father Wolfe ensures that beauty surrounds and inspires the sighted. It is easy to celebrate faith there. His own VE commemoration service last month was resplendent. This cathedral seems too somber and depressing, as though it only welcomes sadness and sacrifice. Look at all those martyrs on the pillars and that painting at the end of our pew of St. Stephen standing on those black rocks. He is depicted as terribly remorseful."

"Ach, Manjula," prodded Kieran. "Don't you know that St. Stephen was the first Christian to be martyred only fifty years after Christ's death? As a spokesperson for the early Christian movement, he had taken the word and works of Christ out into the countryside, particularly outside the formal Jewish temple. He fed the widows and conducted all sorts of charitable works. The Jewish authorities despised Stephen when he questioned their contrary customs so they accused him of blasphemy and stoned him to death. His sainthood came not just from his persecution but from asking, in his last words, that those same persecutors be forgiven by God.

"This church was built in the mid 1800's in St. Stephen's name because he was the very man of God who reached out to all, no matter where or how they lived or worshipped. Remember that during the time of this church's construction, Ireland was experiencing terrible famine and many Ulster women lost their husbands and children. Even more emigrated at that time from the docks below us to the US, Canada and Australia. That's why…"

Kieran could not finish his sentence.

"Tis, true," came a gruff voice behind the two. The couple heard a tone that heralded a gruff figure as well. "St. Stephen's martyrdom tells the universal story of how powerful people rule over those they consider ignorant. They persecute, rather than honor, us. I would like to revenge St. Stephen by raising a stone against anyone today who restricts how or where I worship or, worse yet, how or where I live my life."

Kieran stood up and turned to face a man of defined strength and distinct bluster. "Mr. Campbell, I assume?"

"Aye, 'tis I by whatever name you use," continued the surly voice.

Kieran hesitated. So did the man. Netty's husband was a formidable figure, about six feet tall and thirteen stones wrapped around a chest of considerable width. His shoulders leaned forward at a considerable angle. He appeared to be carrying a load of boulders on his back. Kieran assumed they were formed by years of physical as well as genetic influences. Kieran also realized he had no idea how old this Campbell was as he looked in his eighties, despite Anna saying he was only sixty. What had added decades to this man's exterior and such heaviness to his interior?

"Would you mind sitting with us, sir?" Kieran gestured to a seat in the pew behind him, next to the nave itself. He preferred to give Mr. Campbell enough space to escape if his impatience and resolve dictated a quick departure. Kieran also wanted room for Manjula's and his own defense if needed.

Positioning himself in the pew before Campbell's, Kiernan leaned over it to face this potential adversary. He continued. "I know Mrs. Lawson has spoken to you about our mission today to hear your thoughts about the future of Ireland now that the war is over. Perhaps you would…."

Campbell interrupted Kieran. "Nay, you have it wrong, laddie. The war has not ended. We are just able to focus again on our own battlefield to ensure Ulster is always part of the grand kingdom. "

Manjula had been quietly listening next to Kiernan but could not restrain herself.

"May I ask you to explain a bit what you mean by your term battlefield?" she asked, placing her hand on the top of the pew.

Instead of answering her directly, Campbell looked at Kieran. "Is she your mouthpiece, laddie?"

Kieran hesitated.

"Sir, let me explain that she is my assistant in taking notes during our discussions." Kieran knew Manjula would be furious at him for this description of her role, but felt he had to appease Campbell's blatant prejudice, unsure if it were against women or people of foreign origin. Kieran hoped Manjula would understand. When she leaned back into her own seat, he believed she had and knew they would have much to talk about later that evening.

"Good lad." Campbell seemed to relax. "No woman should have the first nor last word. So, ask me your questions."

Kieran carefully led the hour long conversation avoiding the word "battle", seeking Campbell's past and current beliefs. The past was replete with school boy skirmishes against Catholics in Londonderry's Bogside – stones thrown, windows broken, fires lit to scare Catholics and Protestant Nationalists away from living and working in the center city. While Campbell did not identify the exact group he had joined as a young adult, he referenced many a July 12th Orangeman parade in which he had taken part right up to the past year, over fifty-five parades to be exact. He alluded to various actions taken after each by such phrases as "…and then we showed them…" or "…they learned their place…."

Finally, he mentioned the initials UDV (the Ulster Defense Volunteers) who were part of the local, civil defense system and how well they trained their recruits. "We learned much about protecting our kind that we can use in the future," Campbell offered, referring to the various Ulster clubs in which he was also a member.

"And what do you want for that future?" Kieran asked as he saw Campbell begin to fidget in his seat, almost like a wolf ready to jump on a prey or a fox to run from a hound. Campbell was ready to move as both assailant and victim.

"We Unionists need to stick together for the future of this country, lad. We need to continue what our leaders are telling us: remain within the United Kingdom. We cannot let those Nationalist Socialists overtake our businesses and labor force. We also need to listen to our religious leaders who honor the true Spiritual Kingdom. The Pope and his Catholics have no sense of it. If we must take action on behalf of our beliefs, we will. That will be our future for sure, a time of resolve and action. Tell your readers that we will not surrender."

This final demand returned Campbell to the gruff figure who had first approached Kieran and Manjula. He rose, turned away from them and didn't say another word – no "all the best", "good luck" or "farewell". The couple rose as well and watched his bent figure straighten as he walked down the nave and looked across at the painting of St. Stephen.

Campbell seemed to salute at it, but neither Kieran nor Manjula were sure.

59

Summery of Seasons

Sunday, August 12, 1945

"Like the seasons of the year and the winds over the Belfast Lough on any one morning, there is no rhyme to what we have heard," said Kieran. "I'd say Northern Ireland is back into the middle of a stormy winter or a unusually blistering summer."

"True," agreed Manjula, "but there is reason for either or both. Should I say many reasons? In all we took in, each made sense to the speaker."

The couple and their numerous family members sat comfortably on blankets spread upon the hillside overlooking Helen's Bay. They were a short distance from the formerly named Beastie King Tavern now The Lester and Louisa, managed by the current generation of McCanns, Finbar and his daughter Fiona.

Those culinary wizards had procured all sorts of Irish delicacies or alternatives for this gathering as rationing had not yet been lifted in Northern Ireland town, even the bustling seaside town of Bangor that, in May of the previous year, had harbored General Dwight D. Eisenhower's American warships in preparation for D Day.

Fortunately, American troops were still bivouacked in its strategic harbor and often shared the benefit of their military allowance in the form of cigarettes and chocolate. Only the latter made this union of the McCormick, Smiley and Irvine family a special culinary event. Not one member smoked, but all loved their Urney chocolate.

Among the fifteen relatives who benefitted from the negotiating expertise of Finbar and Fiona, some had been able to reconnoiter their own basement supplies, grocery coupons, and home gardens. They had even brought a few select bones for their favorite canines: Faili, Larger and Grua. There was enough to feed a king and his court, though none would state such colonial evidence as the measure of success. Instead, all considered themselves victorious just to be alive and together. They accepted Father Wolfe's blessing that attributed their earthly riches – potatoes, cabbage and soda bread – to Cernunnos, the Celtic God of Prosperity. Few, alas, accepted Wolfe's additional attribution to God for any spiritual gifts. They had witnessed too much loss to acknowledge them.

Recognizing a growing solemnity after the blessing, Liam interjected his sense of humor. "Hold on, dear Wolfe! With due respect to you as our resident cleric, I thought Cernunnos was the God of Fertility. Are we expecting more than cabbage and potatoes this year?" Liam looked at Kieran, then at Thon, and then at Jon, the youngest men within the family.

"Now, just you hold on there, Master Liam," spoke up Kat. "Why aren't you looking at Rose, Manjula and Anne? You know that new phrase the American soldiers use in Bangor: 'It takes two to tango.' "

Rachel and Ian McNulty, as well as Morna and Robert Smiley, were relieved not be the brunt of this banter, having already added another generation to the family. They watched their contributions playing on the grass around them. Maud McNulty was now four; her brother Patrick, two. The young Smileys had waited for Morna to recover completely from her assault outside the Belfast clinic in '40. Despite suffering from occasional headaches, she had delivered a bulbous, baby boy named Rob who, at three months, rounded out the youngest trio of the extended family.

The six targeted kin took these statements as well-meaning and loving coming from their elders. Thus, they responded with the patience and respect due to those over sixty which, indeed, Liam and Kat were. Only BB reprimanded her husband and sister. "Ach, you both are incorrigible. Please forgive them, young ones!"

"Don't bother with the forgiveness in this crowd. Just get on with your findings," urged Erin McCann as, with pint bottle in hand, he sat down next to Kieran and Manjula. "I'm in need of some mutton for a new play now that the war is over. My head has been longing for the good old days of Irish rebellion and patriotism. It's been too long since I have burrowed into the roots under Irish soil, instead of European, Asian or African."

At the age of forty-nine, Erin knew he had much more to share as the family Thespian, especially when the Dublin, London and New York stage lights would soon be shining again along with sparks of a renewed Irish patriotism in Ulster. He had been careful to write only about Irish myths when the war had impacted all of Ireland, not just the North. That didn't mean he was unaware of the subliminal tensions Kieran and Manjula would soon describe. He, Billie and Liam had forged a strong network of informants within the moribund, but ever so ready to ignite, IRA devotees. Now, Erin wanted confirmation or revision from the two young messengers of his own network's assumptions.

"Come now," scolded Agnes. "Wolfe has given us grace, and we have yet to imbibe. The summer winds may turn brisk before we know it so let us eat while we listen to our resident scholars."

The family settled into their places, some standing with plate in hand, others cross-legged on blankets. The remaining sat on wooden, folding chairs borrowed from their friends at the Bangor barracks. The two dogs, Faili and Grua, lay underneath the chairs. Larger settled next to Wolfe. Human and canine chewed intermittently while listening intently to Kieran and Manjula.

"I'd have to say that the thirty folks willing to chat with us," Kieran started, "seem to fall into four categories, as I said before, like the seasons of the year. Those in the dead of winter are ready to take up the stone or rifle against those whom they label as betrayers to the faith, Catholic against Protestant. Those in the blistering summer heat are ready to ignite fires against those they consider as treasonous, Unionist against Nationalist. Both groups say the war deepened their distrust of each other. With the exclusion of Northern Ireland from mandatory conscription, Unionists and Protestants feel their boys sacrificed too much and Catholics and Nationalists not at all. The bombings of Belfast and mandated food shortages made Catholics and Nationalists feel they had sacrificed as much for a colonizing overlord as they had in historic famines and the Great War. These two groups are diametrically opposed to each other. Their future bodes unwell for Ulster."

Kieran paused, and acknowledged Manjula. "However, my good companion here has some hopeful messages to share about the two other groups. We have entitled them, respectively, the Falling Forward and the Springing Up. She'll explain them."

Manjula stood below a sweeping chestnut tree in front of the nearest blanket. By now, most of the family members had finished their meals and had arraigned themselves in a half circle before her. On the blankets were Maud, Patrick and Rob in the arms of their respective mothers Rachel and Morna plus Rose. Liam, Billie and Erin had joined Ian standing on the left. Robert, Wolfe, Thon and Jon had moved to the back. The remaining grandmothers Agnes, Kat and BB sat on chairs to the right with daughters Katie, Maggie and Liza standing behind, hands placed on their respective mothers' shoulders. The silence of anticipation was accentuated by a gentle breeze flowing upwards from the bay below.

"Kieran and I" began Manjula "were pleased to hear from those who only wanted reconciliation and peace. The first group represented a mixture of our presumed religious stereotypes which we soon found strangely counter to those assumptions. They were Catholics who wanted to befriend their Protestant neighbors and vice-versa. This group we called the Springing Up group as they seem to be like the furze standing out upon the dark green background of our Northern hills with their brilliant yellow. Somehow, they were enlightened not to see religion creating differences. Rather, since both groups believed in one God, they saw it as fostering unity.

"The second group included people with a mix of political stereotypes that also baffled our assumptions. They were Nationalists who were willing to talk with Unionists and vice-versa. They all wanted to form an alliance to address post-war reconstruction Ulster-wide by reassessing the partitioned borders. We call this the Falling Forward group as its members want to jump into a rugby scrum, lean upon each other, and push up-field as one team toward a common goal.

Both groups offer so many positive reasons for building the future of Ulster together." Manjula finished her summary with an audible exhale.

The family was hushed.

Erin was the first to react. "Hear, hear. I envision a new play coming to the stage, perhaps entitled The Four Seasons!" He was secretly gratified to have his own assumptions confirmed, even those about the extreme and oppositional groups, Winter and Summer.

Billie followed next. "Cheers! I hear a possible cross-border agreement coming to Stormont and the Dail." His focus was centered on the groups that could support reconciliation and peace.

Liam nodded his head to both men, but not enthusiastically. He recognized the complexity of dealing with the four seasons, each reflecting differing rhymes and reasons.

Erin's and Billie's initial reactions were soon supplanted by an uproar of clapping followed by numerous exclamations of kudos, bravos, and the Irish Maith Thu ("well done").

The wind began to increase just as the sun dipped below the Carrickfergus hillside opposite the bay. Kat and BB smiled at each other. They sensed that their mother Lizzie and Grandmother Bella had been with them during the afternoon gathering. Evening breezes would soon carry the traditional family kisses that would alight on each and every forehead.

Only the canine trio knew that many others in the Beyond would soon join the ancestral women to comment on the four seasons and influence their impact in the future.

60

Beyond and Before

Sunday, August 19, 1945

Una's Epilogue

Like the hillside overlooking the Lough, the garden in the Beyond welcomed the ancestors of the Smiley/Irvine/McCormick family to its own annual gathering. Since the first in 1886, the garden's Horse Chestnut borders had expanded along with its array of radiant sapphire, ruby and diamond colored flowers. The blue Irises and red Poppies seemed to overshadow the green lawns abutting white sea-shell paths, but the Lilies of the Valley held their floral counterparts at bay. These tiny representatives of purity and humility historically allowed space on the paths for human emissaries to walk justly. Today, in 1945, that ability was going to be needed more than ever.

Despite being free from physical weight, the numerous family members and their distinguished colleagues were heavy in thought and intent. Throughout the Second World War, they had argued ferociously over the purpose, strategies and tactics of the conflict. Some had sided with DeValera on Eire's neutrality. Some had sided with Belfast's IRA Battalion in attempting to sabotage Ulster's relationship with Great Britain. Some aligned with Ulster men – Catholic or Protestant – who joined the Allied armies; some found them treasonous to the Nationalist cause. Many supported Ulster women who secured jobs in previously male designated roles; others criticized the "girls'" independence. Regardless of the differences in strategies and tactics, all knew that the end of violence had to be maintained. Thus, they needed to reconcile conflicting ideas and guide their descendants below toward one goal – sustained peace. Today, they had settled into a quiet, yet subliminally, anxious assembly.

Despite Una's efforts, Uncle Aiden had insisted on being its Chairperson.

"I successfully dispersed opposing boys in the 1886 labor strikes at Belfast's Clarendon docks and, to date, have certainly not lost my power of persuasion," he insisted.

"Aye, ye did calm the boys." Sister Bridgette admonished. "But don't forget, you were killed on the spot after yere last word."

"Tis true," Aiden admitted, a tad sobered by his partner's reminder. "But arriving here and living together, the Dicksons and my family have reconciled, haven't we, Bobbie?"

Bobbie Dickson, standing among the gatherers, bowed his head momentarily in shame, for it was he who had plunged the knife into Aiden's chest in '86 that had taken the elder's mortal life. Although the lad, his grandfather Seamus and Aiden had reconciled their differences in the immortal Beyond, Bobbie still felt some remorse. Only Aiden's forgiveness had lessened it. Thus, Bobbie raised his head and offered a thin, yet sincere, grin to his elder.

Una was grateful for the exchange she had witnessed between Aiden and Bobbie, confirming her belief that, in this garden of the Beyond, reconciliation was possible. She also knew she had to hurry the meeting along. "Let us begin, dear Aiden," she prodded.

He nodded in agreement.

Despite his innate stubbornness or, perhaps, because of it, Aiden had come to know that people sowing fields and reaping crops together with respect and trust would cause Ireland to survive and, eventually, thrive. Hopefully, his darling Bridgette would bring this gathering together toward a common resolution. When previous exchanges had become heated, her interventions always soothed the various family egos and reset discussions on a more productive path. He would depend upon her again today.

I guess she has the power of the Lord on her side to calm the seas and give sight to the blind. He laughed to himself. *I just wish she could change that water into wine or into a small splash of the amber whiskey.*

Just as Una was again ready to nudge Aiden along, he finally raised his cane in the air and shouted out an entreaty in Irish:

"Go n-ardaimis pionta beag comhthola ar son galun mor na siochana. May we raise a wee pint of accord for a grand gallon of peace."

All hands were raised, even those of Molly McKenzie and the Countess Markievicz; Robbie Smiley and Ryan McCormick; Christine O'Leary and Patrick McCann; Parnell, Pearse and Collins. Former adversaries were about to compromise, perhaps not reconcile all of their differences, but, at least, listen to others and accommodate for a cause greater than their partisan beliefs.

So, for over an hour, despite time being immeasurable in the Beyond, many ideas were exchanged. While all agreed that peace below must be maintained, various members disagreed vehemently on the ways by which that could be accomplished. Aiden eventually realized that as many petals as there are on the fluffy headed flower named appropriately Sheep's Bit, there was a myriad of ideas being discussed – too many to summarize, let alone form a common base upon which more than two people could agree.

The cacophony of noise was finally too much for him. He surreptitiously called to his canine companions. He whispered into Bigger's ear who led Sceo and Boru to the front of the garden where all of the humans could see them in a line. The canines

began to howl as in a Gregorian chant. Their synchronized cho-
rus brought individual debates to an end.

"Ach," said Aiden to the baffled group. "Look at who's tell-
ing us to stop and join together. If these dogs can do so in such
beautiful harmony, we can, too. Unlike the Dail, or Stormont
or Parliament, we can do better than their bickering, near-do-
well members. We can follow some semblance of a democratic
process. Come, let's hear each idea and vote on its viability."

Aiden gestured to Will Irvine. "My dear nephew. Lead
us in this exercise. I think we must transform our Sheep's Bit
into what, I have no idea. Ye can weave your lawyer's wit and
wisdom to form an equally comforting, but less intricate, flower
with fewer petals."

Will stepped up and turned to the gathering. Its members
formed semi-circles before him. The pride in the faces of his wife
Lizzie, mother Bella and father William was radiant. "Uncle
Aiden," Will acknowledged. "Bless ye for this opportunity. I
promise all gathered here today that I'll honor yer trust to
respect each one who speaks."

And so, one by one in short time, various ideas were pre-
sented, explained, questioned by any within the gathering, and
then voted upon. Sister Bridgette had only to intervene once
when voices started to interrupt or over speak. She adroitly
quelled them by asking for a moment of prayer.

By the time each idea had been presented, four had received
the most votes.

Will offered them up.

"Among all of our different ideas, we seem to have proposed
four strategies, each building on the next. Tell me what ye think
of them.

"First, I hear the need for openness. We must guide our loved
ones below to seek out those with whom they differ. They may
be folks within similar church groups, work groups, or social

groups. *They may be individuals from different congregations, professions, even opposing sports teams. We can't let our family members stay within their own cocoons, always thinking they have the correct and most righteous beliefs.*

Secondly, I hear the practice of listening, listening to learn from those with whom we differ, not just to confirm our own ideas. We must offer ways by which our loved ones can truly listen. That means we must help them stop assuming they know exactly what others are thinking, believing or acting upon. They must listen to why others believe as they do. We might suggest a trick I learned in the 1870 Court of Chancery. Parnell, I think you knew this, too, when you were balancing the contradictory views of militants and politicians regarding Home Rule. The trick was simple: Don't practice listening at the same time you are formulating your own response. Just listen."

Thirdly, I hear the term compromise. Several of you said we should compromise a bit in the short term so that our greater goals can be met in the long run. We have our Michael Collins and Griffith here to attest to that as a strategy. They compromised during their negotiations with Lloyd George and Churchill on The Anglo-Irish Treaty in '20, not to forget their negotiations with Dev. Despite the short-term pain of that compromise, an Eire independent of Great Britain now exists twenty-five years later."

Collins, never comfortable with others speaking for him, raised his hand, and asked if he could share what he considered a particularly cogent point in support of Will's third suggestion. Will nodded an agreement, but advised. "Please be brief, good sir, or we'll be here debating for hours again."

Michael began. "As God and Sister Bridgette are my witnesses, I will be brief." Many of the assembly members chortled their doubt.

Regardless of the teasing, Collins continued. "I must now

agree with George B. Shaw who once criticized me for saying 'What matter if for Ireland dear we fall'. His words of retort have plagued me over these past twenty three years. I will never forget them. George argued that 'the time has now come for Irishmen to learn to live for their country.' I believe he is right, although I always thought our deaths would bring a better life to our dear Ireland. Being with ye all now, I truly believe we must ensure life without violence, not death with violence. We need to live by reconciling with our enemies, not die by hating them. Will's third strategy is a good way forward."

The assembly clapped in unison. Bravos resounded. Even the dogs howled their agreement.

Will, reluctantly yet determinedly, called for order. Silence was regained.

"Our fourth common idea is one of great complexity. It seeks to pursue peace through various means that may not seem as innately peaceful. These include the reformation of systems, organizations, communities and even families. However, they must be altered non-violently.

In Christianity and other religious faiths, such disruption requires peaceful resistance. Jesus taught about turning ones cheek and loving thy neighbor as thyself – even if the enemy is persecuting ye. The Buddhist faith calls for compassion, not violence. We know leaders, including our own in the past, have promoted such beliefs and actions. Their followers have practiced hunger strikes, labor walk-outs, street marches, Parliamentary debates, and so many other forms of protest. We know that these actions may lead to arrests, physical harm and maybe even death. Tolstoy in Russia and now a young man called Gandhi in India offer us such strategies that we can convey to our beloveds. We will have to advise them carefully, however, since they may suffer dearly, especially from others who espouse violence.

Will concluded his summary.

"All of yer discussions today have raised one common agreement: Violence breeds violence; peace breeds peace. Non-violent
actions will be difficult to foster, but we must convince our loved
ones of our four strategies: first to seek out, not isolate ourselves
from, those different from them; secondly to listen without prejudice; thirdly to compromise as well as possible; and, finally,
to honor non-violence. Only when these four are practiced can
Ireland thrive in peace."

The moment of silence which followed Will's last sentence,
was, as in all timeless places, profound. The family and friends
began to join hands. Semi-circles formed one large round, like
the standing stones of Newgrange.

"Ah, ha," exclaimed Aiden, the clan humorist. "I see our
fuzzy-headed Sheep's Bit has transformed into one, four-leaf
Shamrock held by us all. How symbolic, don't ye think?"

"Aye, indeed" said Padraig Pearse, stepping forward. "Thank
you Una, Aiden and Will for helping us share our ideas so ami-
cably. We have succeeded in determining how we can guide our
next generation in welcoming a new age for Ireland. The next
fifty years of this 20th Century will certainly test their souls,
but we will be with our kin. They will feel our presence in the
wind over the Mourne Mountains, the songs of the Thrushes,
the colors of the wild flowers, and the tides of the loughs.

I wonder if you would mind if I close our gathering together
with one of the most glorious of poems I did not have the chance
to write?"

Guffaws were heard around the circle, for Pearse was not
always known for his modesty nor his praise of others. The
beyond had taught him that.

Una beckoned him to the front. "By all means, dear Padraig,
please recite what ye wish."

"Thank ye, dear Una. Ye, of all among us, would remember
this poem called Mystery by Amerigin, a Milesian prince who

came to Ireland hundreds of years before Christ.

Pearse spoke so eloquently, even the breeze held its breath.

"I am the wind that breathes upon the sea
I am the wave of the ocean
I am the murmur of the billows
I am the ox of the seven combats
I am the vulture upon the rocks
I am a beam of the sun
I am the fairest of plants
I am a wild boar in valour
I am a salmon in the water
I am a lake in the plain
I am a word of science
I am the point of the lance of battle
I am the God who created in the head the fire
Who is it who throws light into the meeting on the
mountain?
Who announces the ages of the moon?
Who teaches the place where couches the sun?
(If not I?)"

The family members and friends parted, honoring Amer-
igin's words in heart and mind. Using the four promises, each
would guide a beloved in the next generation toward the collec-
tive I.

Each knew how critical that guidance would be, for troubles
lay ahead.